BETRAYALS
STAND

SHERRYL D. HANCOCK

Published by Vulpine Press in the United Kingdom in 2018

ISBN 978-1-83919-261-6

Cover by Claire Wood

www.vulpine-press.com

Also in the *MidKnight Blue* series:

CHAPTER 1

Things between Joe and Randy had settled into a routine. He dropped her off at the academy and picked her up in the afternoons. Everything wasn't perfect, but they were working on it together, and in Joe's mind, that's what was important.

Driving home one afternoon after picking Randy up, Joe's phone rang. It was Jessica Harland calling.

"How're you?" he said, grinning widely.

"I'm fine," Jessica said, "and I'll be there tomorrow."

"Tomorrow!" Joe exclaimed, laughing at the same time. It had only been a few days since he suggested Jessica come and spend some time in San Diego. "That's a lot of notice."

"Well, you know how things are. I kept meaning to call and I just forgot. Is it too late to request a pickup at the airport, or should I just go ahead and catch a cab?"

"Like hell you will." Joe glanced over at Randy, who was watching him, smiling. "What time does your flight get in?"

"Four o'clock."

"I'll be there."

"I'll see you then."

Joe hung up and looked over at Randy again. "This is okay with you, isn't it?" he said, his voice indicating that he knew it was too late to ask the question.

"Why wouldn't it be?"

"I don't know… I just thought you might be bothered or somethin'."

"It sounds like she did a pretty good job of looking out for you when I wasn't around, so I don't see why I wouldn't want to meet her," Randy said, smiling.

Joe looked at her for a long moment, trying to detect any hint of anger in her voice, but there was none. Finally, he shrugged. "Okay."

The following day, Joe picked Jessica up at the airport, and once they'd gotten her luggage he escorted her out to his black Jaguar. Jessica eyed it appreciatively. "Nice car, Sergeant."

"This?" Joe said, pointing to the vehicle and shrugging. "It's kind of a backup. I only drive it when I have to pick people up from airports and the like."

"Poor baby," Jessica said, clicking her tongue and shaking her head.

Joe grinned self-consciously. "I guess that did sound a bit stuffed, didn't it?"

"It's okay." Jessica grinned. "You come by it naturally."

"Shut up." They both laughed.

A few minutes later they were on the road. "I thought you said you lived on the beach?" Jessica asked, having noted that he was going east. She raised an eyebrow at him. "Or is that just the weekend mansion?"

Joe rolled his eyes at her. "Smart ass. I've got to pick up Randy at the academy first, if that's alright with you."

"Oh, I suppose you can pick up your wife if you really have to," Jessica said, smiling.

"Gee, thanks."

Jessica looked at him closely. "So you two are really okay now?"

"As best as we can be right now." Realizing she didn't understand what he meant, Joe continued. "We're, uh, not..." He shook his head, not wanting to tell her more than she really needed to know, especially about their sex lives—or lack thereof. "Never mind." He waved away the rest of his statement, but Jessica was nodding wisely.

"No need to explain any further," she said. "I get it."

Joe glanced over at her. "I had almost forgotten how good you are at this."

Jessica nodded, grinning. "But everything else is okay, huh?"

"Yeah."

"And Midnight?"

"Her, I don't know about." Joe looked distressed. "I went and saw her today, and she was real quiet and closed up, and I couldn't get anything out of her. I think I know what it's about, but I don't want to ask directly."

"Is this about Rick?" Jessica didn't want to pry, but she was already worried about Midnight.

3

"Yeah. He's gotten himself in a real jam now, but I don't know if he told Midnight or not. I told him to, but he doesn't always listen to me."

"But if Midnight's gotten really quiet, don't you think he must have told her whatever it is?"

"Not necessarily. I think she might have got some news from the doctor that she didn't want to hear, and that might be it too."

"Would I be being too nosy if I asked what you think that news might have been?"

Joe looked over at her for a long moment. He knew Jessica sometimes saw things more clearly than even he himself did, especially when it came to the women in his life. "I think they told her she can't have any more kids."

Jessica looked surprised. "Shouldn't or can't?" she asked, knowing the difference. Midnight shouldn't have tried to have this second baby, but she had been willing to take the risk.

"Can't," Joe said, his tone definite.

"Oh boy." Jessica blew her breath out in a sigh. "I'll bet that's rough."

"Yeah," Joe said, his expression cynical. "It probably doesn't help much then to hear that your husband's girlfriend might be pregnant."

Jessica's eyes widened. "Oh shit."

"Tell me about it."

"You said might," Jessica said hopefully. "She isn't sure yet?"

"No, and this isn't the first time either."

"She's thought she was pregnant before?" Jessica looked perplexed. "I thought this thing with them hadn't been going on for that long."

"This time, no, but Rick's dated her before, back in England."

"Oh," Jessica said, nodding. "So maybe her trap didn't snare him the first time, and she's rebaited it, huh?"

Joe laughed, shaking his head at her deductive reasoning. "You hit the nail on the head there."

A few minutes later, they pulled up in front of the college. Randy was just coming out of class, and Joe got out of the car, resting his forearms on the roof as he waited for her. She smiled when she saw him, looking pointedly at her watch.

"I'm impressed," she said.

"I get extra credit this time." Joe nodded toward Jessica, who was just getting out of the passenger's seat to make way for Randy.

Randy walked over to the other woman, extending her hand. Jessica took it, smiling. Randy looked over at Joe again. "Why, because you managed to accomplish what you promised?" She raised an eyebrow.

"Hey, I would've had a hell of an excuse to be late, and I'm not," Joe protested, a grin on his face the whole time.

"He's late a lot, huh?" Jessica asked Randy.

"Constantly," Randy said, grimacing. "It is nice to meet you, however."

"Thanks, you too."

Jessica was taken aback by the size and elegance of Joe and Randy's home. She walked out onto the deck and stared at the ocean, a look of sheer astonishment on her face.

"You guys have this view every day?"

"Actually," Joe said, "we have a different one shipped in every day."

Jessica turned and punched him on the arm. "Asshole!"

Joe laughed. "Hey, maybe we should work on your combat techniques while you're here too. That jab could use a little more power behind it."

"You don't want me to really hit you," Jessica said ominously.

"Besides," Randy said, stepping outside and looking at her husband seriously, "maybe we'll gang up on you."

Joe grinned mischievously. "That sounds like an interesting proposition."

"Sinclair!"

"Joe!"

Joe laughed, fending off their advances with his fists raised. Randy got to him first, and he grabbed her around the waist, turning her around and using her to block Jessica.

"Put me down, you shit," Randy said, laughing all the while. Joe wrapped his other arm around her waist, then pulled her back against him in a bear hug. Randy leaned back against him, craning her neck around to look up at him, her smile radiant.

Jessica could see the deep emotion reflected in Randy's and Joe's eyes, and she found herself wishing once again that she could find someone like Joe to love her that much. A few moments later, they looked back at her, but Randy didn't move from Joe's embrace. Joe leaned back against the railing, putting his chin down on Randy's shoulder. His eyes sparkled in the setting sun. "So, Jess," he said. "Whaddya want to do your first night in town?"

"To be honest with you," Jessica said, "what I really want to do is go to bed early and sleep all night long. Things up in Sacramento have been hectic with you gone, and the catch-up time on all my paperwork has been while I was home at night. Do you mind?" she said, wondering belatedly if he'd planned something.

Joe looked at Randy, then back at Jessica. "Nope," he said simply, happy to be able to stay home again. His nights were bound to get longer as he tried desperately to catch up at FORS.

Randy cooked dinner for all of them, welcoming Jessica's help. Joe sat on the center island of the kitchen, observing and making a general nuisance of himself as he drank wine and occasionally reached out to sample vegetables and whatever else they were preparing. Now and again, Randy would stand between his legs, leaning back against him companionably. Joe would kiss the top of her head or lean down to nuzzle her neck.

They ate dinner at the dining room table, and Jessica was again impressed with the elegance of their home. Randy had pulled out the Dresden china, declaring that evening a special occasion. Randy had gotten fairly good at setting a refined table, and Joe was proud of her as she talked to Jessica and made her feel comfortable in their home. He commented on it that evening as they lay on their bed, watching some movie that happened to be on.

"Thanks for being so great to Jessica," he said, smoothing her hair back from her face. She was lying with her back against his chest, her legs stretched out between his.

"I like her. She's really nice."

"Yeah, well, some women wouldn't take kindly to another woman in their domain, ya know."

She glanced up at him. "Is there a reason I should be worried?"

"No." Joe kissed her forehead. "But she is pretty nice looking, and she would tend to cause a little bit of friction with some women."

"Are you trying to tell me that you're attracted to her?" Randy asked, her voice still calm.

"No, that's not what I'm trying to tell you," Joe chided her. "I'm just saying that I think it's great that you're getting along with her."

"Versus what?" Randy had started to sound a lot like Midnight again. Joe couldn't decide if that thought bothered him or not. He had always enjoyed his and Midnight's banter, and having that same type of teasing relationship with his wife was a new twist to their marriage. He just wasn't sure where her quick wit was suddenly coming from.

"Versus you hating her guts and trying to claw her eyes out," he said patiently, grinning down at her.

"Not my style."

"And what is your style?"

"You mean if I thought some other woman was moving in on my man?" Randy asked, her eyes glinting impishly.

Joe shrugged. "Yeah, somethin' like that."

"Well…" Randy sat up slowly and turned to face him, tucking her legs beneath her. "I'd make it so that she wouldn't have a chance."

"Chance to what?" Joe replied, gazing down into her eyes.

"A chance to turn his head," Randy said, staring at him suggestively.

"But what if she didn't back off that easily?"

"Who said I'd be doing anything to her?" Randy moved her hands to the front of his shirt, her eyes never leaving his.

"So you'd be doing something to me then?" Joe said, the tone of his voice indicating that she was getting to him.

"You could say that." She began to unbutton his shirt.

"I see," Joe said, his eyes going to her hands as they reached the last button. Randy pushed the shirt away and placed her hands on his chest, spreading them over his muscles, her nails grazing them slightly as she flexed her fingers. She moved to get in the way of his downward gaze, and when their eyes met, she kissed him. Her hands trailed up to his neck as she pulled him close. It was very obvious from Joe's reaction that he was deeply affected by her actions. They kissed for a long few minutes. Randy pulled back, looking up at him. Joe was watching her closely.

Keeping her eyes on his, Randy reached up and pulled off her shirt, then reached over to remove Joe's. She straddled his hips, and his hands went to her waist as she moved to kiss him again. When their skin made contact, Randy heard Joe's low moan, and it only served to spur her on. Within minutes Joe had his arms wrapped tightly around her, pressing her body to his. When Randy pulled back to look at him, she could see the passion burning in his light blue eyes. She smiled at him, her own breathing ragged from the intensity of their kisses.

"What're you doin?" he said, his voice deep, his accent thick.

"What do you want me to do?" she said, echoing the words he'd asked her on a rainy night so many years before, the first time they'd ever kissed.

"Everything," was Joe's reply, and the look in his eyes told Randy that he had resolved the situation with Midnight and he was hers once again. The thought made Randy want to scream and cheer, but instead she kissed her husband until they were both breathless and unable to control themselves any longer.

Joe made love to her, but he noticed, as did she, that something had definitely changed between them. What astonished Joe the most was that the change was almost imperceptible—but Randy was different, and he was different with her. It bothered him to realize, as they lay entangled a while later, that she reminded him more of Midnight now than she ever had before. He analyzed the thought. It wasn't because he and Midnight had been together so recently, because even that time with Midnight hadn't been the same. They had only made love once, and he knew they had both perceived the difference. He hadn't realized what that difference was until just now—whether he liked it or not, he belonged totally to Randy. Being with Randy now had made him feel complete again, like something that he had once had had been missing, and now it was back. But Randy was different. Her body felt different, her words were different, even the way she kissed him was different—and in a way it bothered him. He liked the changes, but he felt that somehow he shouldn't. It occurred to him that it might have something to do with Dickerson.

When he glanced down, he saw that Randy was watching him.

"What were you thinking about just then?" she asked.

Joe didn't respond right away, and Randy could see that he was trying to decide if he wanted to tell her.

"Tell me, please."

"I was thinking about how different you are now," Joe said quietly, looking into her eyes.

Randy nodded slowly. She had also been thinking that things were not the same between them now. Then she speared him with a look. "You think it's because of Dick, don't you?"

Joe looked at her for a long moment, then nodded slowly, expelling his breath as he did.

"It's not him, Joe," Randy said, unconsciously moving her body closer to his, as if getting closer to him would convince him. "It's you—you make me different now."

Joe looked down at her, confusion clear in his eyes. "How?"

Randy shook her head. "I don't know, really. It's just that I feel so different this time. I feel like we're more equal, like you're more my lover than you are my father figure, you know?" Her voice was soft, but the look in her eyes was intense.

Joe considered what she was saying. "Meaning I was too protective before?" he asked, with no anger in his voice, only curiosity.

"You were protective, but I let you be. I even wanted you to be sometimes, like having you tell me I couldn't or shouldn't do something would let me off the hook."

"Like being a cop?"

"Honestly?" she said. Joe nodded. "Yes, at first I kept thinking that if you'd just tell me you wouldn't allow me to do it, I could just give it up and not have to worry about measuring up."

"But you didn't give it up."

"You never told me you would leave me if I did it," Randy said admonishingly.

"My mistake," Joe said, grinning widely.

"And how," Randy replied, grinning back. "But now, you use the word 'we' when you talk about police work, like I'm already part of your world. It makes me feel more part of you, more your wife and not your ward."

"That doesn't mean I won't still worry about you," Joe said calmly.

"I expect you to worry about me. Don't you think I worry about you all the time?"

"You've never said anything."

"What was the point?" She shrugged. "Were you going to stop doing police work if I told you I was worried about you?"

"No. I would have told you that you had nothing to worry about."

"And you would have been full of shit," Randy retorted. "Not including the time you were shot in the back, or the time you were shot in the shoulder—by the same gang, I might add—but there were plenty of other times when your expected life span looked short, and you think I had nothing to worry about?"

Joe blinked at her small tirade, but he was smiling the whole time, because he knew she was right. "You win. I'm a real risk taker, and you should take out a bigger life insurance policy on me."

"I'd rather just keep you around, if you don't mind."

Joe pulled her body flush with his, looking down into her eyes. "Make love to me again, and we'll discuss it."

"You got it, Sergeant."

They ended up making love half the night, joking back and forth and even making a 3:00 a.m. trip to the refrigerator for a snack, after which they made love again. Six o'clock came very early, but Randy had to be at the shooting range that day. Fortunately it was closer than the college, but she still had to get up. Joe's arm was wrapped tightly around her waist. Randy lay on her back, and Joe on his side. She reached over, shutting off the alarm tiredly. She turned her head, looking up at her husband. Watching him sleep now reminded her of all the times she'd done so before, thinking that he looked so relaxed and calm. She thought of their lovemaking and felt her body respond to the memory. Without hesitating Randy moved closer to him, touching her lips to his neck as she stroked his stomach and reached up with her other hand to brush his hair back from his cheek. Joe moved around a little but didn't wake up. They'd only had about two hours of sleep; he was exhausted. Randy felt guilty for disturbing him, but she couldn't resist the desire to do so. She brushed her lips along his neck and down to his chest. When she moved back up to his lips, she saw that his eyes were open and he was watching her intently.

"Good morning," she said, kissing him sensually. Joe responded immediately.

They ended up rushing around the house an hour later, trying to make it to the range on time. Jessica watched them. She could tell something had changed between them and suspected correctly what that something was. She had been up for an hour, and she'd heard them moving around in the other room, but she had made a point of not listening any closer. Seeing them now, she could tell they hadn't gotten much sleep, but they both looked very happy and kept exchanging private looks. Jessica was happy for them. She had long since admitted to herself that she'd have been happy to be exchanging looks like that with Joseph Michael Sinclair, but she had also come around to the reality that there was only one woman in the world he looked at like that, and she was his wife. Jessica, being the type of person she was, decided that she was happy enough knowing someone like Joe, and knowing that she could count on him as a friend. Joe was like one of those movie stars you adored and watched everything they did with fascination, but you didn't like them any less just because they were in love with their wives. You could still have fantasies about them. Jessica knew Joe would die if he knew she was likening him to a movie star, but that was part of his charm—the fact that he didn't know how gorgeous he was.

"You ready?" Joe asked her, his voice bringing her out of her reflections.

"I've been ready a while, Sinclair," Jessica responded easily, her grin wide. Joe looked almost embarrassed as he realized her powers of deductive reasoning had once again put her one up on him. He smiled broadly.

"What?" Randy said, coming into the room. She put on her watch as she looked between the two of them.

"Oh, nothin'," Joe said, still grinning at Jessica. "Detective Harland was just indicating her readiness to leave."

"Okay…" Randy said, shaking her head and smiling, not sure what Joe was trying to tell her but aware that he and Jessica were sharing a private joke. Then she looked over at her husband. "I'm ready if you are."

"I know that," Joe said, his eyes twinkling mischievously. Randy gave him an impish look of her own.

Twenty-five minutes later, Joe dropped Randy off at Duffy Town, the sheriff's miniature town utilized by trainees and officers to simulate realistic scenarios for their range shoots. "I'll see you later," he said, leaning across to kiss her.

"Okay," Randy said, and got out of the car. She flipped them a wave as Joe drove away.

Randy was surprised when, two hours later, Joe, Jessica, and many of the members of FORS walked onto the range grounds. The class was doing a run-through of the course, and Randy was waiting for her turn. Joe meandered over to her and, standing behind her, leaned down to whisper in her ear, "Fancy meeting you here."

"What are you and your gang doing here?"

"Quarterly training."

"Nice of you to tell me."

"Slipped my mind," Joe said, his husky voice indicating the reason for his negligence.

"I see."

15

It was Randy's turn. Joe watched as she made her run. He could see she was having a hard time holding on to her weapon, and then she cried out, the gun bouncing out of her grasp. Her hand came out to stop the gun from hitting the ground, and she cried out a second time as he started to move toward her. He knew the barrel had been white-hot, and she dropped it again involuntarily.

Joe strode up to her. She looked up at him, holding her hand out. He could see the red mark from the barrel already forming on her palm. He retrieved the weapon from the ground, depressing the magazine release and examining the bullets inside. The training sergeant and range master had walked over, and Joe looked up at the range master accusingly.

"What the fuck is this?" he said, his anger overriding any desire to avoid interfering with the academy training. He held the magazine out to the training sergeant, who took it and shook his head, indicating he didn't know what Joe was referring to. "This load's too fucking hot to run through a Ruger."

The range master, Sergeant Chuck Smith, took the magazine from the training sergeant, looking it over himself. Randy stood by watching, feeling ashamed that she hadn't been able to handle the weapon.

Smith examined the bullets loaded into the ammunition clip. He was surprised, but he disagreed with Joe's assessment. "It's not too hot—it just causes a heavy recoil."

"That's plus P plus, a hundred and fifteen grain, if I'm not mistaken," Joe said, his voice even but his eyes narrowed. "And yeah, it'll go through okay, but it'll beat the shit out of the shooter. These are rookies, you idiot. Half of 'em never handled a gun till today." Joe shook his head disdainfully.

"Well, I agree with you there. This ammo shouldn't have been used—one of my people must have made a mistake. I'll check into it." He looked over at Randy. "Are you okay, cadet?"

Randy nodded solemnly. "I think my pride's had more damage done than anything else."

"Don't worry about it," Sergeant Smith said. "I don't know many cadets that could have held on to that gun as long as you did. Good job." He patted her on the shoulder and turned to walk back toward his offices, the gun in hand.

Randy and Joe walked back over to where the rest of the candidates stood. "I didn't understand all of that," Randy said candidly.

Joe glanced down at her. "The thing is, the ammunition that was in that gun was too heavy for the weapon. It was too strong, and you, being pretty new at this, weren't ready for it just yet. It's not a good training round at all—somebody fucked up." Joe shook his head, his eyes softening as he noticed that she was embarrassed. "Hey, the range master's right. You did real good, considering that load. I'm surprised you not only held on to the gun but managed a couple of pretty fair shots too."

Randy brightened. "Really?" She looked back at the targets and saw that while they weren't excellent shots, they were fair. She grinned. "Must be sleeping with an expert that does it."

"Ya think?" Joe said, grinning back. Randy nodded. The training sergeant announced that the cadets could take a break while Joe's group did their run-throughs.

Randy watched, fascinated, as the members of FORS moved through the course. They would kneel, crouch, and even lie down to get the best angle on the realistic targets. The class clapped as the last of them finished.

Joe ran Jessica through, staying with her the entire time, talking her through each move, telling her when to get lower or when to stand straight. He helped her realign a couple of her shots, so that she hit the target closer to center mass a few times. At the end, Jessica looked up at him and smiled triumphantly, even spontaneously hugging him. Joe grinned at her, congratulating her on her progress. "You're shooting better now," he said, narrowing his eyes at her suspiciously. "You've been practicing."

Jessica shrugged. "Gary's tried to help me out, but he doesn't have your street savvy just yet, ya know?"

"Okay." Joe steered her back over to the group. "Thanks," he said to the training sergeant. "We've been in need of qualifications for months, we just haven't had the time."

"You got it." Sergeant Jones nodded. "But I noted that you didn't do your run-through, Sinclair." The tone in his voice was challenging as he smirked. This was an old game between them; Joe and he had actually attended training together, when Joe had come over from the sheriff's department and was doing some updating and Jones was going through the academy. They'd both been pretty good shots, and who was better had been a joke between them.

Joe nodded toward the course. "You first."

Jones pulled out his sidearm, pulling back the slide and standing at the ready. He nodded to the operator of the course and made his way through. He missed very few targets, and the class, including

Randy, cheered as he finished. The members of FORS stood by, looking very much like a gang, most of them with their arms crossed in front of them. They looked to Joe, and he grinned at them. Pulling out his weapon, Joe depressed the magazine release and checked it out, making sure it was fully loaded. He put the slide back in and held the weapon at the ready. He nodded toward the operator and began his run. Joe moved as if he were serving a search warrant, his motions quick and accurate, his shots dead on. It became very apparent to the class that Joe had come by his reputation of being deadly with a gun honestly. When he finished, he had a perfect score. He'd hit every target perfect center mass and had not shot any of the innocent civilians that were interspersed throughout them.

Randy had yet another new appreciation for her husband's abilities as the class cheered but were outdone by the whoops and hollers from FORS. Joe grinned abashed at the attention, but his expression was victorious as he faced Jones.

Jones shook his head ruefully. "You win."

"I know," Joe said, his grin lopsided.

An hour later, Joe, Randy, and Jessica were in the car, going to lunch. Joe touched Randy's hand lightly, looking over with concern in his eyes. "Is your hand okay?"

"It's fine, Joe. Really."

Joe looked at her for a long moment, and then shook his head, and she knew he wasn't indicating his concern.

"Oh, shut up!" she said, laughing. "It was a reaction, okay?"

"Some reaction," Joe said, his voice holding humor as he rolled his eyes. Jessica started to laugh.

"What should I have done?" Randy asked hotly, but her eyes reflected her embarrassment.

"You should've let the damned thing fall," Joe replied, grinning.

"It's a six-hundred-dollar weapon!"

"Yeah, and your hands are irreplaceable."

"I'm not gonna live this one down, am I?"

Joe shook his head. "Probably not."

Randy smiled over at him. She was glad he wasn't overreacting to her slight injury—she had the distinct impression that a couple of months ago things would have been far different.

They rode along in silence for a while. The radio was on, and Randy heard a song she liked. She reached over and turned it up—Paula Cole's "Where Have All the Cowboys Gone?" She started to sing along, and Jessica joined her on the chorus.

The song addressed the declining attitudes and roles of men in American family life. It traced the decline of a marriage and how the husband didn't seem to care, how he didn't keep up his end of the relationship. She sang about being the woman and wanting her man to be just that, the man. One of the lines was, "I am wearing my new dress tonight, but you don't even notice me." It was true of many marriages in today's society. Randy sang the words with such zest that Joe glanced over at her when the song ended.

"Are you trying to tell me something?" he asked, his lips twisting in a sardonic grin.

"Hardly," Randy replied. "You are the perfect antonym to that song."

"I am, huh?" Joe said disbelievingly.

Randy turned to look at Jessica. "Don't you think so?"

"Most assuredly."

Randy looked back at Joe. "If I wear a little more makeup, a different perfume, part my hair on the other side, anything, you notice. And you say something."

"I was brought up that way."

"I know that, and it's wonderful." Randy smiled at him warmly. "But it's not the norm anymore."

"You want me to change?" Joe asked, smiling at her.

"No!" Randy and Jessica said together, and then started to laugh.

"Don't do that!" Joe said, glancing at Jessica in the rearview mirror and then over at Randy, shivering dramatically. "It's scary."

"Sounding off in stereo, you mean?" Randy said.

"You two haven't known each other long enough, okay?"

"Uh-huh, we know," Jessica said, nodding her head sarcastically.

"And you're ganging up on me," Joe replied hotly.

"You only wish we'd gang up on you," Randy said, the look on her face sly, her eyes sparkling roguishly.

Joe raised his eyebrows suggestively. "Yeah, don't I wish."

Randy looked back at Jessica and both women laughed, as did Joe. Lunch proceeded comfortably after that.

Joe dropped Randy off at the range again, and he and Jessica continued back to FORS. Jessica was very impressed when she walked into the unit's offices. Joe led her to his room, nodding toward Midnight's.

"That's Night's office over there," he said. Jessica nodded, and when they were in Joe's office she looked around with interest. There were some awards and certificates, but most of the souvenirs Joe kept were things like switchblades he'd confiscated that the department didn't care about, or a set of nunchucks that Spider had given him. He had posters from different agencies, even one from the Department of Justice that depicted three agents wearing black raid gear, including Kevlar helmets, and carrying MP5s. It read "Violence Suppression Unit". He also had posters from a number of gun manufacturers, as well as body armor and ammunition companies. It was obvious that he was very serious about the profession he had chosen. Jessica felt that added just a little bit more depth to an already quite interesting person. She looked through the glass into Midnight's office. She noted the Corvette posters as well as the die-cast metal sculpture of a classic red-and-white Corvette on her desk. The wall was covered with plaques and certificates. Jessica tried to read them but couldn't from where she stood. When she turned to look at Joe, she saw that he was watching her, grinning.

"Go on," Joe said.

"What?" she replied, wide-eyed.

"I know you want to go over there and read all her shit—just go." Joe was used to people's reactions to Midnight's achievements.

Jessica shrugged and walked out of the office and over to Midnight's. She came back fifteen minutes later. She sat down in the chair in front of Joe's desk and shook her head. "She's accomplished a lot, hasn't she?" She sounded awed.

Joe inclined his head slightly. "That she has." His words were casual, but the look on his face showed much more. He was very proud to be partners with someone as determined and successful as Midnight.

"So have you," Jessica said, her eyes on his.

"Some."

"Yeah, right." Jessica shook her head at his overly modest attitude.

The rest of the day passed with Joe working on some of the ever-increasing paperwork he'd taken from Midnight's desk. Jessica sat and looked over some of the cases they'd been working on. When she got to the old report file on the Scorpions case, she glanced up at Joe. She had just read the part about Joe being shot in the back and coming very close to dying. He looked up, seeming to sense that she was looking at him. He reached over and with his fingertip flipped the folder up so he could see what the case name was. "Oh, that one," he said, his voice too casual.

"That one?" Jessica said disbelievingly. "It says here that you were almost fatally wounded."

"'Almost' is the key word there."

"Jesus, you guys don't play around down here, do you?"

"Not too often, no," Joe said seriously. "If you read a little bit farther you'll see that that particular gang tried to take out not one but three cops. They tried to take me out twice."

Jessica just stared at him, openmouthed. "Twice?"

Joe nodded.

"How'd they manage to get that close to you twice?" Jessica asked with the slightest bit of rebuke.

"It's a long story, but the gist of it was that a woman I dated wanted me dead, and she helped them out." Joe shrugged, trying to downplay the significance of Tasha's betrayal.

"She wanted you dead?" Jessica repeated, clearly struggling to believe his blasé attitude.

"I told you, it's a long story."

"I guess." Jessica scanned down the report, and again she found herself stunned. She'd come to the section on Midnight's abduction and the medical report on her examination. "Jesus," she breathed, only beginning to imagine what Midnight had experienced when she was taken by the Scorpions. It was every woman's nightmare. Jessica found herself respecting Midnight all the more for what she'd come through. She also had a deeper respect for Joe and the people he worked with.

An hour or so later, Tiny walked into Joe's office.

"What's up?" Joe asked him.

"We got a raid goin' down in a couple of hours. Spider wanted me to let you know, in case you wanted to come along. It could be a good one." Tiny's eyes went to Jessica. He had seen her shoot at the range; he'd also seen how hesitant she had been. "Hi," he said, his voice kind of soft and shy. Tiny was a fairly brawny Samoan—he'd slimmed down somewhat since attending the police academy three years before, but he still stood as tall as Joe and was almost twice as wide with muscle. His jet-black hair was cut short on the top and sides, with a long trail of curls down the back. Jessica glanced up at him and smiled.

"Hello," she said shyly, intimidated by Tiny's size.

Joe looked at the two of them and grinned. "Tiny, this is Jessica Harland. She's a police officer from Sacramento—she's on vacation."

Tiny's eyes never left Jessica's face, but he smiled widely and said, "Some vacation." He looked around Joe's cluttered office and then back to Jessica.

"My travel agent told me this was a great sunbathing spot," she replied, grinning widely.

"This office gets about ten minutes of sun a day. I think you should fire your travel agent."

Jessica laughed, and so did Tiny.

"Tiny," Joe said, his expression indicating that he hated to interrupt, his eyes twinkling. "Tell Spider that I'll be there. Have him call the address into me."

"I can just ride with you," Tiny said, looking at his watch. "We've got about two hours."

Joe looked down at his own watch—it was four o'clock. "Good, that'll give me time to pick up Randy and drop her and Jess off at the house." He stood up, pulling his jacket off the back of his chair. Shrugging into it, he looked up at Jessica. "You ready?"

Jessica nodded and stood. She turned around and just about walked into Tiny, because he had stepped forward to get out of the doorway. He steadied her, holding her by the shoulders. She looked up at him and smiled. "Thanks," she said, and Tiny nodded, smiling back. As she started to step aside to get out of his way, he did the same, trying to move for her. They both laughed. "If we had music…" Jessica said.

"I could hum," Joe put in. Tiny and Jessica looked over at him, and it struck Joe that they'd make a pretty nice-looking couple. Tiny's dark features and his obvious brawn blended nicely with Jessica's tiny frame and auburn hair and fair skin.

They left the office, and Tiny made a point of opening the car door for Jessica. A little while later they pulled up in front of the sheriff's range. Joe got out of the car and perched on the hood. Randy came out a few minutes later. Joe noticed the bandage on her hand immediately, but she waved away his concern. "It's no big deal," she said, moving to kiss him. "I just couldn't shoot without it."

"Mmhmm," Joe muttered, grinning down at her.

"Stop!" she said, laughing. She looked over and saw Tiny in the passenger seat. Her expression changed. Tiny was watching her, his eyes narrowed. Randy knew that everyone in FORS knew about her disloyalty to Joe, and she assumed, correctly, that most of them didn't accept that she and Joe were back together.

Joe realized what she was thinking. "Don't worry about it, they'll get used to it," he said softly.

Randy shook her head, the look in her eyes miserable. "I don't know about that." She walked over to the driver's side of the car and got in the backseat with Jessica. Tiny didn't even turn in her direction. Randy was actually surprised at his coldness; Tiny had always been so nice to her. It really bothered her.

Joe got in. "I gotta drop you ladies off," he said, glancing back at Randy. "I got a raid to go on. I might be pretty late."

"Okay," Randy said, very conscious of every word that she or Joe spoke, in case Tiny should take something the wrong way. Suddenly, their being back together wasn't as easy as it had seemed. Randy was still seeing the effects of her actions, and she wondered how long it would be before anyone would look at her like they had before.

When they got off the freeway, Joe pulled up to a light and stopped. As he and Tiny watched, a woman in a skin-tight black velvet cropped top and retro bell-bottom pants walked by. She was raven-haired with a dark tan. As she strolled past the Jaguar, she glanced inside. She saw Joe and Tiny watching her, and she immediately turned to look at them full on. Joe, with his blond mane and light blue eyes, and Tiny, with his obvious build and dark good looks, sitting in a very expensive-looking car in downtown La Jolla were quite a sight. The girl stared at Joe, her eyes giving him an obvious come-on, but Joe shook his head slowly, holding up his left hand and indicating his wedding band. She shook her head and glanced over at Tiny. "We don't have time, Tiny," Joe said, his grin wide.

"Damn," Tiny said, but both men laughed as the light turned green. The girl walked on but watched the car as it passed her, only then noticing the two women in the back seat. She simply shrugged.

Joe and Tiny exchanged a glance that was obviously an "Oh my God!" look, and then they both burst into laughter.

"Black'll do it every time," Tiny said, shaking his head.

"Tell me," Joe replied. He glanced in the rearview mirror and caught Randy's eye. He smiled at her, and she raised an eyebrow at him, but he could see a gleam of humor in her eyes. "I'm gonna pay for that one, I can see," he said, still watching Randy. She nodded slowly, provocatively. "Might be worth it though," he added.

Later, on the way to the raid, Tiny looked over at Joe, watching him as if trying to figure him out. He and Joe had become pretty good friends over the past seven years. They'd had some run-ins, especially the time that Tiny hadn't backed Midnight up properly and she had gotten hurt. They'd almost come to blows then. There had also been the time when Joe and Rick had gotten into a fight in the office, and Tiny had, at Midnight's request, escorted Joe to the front door. Tiny knew where his loyalties lay, and if it came down to Midnight or Joe, it was always going to be Midnight.

It had been Midnight who had visited him in the hospital when he'd had a fight with another member of his own gang. The guy had literally stabbed him in the back. It was Midnight who had talked to him like a real person. She had been honest with him, telling him that her newly formed unit was targeting his gang. She told him that if he was smart he wouldn't go back to it when he was released from the hospital. He'd mouthed off to her, figuring she was just some broad trying to throw her weight around. Midnight had narrowed her cat-like eyes and told him she'd look forward to taking him down herself if he was stupid enough to ignore her advice. Tiny had found himself taking her seriously from that moment on. Something in her voice had made him see that she was not kidding and she was not someone he wanted to be enemies with. By the end of her visit, Tiny had asked her to come back and see him, if she had time. Midnight had made the time. She'd returned and talked to him, even joked with him. He'd asked her what her story was, and to his surprise she had told him. They had talked about why he was in the gang—mostly because he was so shy that he had to hide out in a gang to scare people out of trying to talk to him. Midnight had found that endearing and had told him so. She'd also told him she thought he'd be a valuable asset to her unit.

"You want me to become a cop?" Tiny had asked her, his voice belying his shock.

"No," Midnight had said, shaking her head and smiling at him. "I want you to become a member of my gang. That's basically what FORS is—it's a gang that's on the right side of the law."

Tiny had taken what she had said to heart. He had thought about her offer for a long time. He had come from a very traditional family and he had known for a long time that his parents were very distressed about his lifestyle. They didn't understand him; they thought he just wanted to be a thug. His mother had tried to talk to him, but he had brushed her off, not wanting to have to explain that he was so painfully shy that he needed to cultivate a tough-looking exterior so people wouldn't try to talk to him. But Midnight had seen through his disguise right away. She hadn't made fun of his shyness, hadn't said anything about it at all after stating she felt that was what was keeping him in the gang. Tiny had felt a kindred spirit in Midnight from day one, and he'd had a crush on her for almost the entire time he'd known her. But over the years the crush had turned to a deeper affection for the tiny blond woman who had basically saved him from himself.

He had come to feel that Joe, too, was a very good friend. Joe had backed him up on so many occasions. He had gone toe to toe with anyone who had put him down, and had even gotten into it once with a higher-up in the department for telling anyone who would listen that Tiny didn't have a right to wear a badge, that he was a disgrace to the uniform because of his weight. The guy had been a jerk, but it had hurt Tiny's feelings enough to make him actually try to turn his badge in. He had gone to Joe, not having the nerve to face Midnight. Tiny found out a few days later that Joe had cornered the lieutenant at a local cop hangout and told the guy that if he ever mouthed off about one of his friends again, he'd personally stuff his lieutenant's bars down his throat. The lieutenant had promptly attempted to have Joe fired, but Midnight had stood up to him and he had backed down, knowing he would look like a real asshole if the truth of what he'd said came out.

"What?" Joe said, catching Tiny's look.

"I just don't get it, that's all."

"What is it that you don't get?" But Joe knew what Tiny was referring to.

"How can you be with her now?" Tiny's voice showed his annoyance at Randy's betrayal.

Joe looked at the other man, shaking his head. "You're right—you don't get it," he said, but with no anger in his voice.

"Joe, she cheated on you! I'm sorry, but in my book that's really fucked up."

Joe shrugged. "Yeah, but then that makes me an asshole too."

"Why?"

"Because I cheated on her too."

Tiny's eyes widened in surprise. "When?" It was obvious he thought Joe was lying to make what Randy had done seem okay.

"When I was in Sacramento."

Tiny's eyes widened further. "You mean with that hot Sacramento cop?"

"Jess?" Joe said, and when Tiny nodded emphatically, he shook his head. "God, no! Jesus, Tiny, she's a kid!"

"No kid I've ever seen has a body like that."

"Well, she's not too much of a kid for you, I guess, but she's even younger than Randy."

"Okay," Tiny said, finally accepting that Joe hadn't slept with Jessica. "Then who?"

Joe didn't say anything for a long moment, and suddenly it came to Tiny. "You slept with Midnight again, didn't you?"

Joe looked chagrined as he nodded slowly.

"I don't believe it!" Tiny almost whooped—it was obvious that he did believe it. "And all that time I felt sorry for her because of Rick's bullshit, and she was with you."

"Whoa!" Joe said, holding his hands up in protest. "No, we weren't together that whole time. Just up in Sacramento, one time."

"But…" Tiny started, confused again.

"We weren't together, Tiny, except one time in Sacramento, right after I found out about Randy and Dickerson."

"So Randy did the deed first," Tiny said, trying to qualify what Joe and Midnight had done. "Same as Rick."

"So that makes it okay—is that what you're saying?"

"Well, yeah. I mean, you didn't cheat on Randy before she cheated on you. It was kind of like, well, uh…"

"Payback?"

"Yeah!" Tiny said triumphantly.

"No," Joe said quietly as he shook his head.

"Bullshit, Joe. She burned you and you were just doing what was fair." Tiny didn't want to give up the argument until Joe was in the right.

"By using Midnight?" Joe raised an eyebrow. He knew he had said the right thing when Tiny sucked in his breath sharply.

"No." The look on Tiny's face showed clearly that he was going through all kinds of processes to make this come out right. "You weren't using her, were you, Joe?" His eyes narrowed just slightly, and Joe knew he was on dangerous ground. He also knew Tiny wouldn't actually kill him, just damage him a little if it turned out that Joe had indeed been improperly using the woman Tiny held in the highest regard.

"No, Tiny." Joe sighed. "I was just trying to make a point. Just because Randy did something stupid, doesn't mean I should go out and do something just as stupid."

"Two wrongs don't make it right and all that crap, yeah?" Tiny nodded, but he still looked affronted at Randy's lack of loyalty.

"Tiny," Joe said, imploring the other man to try and understand, "she's going through a rough time right now. She's trying to grow up, and trying to become independent, and I guess that meant independent of me too. I think the thing with Dickerson was just to put distance between her and me, but now we've closed it again, and I'm tellin' you, she's not getting away from me again." The look in Joe's eyes convinced Tiny there had to be something important going on for Joe to be so determined.

"Okay," he said finally, sighing dramatically. "But I'm warnin' ya, the rest of the unit's just as pissed at her."

Joe looked grim as he nodded. "Yeah, I know." The ironic thing was that FORS was the family Joe had never really had, and now, it was like they disapproved of his wife. He suddenly knew what it felt like to be the wayward son who had brought home the inappropriate date. It bothered him that the rest of FORS was mad at Randy too, and he wondered idly what he could do to change that.

They arrived at the raid site, and Joe didn't have time to think about it anymore.

CHAPTER 2

Randy and Jessica had ended up on the couch after dinner, and they were drinking wine when Randy caught Jessica's sidelong look.

"You want to ask me something?" Randy said with just the merest hint of annoyance.

"It's really none of my business," Jessica said, shaking her head.

"Ask, and if I think it's none of your business, I'll tell you so."

"Fair enough." Jessica nodded. "Do you think you and Joe are going to be okay?"

"In terms of what? Our marriage?"

"To start with, yes."

Randy thought about it for a moment, then nodded slowly. "I'm going to try my damndest to make it work this time."

"What's changed that makes you think it will work this time."

Randy looked at the younger woman sharply, surprised by her directness. "Why do you ask? What's your stake in this?"

"Are you asking me if I'm after your husband?" Jessica said calmly.

"I guess I am."

"To be totally honest with you, the idea of making a play for your husband has occurred to me, although not since I've been here."

"What's been different here?" Randy asked evenly.

"I've seen how much in love he is with you," Jessica said, very matter-of-fact.

Randy shrugged. "It's just as well."

"Why's that?"

"Because I'd fight you tooth and nail for him," Randy said, and it was clear that she meant it.

Jessica smiled, surprising Randy. "Good," she said, and that made Randy take a second look at her.

"Good?"

"Yes, good, Randy." Jessica nodded. "I'm glad to see that Joe's love for you isn't being wasted. And if you're willing to fight for him, then maybe you do deserve him."

"Maybe?"

Jessica shrugged. "You have to admit, your dalliance with that other guy wasn't the smartest move you could have made." There was no accusation in Jessica's words, only friendly observation.

Randy stared at the other woman for a long moment, shocked once more by her directness, but in a way appreciative of it. She knew Midnight would have been more direct, and probably a lot nastier about it, but it was good to have someone to talk to about her relationship with Joe. Someone that was at least partially on her side.

"That," Randy said, "was the stupidest thing I've ever done, and I hope to never make that kind of mistake ever again."

"Good."

Randy smiled at Jessica. She really did like this woman. She had been worried a few minutes ago when the conversation had gone into dangerous grounds, but she realized now that Jessica had, in a way, been testing her. She tilted her head.

"Were you serious about wanting Joe?"

"Oh…" Jessica considered her answer, looking directly into Randy's eyes. "Yes."

Randy just laughed. "You aren't the first, believe me."

"Oh, I do. Like today?"

"Really," Randy said, laughing again. "I was waiting for the woman to climb into the front seat with him. Jesus!"

"I can't even imagine being that forward with a guy, and certainly not with someone like Joe."

"I know," Randy said, agreeing wholeheartedly.

"How'd you bag him?" Jessica had wondered that since the first time Joe had mentioned his wife. How did someone go about catching a man like Joseph Michael Sinclair?

"Actually, he bagged me." Randy shrugged. "More or less. Not that I wasn't just killing myself over him."

"So how'd it happen?" Jessica asked, her eyes wide.

"Well, I was hired as his secretary, and from the first time I saw him, I was in love. But, well, I was really shy, and he was larger than life. He did eventually ask me out. It was all kind of a mess for a while, because of things going on with a really rough case."

"So that's when he fell for you?"

"Well, not really—it's really complicated. Joe was a real mess, and he and Rick were coming to blows over Midnight. It was a really awful time. Then Tim was killed."

"Who's Tim?"

"He was a young man that was trying to help Midnight catch the leader of the Scorpions."

"Wait a minute." Jessica held up her hand. "That was the gang that shot Joe, wasn't it, and they're the ones that took Midnight and… well, you know." Randy nodded somberly. "I read it in a file at Joe's office today."

"Yes, that was the gang that was trying to get rid of FORS altogether. They almost succeeded."

"So what happened? How did you two get together?"

"I took care of Joe after he was shot. He got to go home from the hospital, but the doctors insisted that he have someone with him round the clock. I was the logical choice since I was his secretary, and Midnight already knew I was in love with him…" She trailed off as she remembered the first time Joe had made love to her. He had been so gentle and sweet. The memory made tears come to her eyes.

"Wow," Jessica said. "So did he fall in love with his nurse, then?"

"Well, I guess he had already cared about me a great deal, but he was adamant about not making love to me until he knew he could give me everything he had to give."

"Did he tell you that?" Jessica asked, surprised that a man would be so unselfish.

"Yes, and in fact it was me that demanded that he make love to me. I told him I didn't care if he loved me or not, but that I wanted him to be my first."

"Oh my God, he was your first, too?" Jessica couldn't believe the storybook romance she was hearing. She gave Randy a conspiratorial look. "How was he?"

Randy closed her eyes, as if remembering it again. "Wonderful."

Jessica threw herself back on the couch dramatically. "I just knew it! I knew he'd be one of those real romantic types." She sat up again. "It's kinda hard to tell, with that rough exterior he likes to put on, but every now and then, you see just a glimmer of his gallant ways. Like today, when he showed that girl his wedding band—I thought that was so cool."

"Yeah, me too." Randy felt like a high school girl with her best friend, talking about the boys they thought were just the coolest. It felt good; she'd never really had a lot of girlfriends in school. She'd certainly never discussed sex with anyone, being a virgin and also painfully shy.

"So, he's really sweet and all that?" Jessica asked, dying to know more.

"You have no idea," Randy said, shaking her head. "You know, when he asked me to marry him, he actually handed me that pinky ring he wears. He told me he wanted me to hold on to it for him."

"Why?" Jessica was confused, because the ring Randy wore now was not like Joe's.

"He said he wanted me to hold on to it until he could get a real one. When I asked him a real what, he said, 'An engagement ring,' and then he looked me straight in the eyes and said, 'That is, if you'll marry me.'"

Jessica sighed lustily as she lay back on the couch again. "Why can't I find a man like that?" She looked at Randy. "Does he have any brothers?"

Randy shook her head. "Nope, he's an only child."

"Bummer," Jessica said, shaking her head too.

When Joe walked in late that evening, he looked exhausted. He had yet another bruise on his cheek as well as a nasty gash on his arm. Randy and Jessica were still talking in the living room, and upon seeing Joe, Randy went to him.

"Are you okay?"

Joe nodded, but she could tell he wasn't. Joe had actually fallen asleep in the passenger seat of Spider's car on the way home. Randy led him over to the couch, and Jessica moved to let him lie down. Randy pulled his boots off and looked up at Jessica.

"Can you get me a towel out of that closet over there?" She pointed toward the hallway. Jessica nodded and went to get it.

When she came back Randy had Joe's jacket off. She saw his bloodied forearm and gave him a scathing look. "Yeah, this looks okay, alright. You lie here—I'll be right back." She looked at him sternly, and Joe nodded, clearly tired. Jessica stood watching from behind the couch. She looked down at the man she and Randy had been discussing pretty much all evening. It astounded her how much action he seemed to see. Here she was, put off by a single incident when she had been fired upon—she hadn't even been injured, and she was too scared to return to the street. She couldn't even imagine being in Joe's shoes, getting shot, beaten up, knifed, and all other assorted evils. Jessica realized Joe was looking up at her, watching her face. She could tell he knew what she'd been thinking.

Joe shook his head slowly. "I basically ask for this stuff, Jess. It's not all like this."

Jessica nodded, not believing him. "Sure you do. You're a glutton for punishment."

"Bad guys don't like cops—that's the choice we make."

"I know. It just doesn't look like much fun, that's all."

"What, this?" Joe held up his arm. "This doesn't even hurt."

"That's because you're too damn tired to feel it," Randy said as she reappeared with a bandage and some peroxide.

"And whose fault is that?" Joe said, a lopsided grin on his face.

Randy looked immediately contrite. "Mine."

"Ours," Joe said. "And I wouldn't have given it up for anything—it was worth it." He saw a slow smile start to cross her face and grinned. "So fix me up so I can go get some sleep," he said, his voice lively now.

Randy proceeded to clean the cut, finding that it wasn't as bad as it had looked; his jacket sleeve had just smeared the blood, making it look worse. After she had wrapped the gauze bandage around his arm and taped it off, she helped him up off the couch. He leaned down, kissing the top of her head. "Thanks, Nurse."

"Anytime, Sergeant."

Joe looked over at Jessica and realized she was still thinking about what he had said. "Hey," he said, his lips twisting in a grin.

"Don't blow a gasket or anything—you don't have to make a life decision tonight. We'll talk more tomorrow, okay?"

Jessica nodded, smiling. "I'm glad you're okay."

"I'm always okay," Joe said brightly. Randy led him down the hallway to their bedroom and Jessica watched them go. These people were definitely a different breed. She knew if Joe were her husband and she'd seen him cut up and bleeding, she'd have freaked, but Randy handled it like it was any other night. Jessica realized she could learn a lot from them—that she could learn not to take things so seriously. Life was indeed short, and you had to do something important with it. She went to her room and fell asleep thinking about Joe, Randy, Midnight, and, interestingly enough, Tiny. The last thought she had before drifting off was how Tiny had come through the evening's raid. She doubted seriously that anyone would mess with a man of his apparent strength.

****

Carrie Chevalier was sitting in Midnight's hospital room, watching her daughter as she slept. Her condition had temporarily worsened, and they'd had to go in and do another exploratory surgery on her. They had found yet another slight perforation in her uterus and had repaired it. Midnight was still sleeping off the general anesthetic they had given her. She had not allowed Carrie to call anyone, saying that Joe was just getting back into his life; the last thing he needed was to have to drop everything again and come running to her side. She also

41

told her mother not to call Rick, that she didn't want to see him anyway. Carrie wasn't sure it had been a good idea, but since the surgery had gone well, she had decided it was a moot point.

Watching her daughter now, Carrie could see what a strong will Midnight had, and how much strength of character. Midnight was not wishy-washy; she didn't pine miserably, even though her husband had told her two days before that his girlfriend might be pregnant. Midnight had taken it in her stride, at least outwardly. Carrie suspected the turmoil in Midnight's personal life had in some indirect way caused the new problems in her body. If Carrie had known Midnight better, and if Midnight had been capable of it, she would have known that Midnight would have handled her anguish the same way she always had, by working herself half to death. In fact, when Midnight woke the following morning, the first thing she did was text Joe.

Joe answered from his car phone, on his way to the office after having dropped Randy at the range again.

"Aren't you supposed to be resting?" he said. He had no idea she had had surgery again the day before, and Midnight was not about to tell him.

"Buzz off, Sinclair," Midnight replied irritably. "I have nurses and doctors harassing me about that shit—I don't need you doing it too."

Joe was silent, taken aback by her quick temper. He also didn't know that she and Rick had fought a day and a half before, and that Rick hadn't been back to the hospital since.

"Look," Midnight said after a few moments, "I want you to send someone over with some of the files I've got on my desk. I need some distraction."

"No," Joe said simply, sensing her disposition.

"Don't give me that shit, Joe. I am still the boss, you know." She sounded angry, and Joe could tell her nerves were on edge for some reason; she hadn't pulled rank on him in a long time.

"Yeah," he said evenly. "You're the boss, and you are currently out of commission, and I'm not letting you bury yourself."

"I'll just call someone else," Midnight said, sighing.

"Do it. But they've all been warned, and I'll back it up again this morning that you are not to get any cases or files."

"Don't fuck with me, Joe," Midnight said icily. "I'm not in the mood."

"Don't fuck with me, Midnight. I'm not in the mood either," Joe retorted. Then his voice softened. "I'm not gonna help you kill yourself, Night, so don't ask me to."

"What's reading a few case files going to hurt? You tell me," Midnight said, changing tactics.

"Yeah, first it's two case files, then it's three. Next you're in the office half the day, then all day, and after that you basically live there. I won't let it happen, Midnight. I don't care what I have to do."

"You're a real asshole, you know."

"You got it," Joe said, and promptly hung up on her.

Midnight held the receiver tightly, her knuckles turning white. Joe had never been so immovable before. Of course, she thought, the other times she had tried to bury her problems in work, the problems had been about him, or he hadn't been around, so he hadn't been able to stop her. She did as she had threatened and contacted other members of FORS, but they all staunchly refused to bring her anything. She even resorted to trying to sweet-talk Tiny, who she knew would basically move mountains for her any other time.

"I'm sorry, boss," Tiny had said, sounding anything but. "But Joe says that you're real touch and go, and I'm not going to take any chances."

"What?" Midnight said mockingly. "You afraid Sinclair'll fire you? He can't, you know—I am the boss."

"I'm not afraid he'd fire me," Tiny replied easily. "Shoot me, yes—fire me, no." Midnight could almost see him smile.

"I give you permission to shoot him back," Midnight said, smiling in spite of herself.

"It's not Sinclair I'm worried about, boss—it's you." Tiny sounded so sincere that tears came to Midnight's eyes.

"Don't worry about me, Tiny. I'm okay, really." She was almost imploring him; she hated to have people worry about her, especially in the business they were in—distractions were dangerous.

"And you're going to stay that way."

"Okay, okay," Midnight said, surrendering. "You win, Sinclair wins. Jesus!"

Midnight hung up a few minutes later and looked over at her mother, who had been watching with interest.

"That shit has bullied everyone in my unit," Midnight said.

"I think he told them that you needed to rest. And I think they care so much about you that they don't want to risk it."

Midnight looked at her mother for a long minute, then shrugged. "I guess it could be that too."

****

Two hours later, Rick stood in the doorway to Joe's office. Joe saw the serious look on his face. He put down the report he had been reading and glanced over at Jessica, who had been reading as well. She had noticed Joe's movement and looked up, and then over at Rick.

"I'll go and get some coffee," Jessica said, standing and moving past Rick. She could tell that he and Joe needed to talk.

Rick watched her go distractedly, then looked back over at Joe. He walked into the office and sat down heavily in the chair Jessica had vacated. Joe could see the clouded look in his friend's eyes, and he wondered if Rick had talked to Midnight about Sheila. It was obvious that something had happened. Joe waited, and Rick finally brought his eyes up to meet Joe's. His eyes were bloodshot, and it looked as if he hadn't had much sleep lately. Joe assumed it was because he'd been at the hospital with Midnight.

"I'm goin' back to England," Rick said finally. Joe was so shocked that he just stared at him openmouthed.

"You're what?" Joe asked after a long moment, shaking his head as if not believing his own ears.

"You heard me right," Rick said sullenly.

Joe gave him a knowing look. He shook his head, his lips pressed together into a disapproving line. "In other words, you're gonna run."

"What choice do I have?" Rick retorted, anger flaring. "Midnight hasn't left me any."

"Midnight hasn't been runnin' your life—you have. You're just pissed because you've run it into the fucking ground."

Rick was surprised by Joe's anger, but realized he shouldn't be. Joe was nothing if not Midnight's constant champion—but he was wrong this time. "I tried, Joe," he said harshly. "I told her about Sheila. I told her that I wouldn't marry her. I told her everything, and she didn't care. She told me that she hates me now. What am I supposed to do? Wait around for her to love me again?"

"No." Joe was disgusted that he had to tell Rick what to do. "You should stay here and try to make it up to her."

"Like that's gonna work."

"Well, I guess you won't find out, will ya?"

Rick stood. "No, I guess I won't." He turned and walked out of the office, heading directly to the elevators. Joe watched him go, his face drawn and angry. Jessica walked in a moment later and, noting the look on Joe's face, turned and left again. She didn't know what had happened, but she was sure that it wasn't good.

Two hours later, at lunch, Joe told Randy about it.

"He's just going to leave?" Randy said, shocked.

Joe nodded, his expression full of disgust.

"Jesus," Randy breathed. She didn't know what to say. She had always assumed that Midnight and Rick would get back together.

"What about Mikeyla?" she asked, and Joe realized he didn't know what Rick was going to do about his daughter.

****

That evening, Midnight received a short visit from Rick's parents. They had Mikeyla with them. She ran over and tried to clamber up onto the bed. Carrie lifted her granddaughter up to sit next to her mother. Midnight glanced at Rick's parents. Anabelle looked unhappy, and Robert seemed resigned. Midnight knew instantly that something was up.

"Where's Rick?" she asked, her eyes narrowing.

"He's at the house, dear," Anabelle said hesitantly. She wouldn't meet Midnight's eyes. "He sent us to talk to you, to tell you…" She trailed off, looking to Robert.

"He's coming home with us, Midnight," Robert said as gently as possible.

Midnight stared back at him blankly, as if not understanding.

"He's going back to England?" she said finally, quietly, her shock evident. Then her expression turned wary. "What about Keyla?"

"She's going to go with us," Anabelle said, her voice implying she thought it was for the best.

"Like hell she is!" Midnight said fiercely, putting her arm around her daughter as if to physically keep it from happening.

47

Carrie jumped to her defense, turning to the Debenshires. "What right does he have to take their daughter?"

Robert looked at Carrie, surprised by the woman's sudden defense of the daughter she'd never cared about until recently. "He's not taking permanent custody—it's just a trip."

"Like I'll be able to fight all of you from here," Midnight said, her voice weakening. She hugged Mikeyla close. The child had begun to cry when Midnight yelled. "It's okay, baby," she said, kissing the top of her head gently.

Anabelle stepped closer to Midnight. "Midnight, we aren't trying to take Mikeyla away from you." Her eyes searched Midnight's. "Richard needs time away, and he thinks that being home will help him sort things out. Taking Mikeyla with us will help make your recovery easier."

"And make it easier for him to keep her." Midnight was not convinced, but it was obvious that her fight was leaving her. She was reeling from Rick's apparent abandonment; she just couldn't muster the strength to fight his parents too.

Robert and Anabelle left a little while later, but not before a heart-wrenching goodbye between Midnight and her daughter. Mikeyla had looked up at mother, her eyes wide and innocent.

"So I guess you and Daddy are going on a trip," Midnight said, purposely cheerful.

Mikeyla nodded slowly. "Daddy says we're going to where he came from."

"That's right." Midnight hugged her close, feeling like her heart was being torn out and burned but trying desperately not to let her daughter see it. "And while you're gone, I want you to do something for me."

"What, Mommy?" Mikeyla sensed her mother's unhappiness and wanted to do anything she could to make her smile again.

"I want you to remember every day that I love you very much and know that I'm going to be thinking about you. Can you do that?"

"Yep!" Mikeyla exclaimed, her voice so full of zest that Midnight had to smile. She looked up at Anabelle, her eyes so sad Anabelle wanted to cry.

"You take good care of my baby," she told the older woman.

"We will," Anabelle said, feeling terrible for what Midnight was going through but honestly believing it was for the best. She and Robert had discussed it, and they both knew that Midnight, too, needed some time to sort things through. They weren't pleased with Rick for his decision to go so far away to sort out his feelings, but they were his parents and they felt it was their responsibility to help him through this time in his life, even if they didn't agree with his methods.

As they prepared to leave the room, Robert assured Midnight that Rick taking Mikeyla to England didn't in any way indicate permanent custody. Midnight nodded slowly, still not swayed. Her eyes were already taking on a haunted look. Robert Debenshire left the hospital determined to talk sense into Rick, to make sure his son was very aware that Mikeyla was returning to America, even if Rick himself didn't. Robert would not allow his son's mistakes to ruin two other lives. If Rick decided to stay in England, the consequence would be losing his daughter, even if Robert himself had to draw up the custody papers.

Rick, Mikeyla, and his parents boarded the plane later that evening. Mikeyla was excited and chattered happily for part of the flight, then fell asleep on her father's lap. Rick had been very quiet all day, and now sat staring out at the night sky as the plane grew ever closer to his homeland and ever farther away from the woman he loved. It was clear that he was in great turmoil over his actions and their repercussions.

****

Four days later, Midnight was released from the hospital. Instead of going back to the home she and Rick owned, she went to her own house. She'd never given it up; Rick had told her she should just sell it, but she hadn't wanted to. Selling the house that was her own would be like getting rid of the last of her independence, and she couldn't do it.

She walked in and keyed the code into the alarm system. Carrie looked around the house that Midnight had owned by herself since she was twenty-four. Midnight looked around too, remembering everything that had happened in this house. She remembered the times with Joe; she also remembered the times with Rick. The memory of the night Rick had come home from the hospital, after Daniel Robbins' bullet had felled him. Midnight clamped down viciously on that thought; it had been the night she had told Rick that she loved him, and the memory served as a burning reminder.

Carrie looked over at her daughter and saw the pain flash in her eyes. "What is it, Midnight?" she asked softly.

Midnight shook her head, blinking, as if coming out of a trance. "Memories," she said simply.

They spent the rest of the day moving about the house, uncovering things and just looking around. Midnight's eyes remained haunted. Carrie tried not to bother her too much; she could only imagine what she was remembering. She had no idea that it was in this house that her daughter had been accosted by Daniel Robbins, and that the memory of that experience had triggered a much more painful one of the rape. Everything was so connected in Midnight's life that even the simplest memory led to something about Rick or Joe, and right now both subjects were difficult to think about.

Joe called that evening. Carrie answered the phone; Midnight was sitting out at the edge of the hill in her backyard, looking down at the ocean.

"Hi, Carrie," Joe said. "How's Night doing?"

"Actually," Carrie said hesitantly, "I'm not really sure. I don't know her like you do…" She trailed off as she felt a stab of guilt.

"How's she acting?" Joe asked. He felt bad for not having visited her as much the last few days, but FORS had been taking up a lot of his time, especially with Randy riding along with him—plus having Jessica there at the house and trying to get time to take her over to the range. He felt like he was running on both engines and the tanks were getting low.

"Well," Carrie said, "she's been very quiet, and she goes outside and sits on the hill a lot."

Joe was nodding. "Has she talked about FORS?"

"Actually, no."

"That's not a good sign," Joe said quietly.

"What should I do?" Carrie asked, worried now. She didn't know how to deal with this.

"I'll be there in half an hour."

Twenty-eight minutes later, Joe and Randy stood at the door. Carrie welcomed them in happily.

"Where is she?" Joe asked.

Carrie gestured in the direction of the backyard. Midnight hadn't moved from her spot. Joe leaned over, kissing Randy on the top of the head, and walked outside.

Randy looked at Carrie and realized she hadn't formally met Midnight's mother. She extended her hand to the other woman.

"Hi, I'm Joe's wife, Randy."

Carrie smiled and took her hand. "Would you like to sit down?"

"Sure." Randy glanced around the living room. Her gaze rested on the sliding glass door. "You know, I remember being here so long ago. Everything was so different then."

"Different?"

"Yes. That was when I was new to the group. Joe was always so worried about Midnight. Of course, that was before ..." Randy trailed off—as if Carrie would know what she was talking about.

"Before what?" Carrie asked, curious about anything related to her daughter. Her expression grew serious when Randy looked surprised that Carrie seemed to know nothing about Midnight and subsequently Joe. "Randy, you have to understand," Carrie said, cha-grined, "I don't know my daughter at all, and she's not someone that shares things about herself readily."

Randy nodded, knowing exactly what Carrie meant. "Well, that was a long story, but if you want to know about your daughter, Joe's the one to talk to. They've been so close for so long, I think he knows everything there is to know about her."

Carrie looked surprised. "Are you saying that they…" She ges-tured toward the two figures out in the backyard. Randy nodded, the look on her face not changing at all.

"And now you and Joe are married?" Carrie was very surprised, especially since Randy didn't seem to mind.

"We've been married for over three years. In fact, we were mar-ried in the same ceremony that Rick and Midnight were."

"And Joe and Midnight being together before didn't bother Rick?"

Randy hesitated. "You know, I think it did sometimes. I think women are just better able to understand friendships like Midnight and Joe's." But she looked a little abashed. "Well, usually, I guess." Randy looked out at Midnight and Joe, hoping Joe was making some progress. She could see that Midnight was leaning against him.

Joe walked over to Midnight and sat down next to her. She glanced at him, only a little surprised by his appearance. She'd known her si-lence and uncommunicative demeanor would eventually make it to Joe's ears. But she hadn't had the strength to fake it. She had hoped that since Carrie really didn't know her, she wouldn't know that anything was different. But she had underestimated her mother and her partner again.

"How're you doin'?" Joe asked.

"Great," Midnight said tonelessly. "How 'bout you?"

Joe shrugged. "Don't you want to know what's goin' on at the office?" he asked when she didn't say anything else.

Midnight looked at him for a long minute, then nodded.

Joe launched into a lengthy explanation of the current cases, and halfway through he could see she wasn't even listening. It confirmed that there was indeed a problem.

"And then there was this spaceship, and it came down..." When Midnight continued to nod, he stopped talking altogether, his eyes on her. It took Midnight a few minutes to even realize he wasn't speaking anymore.

"Was that it?" she asked, looking over at him.

"It what?"

"I..." Midnight began, but she realized she'd been caught. She just shook her head, averting her eyes.

Joe reached out, touching her under the chin and turning her back to face him.

Midnight looked so devastated that Joe sucked in his breath sharply, his own eyes filling with such pain that Midnight started to cry, shaking her head.

"He's gone, Joe," she said, moving into his embrace.

"I know, Night. I know." He stroked her hair, silently cursing Rick for his cowardice.

He held her for a long time, but he couldn't think of a damn thing to tell her that would help. He glanced back toward the house at one point and saw Randy watching him. The look on her face was one of concern, and he took heart in the fact that she seemed to understand he needed to be here for Midnight right now. It was as if all of the doubt and trouble between him and his wife of the weeks before had never existed, and it buoyed his spirits.

"What do you want to do, Night?" he asked softly.

"Kill him," she said, and Joe couldn't help but smile.

"Now that sounds a little more like the partner I know and love."

She looked up at him, her face tear-streaked. He wiped the tears away gently with his thumb. "What can I do?" she said, shaking her head miserably.

"I wish I knew, babe. I really do." He shrugged, grinning roguishly. "You could go out and get laid—that might help."

Midnight couldn't hold back a small laugh, but then she looked back up at him and her eyes became shadowed again. "Except my favorite person for doing that has his dance card full now." She regretted saying it a second later, when she saw the desolate look cross Joe's face. She had just indirectly accused him of not being there for her, and she knew it wasn't fair. "God, Joe, I'm sorry. That's not what I meant." But she knew she couldn't take it back now, and she watched as his lips twisted in a self-effacing grimace. "Please, Joe," she begged. "Forget I just said that. You and Randy are finally getting back on track, and I want you to, really." She put every ounce of sincerity she had into her voice, praying it would be enough. She held her breath as she watched him work through the guilt she had caused.

She was thinking she'd pass out when he finally smiled and said, "You had your chance, babe." He sounded his usual jovial self, and she was relieved.

"Yeah, I'm a real idiot, I know. I guess I just picked the wrong Englishman, huh?" Her voice broke on the last word, and Joe pulled her back into his embrace.

"If I could, I'd go over to England right now and kick his ass for you." Joe heard her chuckle.

"Can't you rent a private jet or something?" Her voice was muffled, because her face was buried in his shirt.

"I'll look into it," he said seriously.

Midnight raised her face to his again and smiled. It almost reached her eyes this time, and Joe had a small hope that she was snapping out of her reverie.

Joe ended up staying a few more hours, eventually leading Midnight back into the house. Randy and Carrie just watched, not wanting to get in the way. It did occur to Randy that Midnight might in her upset mention something about how she had gotten injured in the first place, but she told herself she was going to have to face the music at some point, and if this was it, so be it.

Later, though, on their way home, Joe said nothing about it. He was visibly upset about Midnight's condition.

"I think I might have been wrong, Randy."

Randy wasn't sure what he was referring to, but she felt her heart skip a beat as she wondered if he had decided he needed to be with Midnight now. "About what?" she asked, trying to keep her voice as normal as possible.

"About not letting Midnight have any stuff from the office," he said, with no inkling of the direction her thoughts had been heading.

"Why?" Randy said, still recovering her composure.

"I think she needs the distraction right now." He shrugged. "It's like FORS is her family, and being part of it again would be like having her family to comfort her, you know?" He glanced over at Randy and saw a look he didn't understand cross her face, but it was gone a moment later.

"You're probably right," she said, smiling.

"Yeah," Joe said distractedly.

Randy was silent the rest of the ride home, and so was Joe. When they walked in the front door, they were surprised to see Tiny and Jessica sitting on the couch. Tiny stood up, looking almost like a guilty school boy. Joe grinned at him.

"How's Midnight?" Tiny asked.

Joe shrugged. "You know her—it's hard to tell sometimes. She's depressed, but I think she'll snap out of it. I think I'm gonna send her over some of the reports on the current cases."

"But Joe, you told us…"

"I know what I told you!" Joe said sharply. "But I was wrong, okay? This isn't exactly old hat to me, ya know. It ain't every day that my partner's husband takes a powder, leaving me holding the bag."

Tiny just stared back at him, not saying anything. "Look," Joe said, sighing. "I'm sorry. I'm just on edge right now, okay?"

"Yeah, man, no problem," Tiny said, still a little hesitant.

"So, just what are you doing here, anyway?" Joe asked, purposely light this time.

"Oh, yeah! I came to tell ya, we got a call in the office tonight."

"About what?" Joe prompted tiredly as he walked over to the bar and poured a shot of tequila. Randy watched him from the entryway.

"Well, it seems that the chief had a heart attack tonight," Tiny said, just as Joe knocked back the shot and subsequently almost choked.

He coughed viciously for a minute. Randy went to his side, but he held out his hand to halt her. He picked up the bottle of tequila and took a long swig. He looked over at Tiny again. "Is he dead?"

"No! Jesus, don't you think I would have called you if that was the case?"

"Well…" Joe started, holding his hands out in a "Who knows?" gesture.

"Your confidence in me is touching," Tiny said, grinning.

"Sorry," Joe said blandly, but a slow grin was starting on his face as well. "So, do they know how he is yet?"

"Nope, not yet."

Joe nodded, looking very tired suddenly.

"I think you need to head for bed, Joseph," Randy said, eyeing him critically.

Joe looked at her for a long moment, then nodded. "Thanks for comin' to tell me," he said to Tiny, and then with a nod and a short "Night, Jess," he was off down the hall.

Randy looked over at Tiny and then at Jessica, and decided she should take her leave as well. She wished them both goodnight and followed Joe down the hallway.

Tiny looked over at Jessica. "He looks like hell all of a sudden."

"I know," Jessica said, concerned. "I think all of this is starting to get to him."

Tiny nodded. They had spent the evening talking, and he felt that he knew her a little bit better. He had shown up an hour after Joe and Randy had left, and Jessica had told him she didn't know when they were going to be back and politely invited him in to wait. Tiny had accepted after a long moment's hesitation.

Tiny had looked around the living room, once again admiring Joe's house. "Wish I had a place like this."

"Don't we all!" Jessica had replied.

"Where do you live up in Sacramento?" Tiny had asked, surprising himself with his nerve. He usually grew even quieter around beautiful women.

"Still with my parents, I'm afraid." Jessica had looked embarrassed.

Tiny had grinned at her sheepishly. "I'd still live at home if my mom would let me, but she still has three little ones to take care of, so..." He had trailed off as he wondered if he was telling her more than she'd want to know.

"How many brothers and sisters do you have?"

"Two older sisters, two older brothers, and three younger sisters."

"Eight kids?" Jessica had replied, shocked. "And I thought my parents were bad!"

"Why? How many brothers and sisters do you have?"

"Only brothers, I'm afraid—three, all older."

"Must be a rough gig." Tiny had grinned, as if he thought it was anything but. "Being the baby and the only girl."

"Hey!" Jessica had said, laughing. "I came by my own room, my own phone line, stereo, TV, VCR, and computer honestly!" By this time Tiny had been laughing too.

"I'll just bet you did. The closest thing I ever got to my own TV was the time I got real sick and one of my aunts lent me her little itty-bitty black-and-white TV." He held up two fingers about an inch apart to indicate how small it was.

Jessica laughed uproariously, then looked chagrined. "I guess the last thing you want to hear was that my TV was a nineteen-inch color with cable, huh?" She pressed her lips together, trying to suppress the grin.

"You spoiled brat!" Tiny had raged, laughing all the while.

"You're just jealous!" Jessica wagged a finger at him.

"Damn straight!" Tiny had said, and looked immediately apologetic, his face a mask of embarrassment. "Oh, I'm sorry, ma'am," he said, his eyes downcast.

Jessica was taken aback by his sudden change in mannerism. She tilted her head to the side, trying to catch his gaze. "Hey! My mother's said worse than that on a good day. I come from a law enforcement family, Tiny. The last thing you can have in a family like that is a prude's sensibility."

Tiny looked up at her when she said his name, realizing that he liked the sound of her voice when she said it. In fact, he liked her a lot. She seemed really nice, and God knew she was pretty.

They had sat and talked for the rest of the time it had taken Joe and Randy to return home. Now, looking over at Jessica, Tiny wanted desperately to ask her out, but he just didn't know how. He had been so shy for so long, it was nearly impossible for him. He had no idea that Jessica was hoping that he'd ask her. When he said, "I better get going," Jessica felt crestfallen but managed to school her face to keep him from seeing.

"Okay," she said, walking him to the door. Tiny turned to look down at her. She was looking up at him. Her eyes were so beautiful, like deep, rich emeralds. Without hesitating to think, Tiny leaned down and kissed her. To his utter shock, he felt her respond, and when he would have pulled back, recovering from his temporary loss of senses, Jessica grabbed hold of a handful of the front of his jacket. Tiny was sure he had died and gone to heaven. His hands hesitantly went to her waist, and he was pleasantly surprised when she moved in closer to him. When their lips finally parted, Tiny started to avert his eyes shyly.

"Hey!" she said softly. "I'd like to think I'm a better kisser than that." She was grinning up at him.

Tiny found himself smiling as he nodded vehemently.

"Okay then," Jessica said. "So when are we going out, and where are you taking me?"

"Anywhere you want to go," Tiny replied with an abashed smile.

"Well..." Jessica said, turning her eyes skyward as if contemplating the idea. "I guess I'll have to do some research on that." She looked at him. "I guess we'll have to wait till at least tomorrow then."

"I'll clear my calendar," Tiny said sincerely.

"Well, I don't think Joe would like that too much."

"Tough," Tiny said bluntly, but his grin showed that he was just being cavalier.

Jessica laughed. "You better get going," she said, but it was obvious that she didn't want him to leave.

"Yeah." He looked at his watch. It was getting on toward 10:30. "I do have an early raid tomorrow," he said regretfully.

"Well, then I want you to go home and get some sleep," Jessica said, wagging her finger at him. "I don't want you to have the excuse of some little gunshot wound or something to get out of our date."

"No way!" Tiny said, smiling again. He felt like a giddy schoolboy all of a sudden.

"Well, go then," Jessica said, but as he turned to leave, she reached out and grabbed a handful of his jacket, pulling him back to her. Tiny put his arms around her and lifted her up, her slight weight less than half what he used for his forearm curls every day. When her face was even with his, he kissed her gently. Jessica set her forehead against his, feeling much as Tiny had minutes before—like a lovesick teenager. When he set her down, she shooed him to his car, telling him again that he'd better get some sleep.

But Tiny knew as he drove away that he wouldn't sleep a wink that night. He knew he would lie awake in his apartment thinking about her. He was right, but what he didn't know was that Jessica lay in her room at Joe's house doing the exact same thing.

Randy had gone to take a shower. Joe lay down on the bed, fully clothed, only taking the time to kick off his boots and slip his jacket off. Twenty minutes later Randy came out of the bathroom to see that he had dozed off. She knew he would; she had at least expected him to get comfortable. Shrugging to herself, she climbed into bed. Joe's arm, which had been resting above his head, came down almost automatically as she snuggled close to him, but he didn't wake totally. Randy knew he was overdoing it. She had seen first-hand in the last couple of days just how strenuous doing raids and search warrants could be. On top of that, Joe had office paperwork to complete, and he was pretty much riding herd on every member of FORS. It was a lot.

The next day, Joe actually slept in. He hadn't meant to, but Randy purposely didn't wake him. When he did get up, he went to take a shower, and half an hour later he walked into the kitchen fully dressed. Randy and Jessica were discussing Tiny as they drank their coffee.

"Are you two ready to go, or do you need to gossip some more?" he asked, his lips pressed together in distaste.

"Grouch," Jessica muttered.

"Really," Randy seconded, as she stood and walked over to him. She reached up and gave him a quick kiss, smelling the combination of his aftershave and the leather jacket he wore. It was a smell that would always remind her of him—like recognizing his signature.

Later, in the car, she watched him closely. He seemed quiet this morning, as he had the night before. She wondered what was going on with him, but she didn't get a chance to ask—the day was very hectic.

Later that night, Jessica had a date with Tiny, and Joe ended up staying at the office to catch up on paperwork. Randy actually had an evening to herself. She relaxed on the couch, leafing through her training manual, a glass of wine on the coffee table next to her. It seemed strange being in the house alone; she felt a little ill at ease. She jumped when she heard a sound outside on the deck. She walked over to the counter where her holstered sidearm lay and pulled the weapon out. Randy knew she was probably overreacting, but she moved cautiously to the sliding glass doors. As she started to look outside, the doorbell rang. Again, she felt her heart jump. But she walked toward the door, putting her gun in the back waistband of her jeans and pulling her shirt down over it. It wasn't a comfortable feeling, but she ignored it. She looked out the peephole and saw Dick Dickerson standing there. She was taken aback, and not sure if she should answer the door or not. Ever since the incident at the apartment she had avoided any possibility of running into him, and here he was at the house—conveniently the night Joe wasn't home.

"What do you want, Dick?" she called through the door. She felt like a coward, but didn't to open the door.

"I want to talk to you, Randy. Please," Dick said. He sounded apologetic.

"I don't think we need to do that."

"Yes, we do," Dick said doggedly. "Come on, Randy. Let me in."

Randy hesitated for a long time, but finally opened the door. She stepped back as Dick walked inside, watching him carefully. She had decided that if he tried anything she wouldn't hesitate to shoot him.

She walked over to the couch and sat down, careful to keep enough distance around her to be able to draw her weapon if she needed it. She looked up at him. "So, what do you want?" she said, her voice cool.

Dick sat down beside her, a little too close for Randy's comfort. She eyed him suspiciously.

"Randy, we have to talk. I mean, last time…" He shrugged. "Things got way out of hand, and I'm sorry. I guess I was just really upset about losing you, ya know?" His eyes were pleading with her to understand.

"Okay," Randy said, nodding cautiously.

"So," Dick said. He looked concerned now. "Have you talked to Midnight?"

"Why do you ask?" Randy narrowed her eyes. "Afraid she's changed her mind?"

"Randy," Dick said, his voice taking on just the slightest edge. "I'm not the only one that should be worried here. I mean, you were there. If nothing else, it would be considered obstruction of justice. That doesn't look good on a brand-new record," he admonished, as if he were shaking a finger at her. "You know I didn't mean to hurt her that bad. She just, well, she attacked me, and I had to fight back. I guess I just overdid it." He shrugged. "How was I supposed to know she was pregnant. I mean, you couldn't tell or anything."

Randy looked at him for a minute. "How did you know she was pregnant?"

Dick looked at her blankly for a moment, then, as if regaining his composure, he shrugged. "I don't know. I must have heard it somewhere along the way. Maybe you told me." He waved his hand as if it weren't important. "Anyway, I just hope that she doesn't change her mind about pressing charges, because it'll really screw us both up, ya know?"

"You more than anything."

"Yeah," Dick said, nodding. "But, hey, she should be happy. You made up with Sinclair—that should make her feel better, right?" His voice was forcibly cheerful, and Randy could see right through it. It was funny how she could see him very clearly now. He was a macho, egotistical, self-serving man, and she could see it glaringly at that moment. He was worried about preserving his skin, not hers.

"Well, that's true enough. I did make up with Joe," she said, unable to resist the jibe.

"And dumped my ass pretty quick, without even a 'See ya,'" Dick said, his voice taking on that edge again. "I didn't even get a goodbye kiss." He leered at her.

Randy stood up, not wanting to be anywhere near him. "Well, that's just life, Dick," she said, trying to make it sound like a joke. She looked at him seriously. "I think you should go. Joe'll be home anytime now, and I don't want him to see you here."

"What're you afraid of?" Dick stood up and moved toward her. Randy stepped back involuntarily, watching him.

"I'm not afraid of anything," she said, sounding more sure of herself than she felt. "I just don't want you and Joe to get into a nasty fight or something."

"Yeah." Dick stepped closer to her again. His smile was wide, but there was still a smirk in his eyes. "But you said you didn't have to worry about me hurting him, that he'd tear me apart."

Randy nodded, starting to feel a little panicked as he kept advancing on her. Suddenly her training started to run through her head—what to do if a suspect was closing on her.

"Dick, look," she said calmly. "Let's just say that things didn't work out and leave it at that, okay?" Every nerve in her body was taught, but she felt surprisingly composed now.

"Didn't work out?" Dick said, sneering. "You fucked me when you walked out on your husband, and when he crooked his little finger you ran back to him. What was to work out, Randy?" Randy shook her head, noticing to her relief that he had stopped moving toward her. She knew if she needed to, she could draw her weapon on him. He would more than likely be taken by surprise, since he couldn't know she had it at the small of her back. That knowledge calmed her. She didn't want to have to pull her gun, though. She knew that would be the very last resort—he was, after all, a cop. "I think you should just go home, Dick."

"Yeah." Dick sounded angry, but not confrontational anymore. "I'll just bet you think that." Without any warning, he leapt at her, shoving her back against the wall, his arm at her throat. She was pinned, so she had no real hope of getting to her gun. Randy felt panic rising, but she tamped down on the feeling—it wasn't going to help her out of this. Dick was staring angrily. "What does he do for you,

Randy? Huh? Is he really that good in bed? Or is it just the money? I know you miss me, don't you?"

Randy allowed a slow smile to cross her face. "Well…" she said seductively. "Actually, I do. You know these Englishmen—they don't have it where it really counts…"

"Yeah, and you know where I got it, don't you?" Dick said, husky with desire.

"I remember." Randy nodded, her eyes not leaving his. Dick moved to kiss her, and Randy made herself relax against his body. Slowly, Dick moved his arm from her throat and started to pull her close. He didn't notice her reach around behind her—he did, however, feel the cold, hard steel muzzle of her gun as it pressed into his stomach. Surprised, he stepped back, and Randy brought the gun up to point at his head. "Now," she said, her voice strong, "get the fuck out of here."

"You're going to regret this," Dick said coldly.

"You don't get out of here in less than ten seconds and you're going to regret it." Randy nodded toward the door. Dick walked over to it but turned back to her when he got there.

"Remember this moment, Randy," he said imperiously. "It's gonna change your whole life." He turned and walked out.

Randy strode over to the door and locked it, activating the security system as well. She leaned against the wall, taking deep breaths, feeling proud of herself for handling the situation. But as she walked over to the counter to set her gun down, she noticed that her hands were shaking terribly. She went to the bar and poured herself a shot of Joe's favorite, tequila. "Ta kill ya," he liked to call it. When she drank the shot, she realized why—it burned all the way down. She poured another one and drank it down. She picked up the phone and dialed Joe's office number. He answered on the third ring, sounding distracted.

"Hi," she said, trying to keep her voice steady.

"Hi," Joe replied. She could tell he was reading something, because his voice sounded distant.

"How's it going down in gang central?" she asked, wanting to beg him to come home right then. She was haunted by Dick's parting words, but at the same time didn't want to drag Joe away from what he was doing just because of her unfounded fears. Dick had left, and the security system was on—there was no reason to worry. If he came back to the door she'd call the police.

"It's, uh, goin' fine."

"Oh, okay. I just thought I'd check up on you…" Randy trailed off, her nerves still jumpy even after the tequila.

Joe picked up on it. "Randy, what's wrong?" he said, suddenly totally there.

"Nothing," Randy replied automatically. "Well, nothing I couldn't handle, I mean."

"What did you have to handle?"

"I, well… Dick came by." Randy wasn't sure how else to put it.

"He what!" Joe stood up, driven by his fear. "Where the fuck is he?" He was worried that Dick might still be there; his mind was already working on the fastest way to get home.

"He left," Randy said, starting to feel stupid for calling and upsetting him. "I'm okay, Joe. I think he was just drunk or something."

She tried to sound as casual as possible, but she knew it was too late. She could almost feel Joe's tension coming through the phone line.

"I'm coming home, now," Joe said. "Keep the door locked and the alarm on. Do you have your gun?" he asked, as if it was an after-thought.

"Yes," Randy said, patting the weapon. "Right here with me."

"Good, keep it there. And if the bastard comes back, shoot him." Joe's tone was very serious, so Randy didn't laugh, even though it sounded funny to her at this point.

"Okay," she said simply.

Half an hour later, Joe walked through the door, his eyes scanning the house then falling on Randy. She was sitting on the sofa, a shot glass next to her wine glass on the coffee table. He walked over and pulled her up off the couch, into his arms. Randy relaxed against him, feeling much safer now that he was home. Joe pulled back and looked down at her, his eyes narrowed—Randy didn't know why. His hand went to her chin and tilted her head back. "What the fuck did he do to you?"

"What?" Randy walked over to the mirror in the dining room and saw the dark bruise across her throat where Dick's arm had pinned her to the wall. "Oh," she said, not sure what else to say.

"Oh? What happened, Randy? You made it sound like he just talked to you and left amiably." He sounded angry with her now, for holding back part of the story.

Randy looked over at him, suddenly realizing how Midnight must have felt all those times they had gotten into arguments because she had been injured. On the one hand, she felt good about having handled the situation herself, but on the other, she felt comforted by Joe's concern. The two emotions warred with each other. "I didn't see the point in upsetting you. He was gone by that time, and I had the door locked and the alarm on." She shrugged. "I just kind of had the heebie-jeebies, you know, and I thought if you were close to being done…"

"You should have told me to come home that minute." His eyes softened as his concern for her started to override his anger.

"I know, but—"

"But nothing, Randy." His eyes narrowed slightly. "If that son-ofabitch ever comes within ten feet of you again, I want to know about it. As it is, if I see him, he's gonna pay for that." He gestured to her neck as he walked over to put his arms around her, looking at her in the mirror.

Randy smiled at his gallant statement and turned to face him. "I love it when you get all protective," she said, staring up into his eyes.

He smiled. "Yeah?"

"Mmhmm." She nodded.

"Good, 'cause you can't get away from it."

"It, or you?" She raised an eyebrow at him, in a good imitation of his quirked brow.

"Both," Joe said, hugging her close.

That evening when they went to bed, Joe held her just a little bit tighter, and Randy felt just a little safer.

****

71

Jessica and Tiny spent the evening together. He had asked her what she wanted to do, and she had told him anything. Tiny hadn't been sure what to suggest, so he asked Joe. Joe had recommended something fun, like the rollercoaster at Mission Bay Park.

Jessica had absolutely loved the idea. After riding the rollercoaster, they ended up walking along the boardwalk as the sun went down. Jessica stared at the sunset for a long time, not saying anything. Tiny found himself watching her profile. She looked over at him.

"What're you lookin' at?" she asked, smiling.

"You."

"Yeah, but why?" Jessica felt embarrassed for some reason.

"Because you're very beautiful," he said, surprising himself with his boldness.

"You're just saying that because you know I have my own color TV," Jessica chided him, and Tiny started to laugh, nodding.

"With cable, no less," he added, which made Jessica laugh as well.

"I knew it," she said with mock accusation. "I just knew it. All you men are the same—you take a girl out, you wine her and dine her, all so you can take her home and get to her TV set."

"Rats, you figured me out," Tiny said, pretending to be depressed.

Jessica grinned. "The question is, Mr. Asobucco, how far are you willing to go to get to my audio-visual equipment?" She quirked an eyebrow at him.

"Did you get that from Joe?" Tiny said, smiling widely.

Jessica thought about it a minute. "I don't know. I guess I've really always done it, but never on purpose, ya know?"

Tiny nodded, understanding what she meant. "Do you want to sit down?" he asked, looking just a little bit shy again.

"Sure."

Tiny sat down on the grass, and to his surprise and delight, she positioned herself between his legs and leaned back against his chest. After a moment's hesitation he put his arms around her waist and brought his face down beside hers. They sat in silence for a few minutes, then Tiny asked her the question he'd been wanting to ask the whole day.

"What happened in Sacramento?"

Jessica was silent for a moment, then she leaned her head back against his shoulder, still watching the sun sink below the horizon. "I was on patrol with my FTO. It was only my second month on the force, and we got a call that there was some action happening over on Mack Road—"

"Mack Road?"

"It's kind of like your Home Avenue here." Jessica felt him nod, his hair brushing her cheek. "Anyway, we got to the call and we heard gunshots, but we couldn't tell where they were coming from. My FTO got out and told me to call it in, so I did. He went off around this apartment building, and I wasn't sure if I should try and follow him or not. I knew that according to my training I should, but he'd been really weird about me being female and all, so I didn't want him to get pissed at me. But then I heard more gunshots, and I jumped out of the car and headed around the building. Well, there's my FTO lying on the ground—he'd gotten shot in the leg. And the next thing I know, they're shooting at me…"

Tiny could feel her shudder as she remembered the fear that had run through her. He hugged her a little tighter, and she continued her story.

"I radioed in that I had an officer down and that I needed backup code three. They got there within three minutes, the report says, but I was so freaked out that it seemed like forever." She shook her head ruefully. "I've begun to wonder if I'm cut out for this field. Maybe I should have been a doctor or something like my dad wanted."

"Jess, that's a lot to deal with so early in your career, especially if you weren't used to that kind of thing before."

"Before?" Jessica asked, not sure what he meant.

She felt him shrug. "Well, I mean, by the time I was eighteen I'd been shot two times and knifed once, but being in a gang will do that to you."

Jessica turned to look at him. "You know, I'd forgotten that you were in a gang before you were a police officer. It's funny how there doesn't seem to be life before police work."

Tiny grinned. "Oh, I had a life before this. It was destined for really bad things, but I had one."

"How did you come to join FORS?"

"Midnight," Tiny said simply, but when he saw that she didn't understand, he elaborated. "I was laid up, having been stabbed by a guy in my own gang, and Midnight came to see me. Eventually she talked me into coming to FORS. She was so different than other cops, and she was so nice to me." He grinned sheepishly. "I have to admit, I had a major crush on her."

"I'm not surprised," Jessica said, her voice holding no malice at all.

Tiny looked at her for a long moment. "You aren't the jealous type, are you." It was a statement, not a question.

"I can be," Jessica said honestly. "But I really like Midnight, and I can see how any guy would have a crush on her."

Tiny tilted his head, as if measuring her up.

"What?" she said, not sure why he was staring at her.

Tiny shrugged, shaking his head. "Do you want to get some dinner?" he asked, avoiding her question. He'd been wondering why someone as great as her didn't have a boyfriend, but he was too shy to ask.

Jessica nodded. "Okay."

They went to TD Hayes, a restaurant on the beach. Jessica found that Tiny was a pretty good conversationalist once you got a couple of drinks in him. They talked about his family and how they were so happy that he had joined FORS and gotten a respectable life. She told him about her brothers and her father and how they all wanted her to become something other than a police officer. They even talked about Joe and Randy, Midnight and Rick.

"I'm just glad that Midnight's going to be okay," Jessica said. They had been discussing Midnight's "accident." She frowned. "What do you think happened?"

Tiny shook his head, his eyes hooded. "I don't know, but I know if I find out, there's a few of us who're going to beat the guy to death." His voice held so much loyalty that Jessica smiled.

"I just hope that Joe is right, that she's going to bounce back from all this."

"She will—she always does. It's Joe's judgement I'm worried about right now."

"Why? Because of Randy?"

Tiny nodded.

"You know about the affair, I take it?" Again, Tiny nodded. "And you're not sure what her intentions are now, right?"

"I just don't like the way she did it," Tiny said. "I mean, if she was unhappy with Joe, that's one thing—but to turn around and sleep with another cop? Knowing Joe'd hear about it? That's something else totally."

Jessica looked at him for a long moment, thinking about what he'd said. "What if that wasn't her real intention?"

"What do you mean?"

"Well, I've talked to Randy, and she really loves Joe. She was just being stupid and trying to prove her independence when she walked out. She didn't really intend on having an affair… It's like the affair found her."

"So what are you saying? That Dickerson wanted to sleep with her because Joe's a fellow cop?" He shook his head. "That's not how we usually operate."

"I know, believe me," Jessica said, her brows drawn together as her mind clicked away. "It just seems strange that she'd do something that she knew would get back to Joe, especially if she still loved him as much as she does."

"Well, I think she wasn't thinking, and she just did what she wanted and didn't think about the consequences. And that's why I'm still mad at her."

Jessica looked at him for a long moment, still thinking about it, but eventually she shrugged it off.

The rest of the date proceeded casually. Eventually Tiny dropped Jessica off at Joe and Randy's. He walked her to the door and stopped, unsure whether or not to kiss her goodnight. Jessica helped him out by reaching up to kiss him.

Tiny was once again surprised at her forthright actions, but pleased by them as well, because he had a feeling their relationship wouldn't get very far if it weren't for her willingness to take some of the first steps. Tiny hadn't gotten used to the fact that he was trimmer now than he'd ever been. His weight and height had always made him feel self-conscious—although it had come in handy in the gang, it made talking to girls, and subsequently women, near impossible. He needed someone like Jess to make it easier for him. Once he was aware she was open to him, he could take it from there.

And he did. His kiss was much more relaxed this time, his hand coming up to touch her face gently, his other holding her waist. Jessica felt a jolt of excitement when he touched her. His hand was smooth on her skin, not like she had expected it to be at all. When he moved that hand to her hair, holding the base of her neck, his lips more ardent on hers, she moved in close to his body, reaching into his jacket to slide her hands up his sides to his back. She felt the shoulder holster that he wore, and for some reason that excited her just a little bit more. It was like being reminded that he was a police officer, just like her, made them more right for each other.

When their lips finally parted, Tiny looked down at her, his eyes widening melodramatically. "I guess you were holding back last night, huh?"

"You should talk," Jessica admonished.

Tiny shrugged, looking a little abashed. "Making moves on women is not my strong suit." He sounded uncomfortable and averted his eyes.

"Hey!" Jessica said, ducking under his gaze—not hard to do, since he was over half a foot taller than her. "That's okay with me. A man who's willing to let me make the first move is so much better than a guy who climbs all over me, waiting for me to tell him to stop."

"Really?" Tiny said, his voice full of wonder—he sounded very young. "I always thought it made me seem... chicken."

"More like a gentleman," Jessica said confidently.

"No one's ever accused me of that before." Tiny grinned. "Joe, yes—me, no."

"Consider yourself accused, then." Jessica stood on her tiptoes to give him a quick kiss on the lips.

Tiny left a little while later, and Jessica went into the house, using the key Joe had given her, after taking a few minutes to bring her heart rate down long enough to remember the access code. She went to her room—Joe and Randy had long since gone to bed—and after undressing and putting on a night shirt, she lay in bed thinking about Tiny. It took her a long time to fall asleep.

CHAPTER 3

The next morning, halfway into the office, Joe realized he hadn't called Midnight about the chief's heart attack and promptly dialed her number. There was no answer. He tried again, thinking he might have dialed wrong. As a last resort he tried her car phone. She answered on the second ring.

"'Lo."

Joe could hear the radio in the background. Midnight didn't go anywhere without some type of music on—anyone who knew her knew that.

"Where the hell do you think you're going?"

"Good morning, Joseph. I'm just fine, and how are you?" Midnight said, upbeat. Well, Joe thought, at least this was a change from yesterday. "Spider knew I was coming in. I talked to him yesterday. Don't you check your voicemail?" she asked.

"Sue me," Joe said lightly. "I called because I forgot to tell yo—"

"The chief had a heart attack, I know."

"How? Who?" Joe stammered.

"I got a call from the assistant chief yesterday. He wants to have a meeting."

"What for?" Joe asked suspiciously.

"Got me," Midnight said, shrugging. "Maybe he just wants to give us the chief's status and his game plan for the next couple of months, or something."

"Yeah, maybe."

"You are such a pessimist, you know that? I don't meet with him till eleven, so I'll be in when you get there. Maybe you can bring me up to speed."

"You got it," Joe said, smiling. He was happy that his partner was back, at least in some way.

They hung up, and Joe looked over at Randy. "Hopeless."

"No worse than you," Randy said, and Jessica laughed from the backseat.

Joe glanced up at her in the rearview mirror. "You be quiet back there, or I'll start drillin' you on your date last night."

Jessica quieted immediately, giving him a mock salute. Randy had already gotten the details that morning while Joe showered. She knew Joe was happy about the match between Tiny and Jessica—he thought they'd make a pretty good couple. Jessica was the right amount of outgoing for Tiny without being too much for him, and Tiny would be a nice, stable but strong person for Jessica. He knew Tiny could hold his own once he was comfortable with a woman; he didn't doubt that he could woo Jessica if he wanted to. It was Joe's intention to find out if Tiny was so disposed.

Midnight hung up her cell phone with a grin, looking over at Carrie. She had offered her mother a ride home, since she didn't expect to be going back for a while. Carrie had agreed, but she had also told her she didn't think it was a good idea for Midnight to go in so soon. Midnight had shrugged. "I really don't have a lot of choices. If the assistant chief wants to see me, I gotta go in."

Her cell went off, beeping incessantly. She pulled it off her belt, and when she saw the numbers in the message she started to grin. A few minutes later she got another text. Her grin got wider. When the third text arrived and a fourth right after it, she started to laugh out loud. Carrie, who had been thinking her daughter must be important to receive so many messages on her first day back, looked over at her.

"What is it?" she asked as the fifth text went off.

"It's my crew," Midnight said, grinning. "They're welcoming me back to work."

Carrie looked perplexed. "How?"

They came to a stop in traffic, and Midnight held up the phone. "See, they're putting in a ten, a space, and then a ten-eight. I'm the first ten, and ten-eight means 'on duty.'"

"So what are the other two numbers?" Carrie asked, noticing as Midnight scrolled through the texts that they all had two-digit numbers following each "10 10 8."

"That's their radio call numbers." Midnight looked at her mother and realized Carrie had no idea what she was saying. "A radio call number is a two-digit number that identifies the officer for the dispatcher to call back to. I'm Lincoln ten. The Lincoln is the phonetic word for 'L,' which identifies me as a lieutenant. The ten is my identifier number—probably the tenth lieutenant in the department, for all I know. Anyway, Joe is Sam twenty-two, standing for sergeant." She looked at Carrie again. "Does that make any sense?"

"Actually, yes, it does. You're a lieutenant?" Carrie hadn't realized her daughter had a rank.

"Yeah." Midnight shrugged as she switched her cell over to vibrate so she wouldn't have to hear the beeps. She clipped it to her belt so she'd feel it if it went off again, which it did. "I'm on the captain's list, but they're not promoting anyone right now." What she didn't tell her mother was that she was number one on the list, much to the mortification of many men in the department.

"Will I ever know everything about you?" Carrie asked, sighing.

"Probably not," Midnight said, with just a little bit of an edge. She was enjoying her time with her mother, but her heart wouldn't let her totally forget her lost childhood, or what had happened to Thomas because of their neglect. Jack had avoided the hospital as much as possible, showing up mostly just to pick his wife up. He couldn't handle the guilt seeing his daughter caused. His sponsor had told him that the best thing would be to avoid the conflict if he thought it might make him slip up. So that's what Jack Chevalier did. Carrie didn't like it, but she understood that Jack had to choose his own way to do things, and pushing him to see Midnight wouldn't be the best for any of them. So Carrie made the most of her time with her daughter, trying constantly to understand the complex woman she had become.

Midnight dropped Carrie off at her and Jack's home. It was a different house than the one Midnight had lived in as a teenager. It looked nice, and clean. Midnight imagined that her father was the one who kept up the yard. She had long since remembered how compulsive he had been about that type of thing when she was little. They had spent almost every other weekend in the yard, weeding, fertilizing, watering, and the rest. Midnight had remembered a lot of things from her childhood since she and Carrie had become uneasy friends again. Many times she'd ask Carrie about this or that, and Carrie would be amazed at Midnight's memory.

Now, as Midnight drove away, she looked up into her rearview mirror. Her mother stood at the curb, waving. It was strange, the twists that fate could take. Here she was, thirty years old, and she was finally getting to know her mother. But then the pain started, the stab in her heart that reminded her that her husband and daughter were in England and she had no idea when she'd see either of them. She planned to call the Debenshires that day to try and talk to Robert, to see if he knew when Mikeyla would be coming home. She had no desire whatsoever to talk to Rick. Whenever she thought about him her blood ran hot and cold. She missed him like crazy, but the pain was subsiding little by little each day. She didn't want to talk to him and have it all come back again.

Reaching over, Midnight popped a CD into her stereo—No Doubt. She'd bought the CD for one song, unable to find it as a single, but had ended up liking a lot of the tracks on it. But the one that was playing now, as she turned up the volume, was the song she had liked from the first time she'd heard it a month before. It was called "Don't Speak," and she felt it was very appropriate for her life at the moment. She always liked songs better if they meant something to her. She sang along, feeling every word.

As the music faded away, Midnight glanced down at her left hand on the steering wheel. It was bare. Serves him right, she thought as she drove on toward the office. She was comforted by the feeling of her cell as it vibrated over and over—she knew it was her other family welcoming her home, and that made her feel really good.

Joe walked into Midnight's office a half hour later. Randy and Jessica were with him, and both stood hesitantly at the door. Midnight glanced up, smiling at Jessica as she stood and walked around her desk. "I heard you were here. How are you?" She extended her hand to the other woman.

"I'm fine, Midnight," Jessica said, returning Midnight's smile with a warm one of her own.

"She's better than fine," Randy put in, grinning at Joe.

Midnight glanced at her, raising an eyebrow as she looked back over to Jessica. "What's going on?"

Jessica grinned. "Oh, nothing really…"

"She's seeing Tiny," Joe said.

Midnight looked surprised. "Really?" she said, a wide smile on her face. She looked Jessica over, as if trying to size her up, then nodded approvingly and glanced over her shoulder at Joe. "Perfect choice, huh?" Joe nodded in agreement. She looked over at Randy. "And how's the academy going?"

"Good," Randy said simply.

"So why aren't you there?" Midnight asked, sounding a little bit like a mother.

Randy looked uncomfortable as she glanced over at Joe.

"That's, uh, somethin' I was going to talk to you about," Joe said, looking a little uncomfortable himself. "Randy, why don't you two go and check out those reports we requested yesterday?"

Randy gave him a measured look, aware that he was about to take a lot of flak for his decision to counter Midnight's denial. Midnight already had her eyes narrowed at him.

Randy and Jessica beat a hasty retreat, and Midnight closed the door to her office. She walked over to her chair and sat down, leaning back and putting her booted feet up on the credenza behind the desk. She glanced back over her shoulder at him.

"I'm listening," she said, her voice a little chilly.

"Well," Joe said, shrugging as he moved to sit sideways in the chair in front of her desk, extending his long legs to rest on the chair next to it. "Randy needed to do a ride-along, and I wanted her safe. It's pretty simple, really."

Midnight was silent for a few minutes. He could tell she was trying to reign in her temper, because her foot was moving agitatedly. It was a habit she had picked up over the last couple of years, that and tapping her pen when she was irritated. "I denied that request almost a month ago," she said.

"Yeah." Joe nodded, keeping his voice even. "But that was when Randy was screwing around with Dickerson and you were pissed at her."

Midnight's foot stopped moving. She twisted around to look at him with narrowed eyes. "Are you trying to say that I let my feelings cloud my judgement?"

"Are you trying to say that they didn't?" Joe said calmly.

Midnight looked at him for a long moment. "Maybe," she acquiesced, but her tone hadn't changed much. "But I don't think Randy riding along with you is the best idea either."

"Why not?" Joe was starting to get a little irritated himself.

"Duh, Sinclair. Maybe for the same reason that you and I never stayed together too long. You have this bad habit of smothering people and making them too careful, remember?"

"Randy's not undercover, Midnight."

"No, but she's not a fully trained peace officer either."

Joe was silent. He knew she was right, but he hadn't thought about it in that way before. "So, you're saying you don't mind her here at FORS, but you don't want her with me?"

"You got it."

"Well, there's one little problem with that." Joe pressed his lips together.

"What's that?"

"They're mad at her."

"What? Why?"

Joe looked at her as if she was an idiot. "Duh, Midnight." The words Midnight so liked to use on him sounded strange in an English accent, and she found herself laughing.

She made a face. "Hadn't thought about that," she said honestly. Standing up, she looked into the outer office. "Hold on," she said, holding up one finger to Joe. She went to the door and opened it.

"Kana, Spider, Tiny, and Dibbs—front and center!" she bellowed. She turned around and looked at Joe as they moved toward her office. She tilted her head to indicate that he should leave. Joe stood up, his face showing his lack of understanding, but he left. The four senior members of FORS entered her office and took up positions. Spider and Dibbs sat in the two chairs, Kana leaned against the table in the corner, and Tiny perched on her credenza.

"It's nice to have you back, boss," Spider said. The others nodded in agreement.

"Well, thanks for the sentiment," Midnight said, making a face. "But I called you in here to chew on you a little bit, so let me do that before we have the group hug, okay?" Her tone was light, and the other four knew she appreciated their support, but she wasn't one for great shows of emotion. "I did, however, appreciate the twenty-one-text salute this morning." She grinned at them then, as all four smiled widely.

"So what else did we do this time?" Tiny asked, suspecting he knew what she was going to say.

Midnight looked at them seriously then. "I want you to lay off Joe and Randy."

There were snickers and coughs. It was obvious they didn't like the idea.

"Is that how you'd react if I got back together with Rick?" she said, the look on her face indicating the remoteness of that possibility.

"It's not the same thing," Kana said, her eyes narrowed.

"Why not?" Midnight asked, without any anger.

"Because Rick screwed up, but it wasn't with another cop—that makes it different," Dibbs said.

"Come on," Midnight said, shaking her head. "I know she fucked up, believe me. I wasn't real pleased with her actions either…"

She trailed off, knowing they had no idea how much Randy's actions had affected her personally. "But here's the thing. Joe loves her, and they're back together. That's what counts in the end, isn't it?"

"Not really," Spider said.

They weren't giving an inch. Midnight grinned. They really were like a family. Joe and Midnight were the parents, and they were the stubborn children. When one of their parents made what they perceived as a bad choice, they dug their heels in and wouldn't let up.

"Oh, come on, guys!" she said, exasperated. "Haven't you seen the guy? He's happy as hell, and it makes me sick, but none of you saw how unhappy he was up in Sacramento." She shook her head. "I don't ever want to see him that bad off again, and if Randy makes him happy, what right do we have to tell him he's wrong?"

Tiny was looking at her, and she stared back at him. "What, Tiny?" It felt like she was under a microscope.

"I heard about Sacramento," he said, and Midnight knew exactly what he was talking about. She wondered mildly if the other three did too. She realized they didn't seem to—but they wanted to now.

"Shit," she said, and went to sit at her desk. She looked up at Tiny. "Joe tell you, or did Jessica?"

Tiny grinned shyly when she mentioned Jess, but he shook his head. "No, Joe told me. Jess wouldn't tell me something like that. She knows it's private."

"Yeah," Midnight said. "Well, Sinclair's got a big mouth."

"Excuse me," Spider said, looking between her and Tiny. "What're we talking about here?" He looked hopeful.

Tiny nodded, confirming what Spider was thinking. The other two got it shortly after that.

"So how come you two didn't stay together?" Kana asked, sounding to Midnight like a kid asking about her divorced parents getting back together. "That way you could get rid of both pieces of deadwood in one shot."

Kana had always liked Rick, but she didn't like what he had done to Midnight, and for that reason she had changed her mind. It was that easy with gang members—your friend one day, your mortal enemy the next.

"Kana," Midnight said, with a warning note in her voice. Then she looked at the others. "Look, we have to work together here, and Joe's getting a lot of negative shit coming his way, and he doesn't need it right now. Okay?" She looked at them sternly. "And I want it to stop." Her eyes pinned each of them in turn. "Now."

"We have no control over the other members," Dibbs said, sounding rebellious.

Midnight flashed him a nasty look. "Don't play dumb with me, Dibbs. They'll follow you fours' lead, and I want you to lead them down the happy-go-lucky members path. You got it?"

All four of them moaned, shaking their heads or looking up at the ceiling.

"Hey," Midnight said, her tone softening. "I'm askin' here, okay?" She knew she couldn't issue an order that they all play nice, but that if she did, they'd follow it without question—and if that was what it took… But they were nodding now, guilted into agreeing. "Oh, what good boys and girls I have." Midnight smiled as they started to grin at her. She looked down at her watch. "Ah, shit. I gotta go."

"Where to?" Spider asked as the other three moved toward the door.

"Meeting with the assistant chief." Midnight made a face.

"So important," Spider said with a sardonic grin.

"Yeah, right." Midnight grabbed her jacket off the back of the chair.

Spider noticed that Midnight was wearing black cotton slacks with a white cotton button-up shirt, but she was wearing her usual black boots, with the tapered legs of her pants reaching just to the back and top of the heels—what Midnight would consider regulation. The jacket she shrugged into was the same heavier black cotton as the pants, and tailored so that it stopped right at her waist and cut in like a matador's coat.

Spider whistled. "Impressive."

Midnight slapped him on the arm. "Can't go totally casual, can I?"

An hour later, Midnight left the assistant chief's office, her face drawn and angry. She leaned against the wall just outside, trying to keep from going back in and shooting him. When she stepped away, intent on heading back to her office, she ran into someone coming the other way. She looked up, and her apology died on her lips. Dick Dickerson looked down at her as if surprised that she was there, but then his expression turned into a leer as Midnight's eyes narrowed at him.

"Well, little Midnight," Dick said, his voice low. "How are things going?"

Midnight nodded, looking daggers at him. "You and I have a date, Dickerson," she said, deadly quiet.

"Really?" He glanced down at his watch. "Well, I can't make it right now, honey, but we'll do it real soon." He reached out to pat her hand but was surprised when she grabbed his wrist and twisted his arm up and around behind his back, slamming him face first into the wall.

"You touch me again, and you'll wish you hadn't," Midnight said, her voice a harsh whisper.

The assistant chief's secretary came running out of the office, having heard the commotion. Midnight looked at the woman for a long moment, her cat-green eyes all but shooting fire, then she let Dickerson go with such abruptness that he stumbled sideways.

"You'll pay for that, Chevalier!" he yelled as she started down the hallway.

Midnight turned around. She was a striking figure in black and white, her copper-blond hair a sharp contrast. "I already have, ten times over," she said, her tone indicating that she could tell everyone who cared to hear just how.

Dickerson shut up, realizing he was taking too many chances.

Midnight nodded condescendingly. "Oh, and don't think for a minute that this is over, 'cause it's not." She turned on her heel and headed for the elevators.

By the time she reached FORS' floor she still hadn't managed to calm down. Her hands were shaking as she reached for the door to her office. Spider noticed and went to find Joe; he, Randy, and Jessica were in one of the briefing rooms, looking over reports. Glancing over his shoulder, Spider saw Midnight heading back toward the elevator with keys in hand. He picked up his pace, all but running to the briefing room, and skidded to a halt in the doorway.

"Joe!"

Joe's head snapped up.

"You gotta go after Midnight."

"What happened?" Joe asked, standing and moving toward the door.

"I don't know," Spider said, leading the way, both of them taking long strides. "But she came back from her meeting with the AC and she didn't look good at all." He glanced at Joe as he punched the button for the elevator. "She had her keys, man. I don't think she should be alone."

Joe looked at him sharply. "Fuck this," he said, gesturing to the elevator, and headed for the stairwell.

Joe took the stairs two and three at a time and managed to get to Midnight's Corvette just as she did. He leaned against it casually.

"Where're you goin'?" he asked, eyeing her. She did look very shaken up.

"Out." She gestured for him to get out of the way.

"Well, I'm going with," he said, his tone allowing no argument.

"Fine," Midnight said tonelessly.

A few minutes later, Midnight drove out of the parking lot, leaving black tracks on the pavement as she accelerated down the street.

Joe watched her, wondering if he should have made her let him drive, but he knew Midnight found driving therapeutic.

She was once again listening to No Doubt. "Just a Girl" came on, and she cranked the volume, her way of saying she didn't want to talk just yet. As Joe listened, he began to really wonder what had happened with the assistant chief. He didn't like that Midnight was singing the words with such intensity. He didn't like the lyrics—they related to women's place in society, and he knew that Midnight meant every word as sarcastically as the lead singer of the band did.

"I take it the meeting didn't go well," he said as Midnight reached over to turn the volume back down.

She shook her head, her face a mask of cynical anger. "Not well would be a pretty safe description," she said coldly.

"What'd he say?"

Midnight shook her head again, her eyes narrowed. "It wasn't so much what he said, as what he didn't say. No—come to think of it, what he said pissed me off just as much."

"Well, let's hear it." Joe could see the anger building in her, and he knew she needed to vent.

"Well, let's see," Midnight said, like she was getting ready to rattle off a grocery list. "First of all, he told me that the chief'll be out for at least six months, maybe longer, maybe forever." She looked over at Joe, and he nodded, his face solemn, but he knew this wasn't the main point. "Oh, yeah," she said, as if in afterthought. "He also told me that he was aware that my program had always been treated with a lot a favoritism, since I had managed to ingratiate myself with the chief…" She trailed off as she let her words sink in.

"Ingratiate?" Joe said, his mouth agape, the look on his face reflecting his shock. "He said that to you?"

"Yeah," Midnight said, her expression showing her rage.

"He used the word 'ingratiate'?"

"Yep," Midnight said, shrugging and giving him a hurt, angry look. "I guess 'fucked your way to the top' was too indecent for him."

"Sonofabitch!" Joe yelled, balling his hand into a fist. A lethal look came over his face. "I'll kill him."

"Oh, no," Midnight said seriously. "No, I need you with me, Joe, and getting your ass fired and thrown in jail won't help."

Joe looked at her for a long moment, not even able to guess how she was feeling. He nodded. "You're right."

"Oh, there is good news," Midnight said, but she was clearly still being sarcastic.

"What's that?"

"Well, he made it clear that his career ladder was open to my agenda if I'm so inclined."

Joe just stared at her, not believing what he was hearing. "Jesus, Midnight," he said, a mere whisper. "Who is this guy?"

"I don't know, but he's gunning for us, and we have to be ready to shoot back."

Joe could see she was trying to shrug off the impact of what she was saying. He could also see that it was affecting her deeply. He once again cursed Rick for not being there. Midnight needed the man she loved right now, and he was in England, licking his wounds.

"Oh, we'll shoot back alright," he said, his voice deadly serious.

"Hey." Midnight shrugged. "Maybe I'll make captain yet, huh?" Her words were light, but the look in her eyes was one of deep pain.

"Not funny."

Midnight drove in silence for a while. Joe knew she was angry and hurt, and he knew that what had just happened to her was the polarization of all her fears and angst over her career. To have someone dismiss everything she had accomplished with a few simple words, one in particular. Joe wanted to kill the guy, to beat him to a pulp, but he knew Midnight was right—there was nothing he could do and still be there for her.

He found himself looking at her left hand, and noticed it was bare. "You took it off?"

Midnight glanced over at him, and when she saw where he was looking, she looked back out at the road again. Her eyes narrowed just slightly. "I sent it to him," she said coldly.

"Ouch," Joe said, his eyes on her. It amazed him once again how strong she was. She didn't let anything get her down for too long; she always fought her way back. It was astounding. He had no idea that she was thinking about how badly she wanted a really stiff drink right then—a lot of them. It wouldn't diminish Joe's faith in her; it would, however, mean he had to get drunk with her. It had become an unspoken rule with them—if they were in the same town, one couldn't get drunk without the other one present. Midnight didn't want him there, though. She knew he was still repairing his relationship with Randy, plus he had Jessica there now too, and she didn't want to be another problem for him.

Back at the office, they spent the rest of the day trying to get together stats and information on current cases. The assistant chief wanted them on his desk by the next morning. At one point Midnight looked up at Joe, Randy, and Jessica, who were in her office going through stacks of paperwork.

"Why don't we just give the asshole a list of zeros," she said. "It's all he's going to see anyway."

Joe looked at her pointedly. "Let's all quit then."

Midnight's eyes showed her exhaustion. He didn't know that her head had started to ache a couple of hours before, and that she felt like someone had beaten her up all over again. Without saying a word, she went back to work. Joe caught Randy's eye, and they exchanged a worried look.

Three hours later Joe stood, stretching. "I'm takin' you home," he said to Midnight. When she started to shake her head, he pinned her with a look. "Don't give me any shit, Midnight. I'll get the rest of this pulled together, okay?"

Midnight nodded. She knew Joe could do it just as well as she could; they'd been working together long enough to know that.

Joe looked over at Randy. "You follow me, okay?" Randy nodded.

Half an hour later, Joe escorted Midnight into her house and made sure everything was okay. She turned to him, her eyes reflecting the day's events. Without a word, Joe took her into his arms, hugging her close.

"It'll be okay, Night. We'll kick this guy's ass."

Midnight smiled at the conviction there. Her fights were always his; it was good to have someone to count on all the time. Joe left a few minutes later. After making sure the house was secure and locked up tight, with the alarm on, Midnight headed over to the bar. She spent the next three hours drinking as she sat staring off into space. The house was quiet, too quiet, so she turned on the stereo, but even that she kept low.

****

Rick was doing much the same thing five thousand miles away. He was sitting in a night club, wondering vaguely what he was doing there. He had passed the week at home, just spending time with Mikeyla and moving as if in a dream. But today, he had received by priority overnight mail the emerald-and-diamond ring he had given Midnight a little less than four years before. He had stared down at it as if he couldn't imagine where it had come from, then closed his hand over it so tightly that it had cut into his palm, drawing blood. Now, he gazed down at the cuts as he lifted a shot of whiskey to his lips.

His sister Allison had dragged him here, hoping to cheer him up. Allison, who had been engaged to one of the barristers at their father's law firm when he had met Midnight, had gotten married and subsequently broken up with the young man. She told Rick that she had seen how much in love he and Midnight had been, and Joe and Randy as well, and she wanted to wait for love like that. Rick had reminded her tonight, on the way to the club, just how great love was, his voice sharp and angry.

Now he looked out over the dance floor, searching for his sister. She was dancing with some guy, and it looked like she was having a good time. Rick wondered idly if he could leave without her getting mad at him. The DJ started to mix in a new song, and a lot of people started to move to the dance floor, but Allison was heading to the table. Rick leaned back in his chair, his leg up on another one. Unknowingly, he looked a lot like Joe had many years before in the pub the Black Knights had hung out in. He was dressed all in black, his light brown curls as long as ever, his handsome face and deep blue eyes closed off to any approach. The only point of lightness was the gold wedding band he still wore on his left ring finger. It was as if taking it off would sever his and Midnight's connection forever.

Rick found himself listening to the words of the song. It was an upbeat dance track, something he knew Midnight would like. But the lyrics made him think of her; his hand tightened on the bottle of beer he now held as he closed his eyes, just like in the words of the song. The fresh pain that flooded him felt almost exquisite in its purity. The song played on, and Rick felt each word.

Allison watched her brother, and she knew he was thinking of Midnight. It depressed her to see him this way. She'd never seen her brother so unhappy, not even when Sheila had told him she might be pregnant. The first time, Allison reminded herself. It had eventually come out that Sheila had told him once again that she thought she was pregnant. Allison couldn't believe it—she knew her brother was smarter than that.

"I have the CD if you like this song," she said. He opened his eyes, and his lips twitched in a slight smile. He knew she was trying desperately to cheer him up; he also knew her mission was hopeless. But he nodded at her offer. He knew hearing the song over and over would depress him more, but he felt the need to wallow in his dejection.

"Well," said a voice from behind him. "Look who's here."

Rick turned. Teddy Anne stood looking down at him. She took in the look in his eyes, but also the wedding ring he still wore. She leaned down and kissed him on the cheek. Allison, ever polite, invited her to join them. Rick's eyes flickered over to his sister, but he didn't show any real reaction. Allison knew Rick didn't want anyone to join them, that he wanted to sit and get drunk and stick to himself. But she figured that if nothing else, he wouldn't be rude enough to walk out with Teddy Anne sitting at the table too.

Allison was asked to dance again a few minutes later, and she went off. Rick ordered another shot of whiskey. "On second thoughts," he said, reaching into his shirt pocket and pulling out an American hundred-dollar bill. He dropped it on the waitress' tray. "Bring the whole bottle."

The waitress' eyes opened wide—he had just given her a sizeable tip. Megan Jones smiled widely. She'd already decided that he was probably one of the best-looking men she'd ever seen. She even considered making a pass at him. As a rule, Megan didn't date the men in the bar—at twenty-four, her attractive body and pretty face brought her a lot of attention, especially with the short, tight skirt she wore, with sheer black stockings and three-inch black heels. Her shirt was brown velvet and cropped an inch under her breasts—which were also eye-catching. Rick didn't even notice; he was busy looking out over the crowd again, ignoring Teddy Anne completely.

Teddy Anne watched him. She was wearing a white silk sleeveless blouse, open invitingly just above her breasts, and skin-tight black pants with a chain belt that accentuated her slim figure. She had gotten even more rowdy since Rick and Midnight's engagement party. Rick's rejection had sent her into a tailspin. Just when she'd gotten over him, here he was again. His dark, brooding silence served to attract rather than repel her. She moved to sit next to him. His deep blue eyes fell on her, but there was no interest in them.

"So what are you doing home?" she asked. She had to put her lips up to his ear so he could hear her over the music. She inhaled the smell of him. He always wore the same cologne; it was spicy, but very masculine, and combined with the smell of the leather jacket he wore, it was a heady scent. Teddy discovered that she still wasn't immune to this man. She never had been able to get used to his sharp good looks or the way he spoke, or the way his eyes could look right inside her. He wasn't looking at her now, and she found herself wanting to make him, so she could feel the electricity of his gaze again.

"Visiting," he said simply.

"I see." Teddy nodded. She knew something had to be going on in America for him to be back and looking as morose as he did. She hoped that his marriage was over. Her pride was still injured from her and Midnight's confrontation the night of the engagement party. Midnight had challenged Teddy to try and take Rick back. Teddy had thought it would be easy—she'd been very wrong. Rick had ended up wounding her deeply, a wound that had just started to heal. Now Teddy figured she had another chance to win him back. She watched as Rick set down the empty beer bottle, and saw the cuts on his hand.

"Good lord, Richard," she said, reaching out to take his hand and looking more closely at his palm. "What have you done to yourself?" She looked up at him. He was gazing down at the cuts as if he didn't really know how they'd gotten there. "Does it hurt?" she asked. The gashes were surprisingly deep, the solitaire stone having ground into his hand—he hadn't felt it at the time.

Even now, he looked down at his hand with only mild curiosity. He opened and closed it, as if checking to see if it hurt. It did when he made a fist or opened his hand too wide. The sharp pain felt good. It was as if by inflicting it on himself, he was somehow atoning for the pain he was causing Midnight and Mikeyla. His daughter asked about her mother frequently, and it hurt Rick every time. He knew that taking her all the way to England had been an asshole thing to do, but he'd managed to convince himself that it would be for the best. Now, as he looked up at Teddy and saw the concern mixed with desire in her eyes, he felt himself sink a little deeper into the mire.

The waitress showed up with the bottle of Jack Daniels, and Rick looked up at her gratefully. He broke the seal on the bottle and, taking the glass the waitress had set down on the table, proceeded to pour shot after shot, drinking them down in succession. When he looked at Teddy again, he felt the beginnings of the numbness he was searching for. Teddy's eyes reflected surprise at his disposition—she'd never seen him drink himself into a stupor. They'd always drunk together, but Rick never overindulged, always wary of losing his edge. He had always been happy and gregarious, drunk or not.

"What has that woman done to you?" she said.

"Done?" Rick's eyes were on her again, but she could tell he wasn't really seeing her.

"Yes, done, Richard." She reached out to touch his hand, ironically brushing the cold metal of his wedding ring. "You've never been like this. She's changed you."

Rick didn't say anything. His eyes had gone to her fingers on his. He idly compared her highly manicured hand to Midnight's small, unpolished hands. Rick knew he was drunk, and that if he continued

101

to drink he wouldn't feel anything anymore. That was his goal, and Teddy was distracting him.

"Teddy," he said, his voice low, his lips right next to her ear. "Don't you have somewhere to go?"

Teddy's breath caught in her throat at his sudden nearness. She could feel his breath on her ear, and she could smell the whiskey on it. But it made her almost shudder with yearning for him. Turning her head just slightly, she looked into his eyes. His face was so close to hers, and she wanted him so much. "Anywhere you are, Richard," she said, her eyes telling him everything her body was screaming at her.

Rick sucked in his breath sharply, seeing her naked desire. It had been so long since he'd been with Midnight, or even Sheila. His body responded even as his heart backpedaled. Without a word he stood and, taking Teddy's hand, led her from the club. Once in the parking lot, she guided him to her car—she knew he was in no condition to drive. She turned to him, looking up into his eyes. She started to speak, but Rick's lips silenced her. After that, she couldn't catch her breath long enough to try to talk.

Rick shoved her roughly against the passenger door of her car, his lips bruising hers in his fervor. He didn't want her to say anything—he didn't want to think about what he was doing and what it would mean. He felt her hands in his hair, and he reached up, taking them and bringing them back down, holding them to her sides. Midnight always entwined her hands in his hair when they kissed, and he didn't want to be reminded of that.

Keeping her hands where they were, he pressed his body pressed against her, and his lips devoured hers. Teddy wanted him more than she had ever wanted a man, including when they had been together before. His intensity was almost frightening, but it was exciting too. She found herself identifying with those women who liked the "rough stuff," and when Rick's hands released hers and clutched her upper arms, his fingers digging into the delicate skin, she almost gasped at the contact.

"Do it, Richard," she whispered harshly, all control gone now. "Do it, now, here." She was writhing with the desire for him to touch her further. She cried out when he stepped back and looked down at her. It was as if someone had thrown cold water in his face. Within moments he was scowling, his eyes reflecting the frustration he felt.

When she had spoken his name, her voice so full of passion, it had made him think of Midnight and how she sounded when they made love. It had been a glaring difference, and it had made him feel the sharp guilt instantly. Now the idea of what he had been about to do made him feel absolutely sick. He turned away from Teddy and strode off, not looking back. He blindly walked down the streets of London. He didn't pay any attention to where he was going—he just walked. He was still feeling the effects of the alcohol, but his mind was turning over and over with the thoughts of his wife. His hands were clenched into fists and stuffed into the pockets of his leather jacket. Ironically, he had pulled out his Black Knights jacket that evening, having felt nostalgic when he found it in his closet.

Rick was surprised when he walked into someone coming the opposite way. He raised his eyes to look into the face of a much younger man. The boy reached out and attempted to shove Rick backward; Rick took one step back, but didn't stumble backward as the young man had expected. Rick looked him over. He was wearing ripped jeans, a dirty-looking T-shirt, and an equally dirty jean jacket with a chain running down the front left side. He looked like all the kids he'd dealt with in the gangs in America.

Kevin Clark looked at the man whose path he had purposely stood in. He didn't know who the fuck this guy thought he was, but he was on the Coyotes' turf, and Kevin meant to teach him a lesson.

As Rick watched, the young man drew out a switchblade. Rick grinned openly, shaking his head at the irony. Here he was, five thousand miles from FORS, and he was facing a gang member again.

"Kid…" Rick said, narrowing his eyes. He saw that more men were moving toward him, and he found himself wishing he could legally carry here. Not that it mattered whether or not it was legal—he still had his gun placed snugly in its holster at the small of his back. But if he actually had to shoot someone, his dad would be bailing him out of jail later, and it wouldn't do a lot for his law enforcement career in America.

"You think you can take me, man?" the young man said, brandishing his knife. Rick moved so that his back was against the nearest wall, so no one could get behind him. His police training was kicking in automatically.

"I don't think I can, kid," he said confidently. "I know."

"Bullshit!" the kid yelled, and charged at Rick. Rick simply waited, then stepped aside at the last minute, bringing his fist up under the outstretched knife and punching the kid in the stomach.

Kevin fell to the ground coughing, in shock. He had figured the older man for an easy mark. He lashed out with the knife, catching Rick on the leg but only slicing his pants as Rick jumped back.

Someone grabbed Rick from behind. In moving away from Kevin, he had mistakenly turned his back on someone else. Rick relaxed just enough for the person holding him to think he wasn't going to fight, and then jammed his elbow into their ribs. He heard the man yelp, and Rick grabbed one of the arms still holding him and flipped the man over his shoulder. He looked around him, and was just turning to grapple with yet another young man when he heard his name.

"Rick Debenshire, what the hell?"

Rick turned, looking back at the man he had just felled. His eyes narrowed for a minute, and then he began to smile. "Tom Allen! Sonofabitch!" He held his hand out to the other man, helping him up off the ground. Tom was holding his ribs gingerly, but he was smiling. He held his hand up to the other members of the gang, who had paused.

"It's okay," Tom said, his accent thick. "He's cool—known him for years."

"So he'll give us his wallet without a fight," Kevin said, eyeing Rick angrily, pissed about being taken out so easily.

Tom looked over at Kevin sharply. "Kev, I think if you're smart, you'll be backin' off now. Rick here could take you, me, and half the gang without battin' an eyelash."

Rick was grinning at the other man.

"An' just how do you know?" Kevin said, loath to let go of his anger.

"'Cause I was in the Knights with him, Kev. Now shut up!" Tom said. The rest of the gang looked sufficiently cowed. He glanced over at Rick. "Heard you became a cop. That true?"

Rick nodded. "In the States, yeah."

Tom looked at him for a long moment, as if trying to decide how to take the fact that his former friend was a police officer now. Then he inclined his head, indicating a bar a few doors down. "Come on."

They spent the next hour catching up. Tom Allen had actually been a very junior member of the Knights, having only been fifteen at the time. Now, at twenty-five, he ran the Coyotes, but he assured Rick that they just dabbled in the light stuff, much like the Knights had. "I don't go for all that drug dealin' an' shit."

Rick nodded. "Good thing." His voice was serious, but his eyes showed humor. He was pretty far gone, after sharing a bottle of Jack Daniels with Allen. Tom's eyes fell on Rick's wedding band.

"You married, man?"

Rick looked as if he were considering the question for a moment. "For now," he said finally.

"An' what's that supposed to mean?"

"Things aren't workin' out." He didn't really want to talk about it.

"She get fat or somethin'?" Tom said, grinning. "You were always into the ladies. Can't imagine one that could hold you down."

Rick gave the other man a measured look. He pulled out his billfold and flipped to a picture of Joe and Midnight. The photo had been taken at a party a couple of years back. Midnight was wearing all black—jeans, boots, and a satin shirt. Her hair was wild, and she and Joe were laughing. He showed the picture to Tom.

Tom whistled, his eyes almost bugging out of his head. "An' she's in the States?" Rick nodded. "What the fuck're you doin' here?" Then he looked at the picture again. "That Joe?"

"Yeah."

"How's he doin'?" Tom asked, surprised to see the former leader of the Knights with Rick's wife.

"He's good—he's married too." He showed Tom a picture of Randy and Joe.

"Nice piece." Tom said, grinning.

"Yeah," Rick said, his face serious. "Anyway, he's a cop too. In fact, he's my boss, and Midnight's his."

"Midnight?"

"My wife."

"She's your boss too, then?" Tom looked shocked.

"Yeah. Scary, ain't it?" Rick said, his eyes bleak.

"Incredible's more like it." Tom leaned back in his chair and looked Rick over. "So what's goin' on with you and her?"

Rick shrugged. "It's a long story, man. Let's just say we don't see eye to eye on anythin' these days."

"You love her?" Tom asked, surprising even himself with the question.

"Too goddamned much," Rick said, shaking his head ruefully.

Tom looked back at his longtime friend, surprised by the vehemence in his voice. He had never seen Rick Debenshire in love, and he could tell Rick was definitely in deep with this one.

They spent another hour talking and drinking. Finally, Tom called him a cab and sent him home safe and sound. Rick thought about the old days on the ride back to his parents' house. He remembered Tom as a pretty nice kid, but he hoped the man didn't plan to make the gang his life. Rick knew better than anyone, with the exception of Joe and Midnight, that being in a gang could be hazardous to one's health.

When he walked in, it was four o'clock in the morning. He moved as quietly as possible, getting undressed. But once he lay in bed, he found he couldn't stop thinking about Midnight. He thought about the scene with Teddy, and it made his blood start to pump again, realizing how close he had come. His body even now protested the denial of what it had wanted so badly for a few intense minutes. Thinking about sex, his mind moved directly to thoughts of Midnight. The way she looked when she wore one of his shirts and nothing else, the way she looked during their lovemaking. Her voice, her hands on his skin and entwined in his hair. Without stopping to think, he reached over and picked up the phone. He dialed their number. There was no answer, and he hung up. After a few minutes he picked up the phone again and dialed the number for Midnight's house. She answered on the fourth ring.

"Yes?" She sounded a little out of it, but not sleepy. Rick closed his eyes at the sound of her voice—it made him ache all over again.

"Midnight," he said, his voice husky from the barely contained lust he felt. He knew it was a combination of frustration and alcohol, but he didn't care.

"What do you want?" she said, her voice taking on an edge.

"You," he said simply, and heard her sharp intake of breath.

Midnight had heard the desire in his voice, and her body had responded automatically. She had to fight to hold on to her anger. "Don't, Rick. Not now."

"I can't exactly do anything from here, can I?" he said wryly, but the ache in his voice hadn't receded.

"Please," Midnight breathed, closing her eyes against the tears that sprang to them. She knew she should hang up, but didn't.

"Please what?" he said, his voice full of innuendo.

"Don't, okay. Just don't." It was obvious to him that she was trying desperately to hold on to her control.

"Don't what?" he asked softly. "Don't talk to you, don't think about you... don't think about us, together?" He sounded more intense with each word, and Midnight found herself shaking.

She was silent for a long moment, fighting to get control of her emotions. "Rick, I—"

"That's it," Rick said, his voice deep.

"That's what?"

"The way you say my name when you want me—that's what has me hooked. No one else does that to me, just you." His voice held all the pent-up passion and need that his body had been awoken to earlier that evening.

"Does what to you?" Midnight asked, turning things around on him.

"Jesus," Rick said, closing his eyes. "I miss you so much, your body, your lips—everythin'."

"But my body particularly at this moment," she said knowingly.

"God, yes. I want you, like no one else I've ever wanted."

"Do you?" she said, close to regaining her composure. Rick could sense it, and he didn't want it to happen, but he had no idea how to stop it. If he'd been there in front of her, he'd have been able to make her lose her self-control. He cursed the miles between them, and cursed himself for putting them there.

"Midnight…"

"Richard," she said, purposely using his full name. He felt the jab from five thousand miles away.

"Damn it, don't do that," he said, anger starting to creep in.

"Use your name? Why not?" She sounded perfectly normal now.

"You know what I mean. By the way, I got your package today."

"Oh, good," Midnight said lightly. "I had it insured, in case you were worried."

"I wasn't." Midnight was silent. "Why?" he asked, hurt now.

"It doesn't mean anything anymore, Rick. It's just a ring now. I didn't want it on my finger, and I didn't want it in my house." He could almost see her shrug. "I figured your family'd want it back."

"I want it back," Rick said, his voice strong and sure. "On your finger."

"I wouldn't hold your breath," Midnight said, then hung up.

Rick lay back, looking up at the ceiling as he listened to the hum of the dial tone. He knew his phone call had accomplished nothing. He had hoped to sweet-talk her into coming to England so they could have some time together, or something. But now they were even farther away from each other than before.

The next morning, Rick talked to his father about the divorce papers Midnight had filed. Robert told him that even if Rick contested the divorce, if Midnight acquiesced to his demands, in less than five months their marriage would be over. It made Rick almost sick to think about it. Over the next few days, his heart hardened into stone. He spent time with Mikeyla during the days and went out at night. He drank and ran around. He wasn't the same gregarious person he had always been, but women were attracted to him just the same. He always stopped just short of sleeping with them, as if crossing that final line would be the real end to his marriage.

CHAPTER 4

Four days after her encounter with the assistant chief, Midnight found herself in yet another meeting with him. Greg Dearborn had taken to calling himself the acting chief. He was a slick politician, and she hated his guts. Even now, he was looking at her like she was some kind of prize.

"Look, Dearborn," she said tiredly.

"Chief."

"You aren't the chief."

"For what you need, I am," he said, leering at her.

Midnight narrowed her eyes at him. "I'd watch your step if I were you, sir. The press just loves sexual harassment cases these days."

"Am I harassing you, Lieutenant?" Dearborn said, feigning a look of surprise.

"Just give me the approval I need and let me get out of here." Midnight wished idly that she had her baton. She'd love to accidentally cave his skull in for him.

"In a hurry, are we?"

"Look." Midnight stood. He watched her every movement. "Just call one of my people when you have my answer, okay?" She turned and stalked out of the office, slamming the door behind her.

Greg Dearborn sat staring at the space where she'd been. She was one hot-looking woman, and he'd be very happy to make her a captain—if she'd make him happy. As his secretary tapped on his door, he schooled his features, feigning pleasant, business-like manners.

Greg Dearborn had come up through the ranks stepping on anyone that got in his way. He was what would be considered an old-time cop. He thought women didn't belong in the business; he basically thought women belonged in one place, and that was under a man. Literally. But he was very good at hiding his opinions and playing the game. That's how he'd made it all the way to assistant chief. And now he had his eye on the chief's position—if the old coot would just die, it would make things easier. Dearborn had high aspirations; he expected to make governor within the next fifteen years, and being the chief of the San Diego Police Department was going to get him there.

He'd disliked Midnight Chevalier's unit for a long time, since they seemed to receive much more notoriety than his own unit—vice. For many years, after the advent of television shows like Miami Vice, his team had received a lot of critical acclaim. But then this broad from a gang had made a lot of noise and turned a lot of heads—with her ass, Greg figured. For years now, his unit had been losing money while Midnight's had gotten more and more. When he'd made assistant chief two years before, he had tried to tell the chief that Lieutenant Chevalier had outlived her usefulness, that she wasn't producing as many results as she had before. The chief had been adamant about upgrading Midnight's budget each year, saying that even if her results had slowed ever so slightly, the notoriety that her unit was bringing to the department was invaluable.

Greg Dearborn had set his sights on Midnight Chevalier. He had two goals where she was concerned—he wanted to nail her, and then he wanted to fire her.

Back in her office, Midnight threw herself down in her chair and put her booted feet up on the desk.

"Good news?" Joe asked, standing in her doorway.

"That asshole! Now he's fucking with requests that used to get rubber-stamped." She shook her head. "I don't know, Joe. I may kill him if he keeps it up."

"Do it," Joe said, his voice serious. "I'll testify on your behalf."

Midnight grinned at him, closing her eyes for a moment. She glanced past him out the door and saw Tiny talking to Jessica about a case he was working on. They seemed very comfortable together now. As she watched, Tiny put his hand on her leg and looked into her eyes, and Jessica smiled up at him.

"What's the deal with Jess?" she said. "When's she supposed to go home?"

Joe shrugged. "Tomorrow, I think, but I'm beginning to wonder if she's thinkin' about stayin'."

Midnight looked at him, then out at Jessica again. "She'd be a great addition to the department." She rolled her eyes. "Any other time, I'd be the first to make a recommendation, but I think my recommendation would fall on deaf ears right now. Hell, it might even keep her from getting hired."

"She can apply," Joe said, shrugging.

"Randy back at the academy today?" Midnight asked, seeing the slight look of loss in Joe's eyes.

"Yeah," he said, knowing what she was thinking.

"You liked having her around, didn't you?" Joe nodded. "Yeah, but do you like the idea of her being a cop now?" Midnight continued, keeping her eyes on him.

"Ya know," Joe said, looking surprised at his own thoughts, "I'm gettin' used to it, and in a way we're closer now, because she understands me better. It's weird."

"It's not weird, Joe. We cops are a different breed, and it takes other cops sometimes to understand us."

"I guess."

"Trust me," Midnight said, looking weary.

"You gettin' enough sleep?" he said, taking in her appearance.

"Probably not."

"You talk to Rick again?" She had told him about Rick's phone call four nights ago. Most of it, anyway.

"Hell no," Midnight said, looking at him sharply. "I did talk to Anabelle though, and she let me talk to Keyla." She shook her head, tears springing to her eyes. "I miss her so much, Joe. I didn't think I'd ever be dependent on such a little person before."

Joe grinned at his partner, never having thought she would either. "Did Belle say anything about when they'd be sending her home?"

"No, I didn't ask. I think I was afraid she'd tell me never."

"She say anything about Rick?"

"I didn't ask about him either—I think she got the hint."

Joe nodded.

Later that day, Midnight was heading to the courthouse to pick up some warrants she'd applied for when her car phone rang.

"Yeah?" she said, hitting the button for hands-free.

"Midnight?" Phil Griffin said, glad to have gotten ahold of her.

"Griff! How's it goin'?"

"It's goin' okay, Midnight. How're you?"

"Oh, busy as ever."

"Good, I like to hear that. I was worried about you for a while there."

"I know, Griff, and I appreciate it. So what's up?"

"Well, I got something here I think you should see," Griff said, his voice taking on a funny tone.

"What is it?"

"Well, some of our VSU guys hit a house this morning, and the lead agent just brought some stuff in to me that they recovered. I thought you should see it."

"Okay…" Midnight said, the hairs on the back of her neck standing up. She looked down at her watch. "I'll be there in an hour."

The receptionist at the BNE offices knew her and buzzed her in automatically, paging Phil to go back to his office. Midnight and Phil reached his door at the same time.

"Hey!" Griff said, reaching out to hug her. Midnight moved easily into his embrace. Griff let her go a few moments later and motioned for her to precede him into his office. Once he was seated behind his desked, he looked over at her. "So, how're things at SDPD? I heard the chief had a heart attack—how is he?"

Midnight made a face. "He's alright, I guess. Of course, I'm not exactly getting updates. The assistant's too busy busting my chops to give me any important information."

"Who's the assistant chief right now?" Griff didn't like what he heard in Midnight's voice, and knew there was a lot more to it than what she had just said.

"Greg Dearborn. Ever heard of him?"

Griff thought for a few moments. "Nope. What's he up to?"

Midnight didn't answer for a long moment, but then she shook her head. "Never mind. I don't want to get into interagency gossiping right now. Just suffice it to say, he's making my life difficult at the moment."

"Okay…" Griff wasn't really satisfied with her answer, but he knew Midnight was the last person to ever complain about her own plight.

"So what's this stuff you wanted me to see?" she asked.

Griff reached down and picked up a small box. He dropped it on the desk between them. Midnight reached over and gingerly picked up some of the papers it contained. She scanned the writing, narrowing her eyes as she realized what she was reading. She looked up at Griff sharply. "DMV printouts?" she said, her voice deathly serious. The one she held was on Spider.

Griff nodded. "Why do you think I wanted you to see it?"

Midnight looked at the sheet more closely. "This one's old. Spider doesn't live there anymore. But…" She trailed off as she thought about the possibilities. She didn't like any of the thoughts that came back to her. "Shit," she said, and Griff nodded, his expression very serious.

Later that day, Midnight and Joe went through all of the papers in the box Griff had given her. Much of it was basically junk—it was like they'd been searching through computer files with no results. Some of the papers contained a lot of machine language, as if someone had been trying to write a program or something.

There was a printout in the file for Midnight, and what bothered her was that it had her and Rick's house listed as her address—that was more current than it should be. Joe had looked up at her sharply when she'd handed that printout to him, after reading the name and address on it. Midnight had returned the stare, her eyes very serious.

"What does all this mean?" she said, scrubbing her face tiredly.

"Who had this stuff?"

"A gang called Perros Locos," Midnight replied, her accent perfect on the Spanish words.

"Which means what?"

"Crazy Dogs."

Joe grinned. "Sounds more impressive in Spanish."

Midnight laughed. "Yeah, it does."

"Think we should talk to them?"

Midnight thought about it for a minute, but then shook her head. "Let BNE finish up their investigation first. I don't want to tip them off that we have this stuff just yet."

Joe nodded, always trusting her judgement on these things.

****

A week later, Jessica had indeed stayed in San Diego. She had even gone so far as to look for an apartment. Joe had told her he'd be happy to help her with deposits or whatever, or she could just keep staying with him and Randy. Jessica had smiled at him, but shaken her head. "I think you two need to be alone a little more right now."

Joe had returned the smile. He knew she and Randy talked all the time. "Fine," he said, shrugging.

Later that night, he and Randy were alone, since Tiny and Jessica were out on yet another date. They spent a quiet evening together, part of which was spent on the deck, watching the sun go down. Randy had made dinner and they took their time eating, enjoying each other's company. Randy told him about her progress at the academy. They'd had another range shoot, and her score had been downright respectable. She'd learned a number of things from Joe. He'd taken her to the range with him and taught her how to line up her shots, and how to keep the muzzle of the gun from jumping up every time she fired. It pleased her to no end that he cared enough about her career now to help her and teach her things that he had never imagined she'd ever need to learn. It was a different experience for Joe as well. He found that he enjoyed being able to talk to Randy

119

about police work. It was almost fun to have someone to teach and talk to that would understand everything he talked about, or would try to.

They ended up staying up late, watching Braveheart, a three-hour movie, on HBO. They fell asleep fully clothed on top of the covers with the TV still on. They never heard the intruder.

****

Rick sat in a night club with Teddy and some of her friends. Teddy had not really forgiven him for walking out on her that first night, but she was determined to get him into bed now. Her friend Romi had been eyeing him too, and Teddy was busy trying to fend her off.

"So Teddy says you live in America?" said Romi, a dark-haired, dark-eyed Mexican girl, her voice sultry.

"Yes, I live and work there."

"What do you do?" Romi asked suggestively.

"I'm a cop," he said, deadpan.

Romi looked taken aback. "But your family—they have money, no?" She looked over at Teddy, as if trying to decide if her friend had lied to her.

"Yeah, my family does, but I don't." Rick was growing weary of playing these little games. He'd forgotten how tiring being with society women could be.

"So where in the States do you work?" Romi looked mildly interested.

"California, in San Diego."

"Really? I just love San Diego. A lot of places to sunbathe and buy good dust."

"Dust?" Rick eyed the woman, sure he knew what she was referring to.

"Cocaine, you know," Romi said, elbowing him.

Rick didn't even smile. "Yeah, I know."

"You don't work narcotics, do you?" Romi was suddenly aware that she might be saying something she shouldn't.

"No, gangs." Rick was ready to end the conversation there, but Romi looked surprised.

"What place?"

"Place?"

"You know—place…" She trailed off as she tried to think of the right word. "What is the word… Ay, dios mío. Place… ah, unit?"

"I work with FORS. Why?"

"Ay, es muy bien that you don't work there now then." Romi nodded meaningfully.

"And why's that?" Rick said, getting bored with the woman's game.

"I was with this guy a while back, and he was a real nasty one. He wanted a couple of policías dead in the worst way, you know." She looked at him to see if he caught her meaning. When Rick nodded she continued. "I wouldn't want to mess with him—he's dangerous." She shook her head, the look in her eyes suggesting she was remembering just how bad the guy was.

"What was his name?" Rick asked, mildly interested again.

"Carlos, but he wasn't doin' the hit. He had someone else. He was too high up. But he had plans for one policía in particular."

"Was this guy's last name Rivera?" Rick was sure she was talking about when they'd used the Scorpions to try to get rid of FORS.

"Yeah, that was him. How do you know?"

"'Cause he already tried to get rid of FORS, but his little hit squad failed."

"Oh." Romi nodded. "I didn't think he was ready yet." She shrugged. "But I could be wrong."

"Ready yet?" Rick said, thinking the woman had inhaled too much cocaine in her time. "This happened almost four years ago."

Romi looked at him for a long moment and then started to shake her head. "Then we're thinking of different people."

"No," Rick said, looking confused. "It was the Riveras—we never got to them, but we knew it 'cause Daniel Robbins told us before he ended up dead."

"Who's Daniel Robbins?" Romi said.

"He's the guy that the Riveras sent after FORS." He looked at her. "You didn't know much about their little plan, did you?" he said somewhat scornfully—some informant she'd make. "Daniel Robbins ran a gang called the Scorpions, and they were the ones that tried to take out FORS, but we got them in the end."

"Well, I'm not sure who Daniel Robbins is, or these Scorpions, but that isn't who Carlos was working with."

"How long ago were you with this guy?" Rick said, irritated by her obvious confusion.

"Last month."

Rick's blood ran cold. He was up and searching for a phone a moment later.

He ordered the bartender to let him into the small office behind the bar, identifying himself as a police officer. "Not here, you aren't," the man said, not recognizing the badge Rick showed him.

Rick pulled out his gun and stuck it under the man's chin. "I am a San Diego police officer, from the United States, and if you don't open the fucking door, I'll kill you." His voice was deadly serious, and the man did as he was told.

Rick dialed Midnight's number. When there was no answer he did a quick calculation of the time difference. It was 10:00 p.m. in England, so it was two in the afternoon in San Diego. He called Midnight's office phone.

Midnight answered on the third ring, sounding very distracted.

"Night, FORS is in danger. I think the Riveras might be gunnin' for us again," he said without preamble.

Midnight gripped the phone tightly. The office around her was full of frantic action. "Rick," she said, forcing herself to stay calm. "Joe disappeared ten hours ago."

"What!" Rick yelled. "Why didn't you call me?" He could have been back there by now.

"You aren't a member of FORS anymore—why should I call you?" she said tonelessly.

"Like hell I'm not. I'll be there in ten hours." Rick hung up.

Midnight stood amid the mass confusion. Hanging up the phone, she dismissed Rick's ire, as well as his statement that he'd be there so quickly. She'd heard what he'd been doing. She had talked to her daughter in the last week and Rick was never there. He was always out. She had finally spoken to Allison and gotten the whole story. Rick was hanging out with Teddy Anne Emerson again. Midnight figured he didn't want to mess with Sheila anymore, so he had picked up with his old fiancée.

She looked over to where Randy was sitting, reliving the last ten hours. From what she had gathered, Joe and Randy had gone to bed at about one thirty. Randy had woken to find Joe wasn't there. She had felt very groggy, and when she sat up she saw blood on Joe's side of the bed. She had screamed, which had brought Jessica running. They had looked for Joe, but he was nowhere to be found. Randy didn't know anything. She was checked out at the hospital and was believed to have inhaled ether, probably keeping her from hearing the gunshot that had left Joe's blood on the bed—it had been determined that one, it was Joe's blood, and two, he'd been shot, because there were powder burns on the sheets. It was assumed that since Jessica hadn't heard the shot, a silencer had been used to muffle the sound.

Randy and Jessica had called Midnight immediately. It was a little after 4:00 a.m. Midnight had arrived at the house less than half an hour later, followed closely by two black-and-whites and the crime scene investigators. Randy was questioned, as was Jessica, but neither woman knew anything. The crime scene team had managed to lift a partial print from the keypad, but it was only the uppermost portion of one and probably not much use.

Randy had been beside herself with worry the entire time. She apologized to Midnight for not knowing more. Midnight had nodded, her mind already working. She had headed to the office and put out a 911 text to all members. They knew the text meant they were to report in as soon as possible, and within half an hour, every member of FORS had arrived. Midnight briefed them as a group, telling them what little they had. Most of them had looked stunned. It was unreal that Joe had been taken. His life had been in danger so many times, and they couldn't believe it was happening again.

"This is important, boys and girls, so let's get to work," Midnight had said. Everyone moved toward their offices. This time there had been no threats, no imminent danger, nothing. It had happened suddenly, and that was what worried Midnight the most. There was a cold knot in her stomach as she silently prayed that Joe wasn't already dead. There'd been no phone call to demand anything, and the more time went on without one, the less likely it was that Joe was still alive.

At one point Jessica came over. "How are you?" she asked, knowing Midnight wasn't fully recovered from her miscarriage, especially since she'd come back to work a week or two too early. Midnight looked haggard and utterly on edge. Jessica understood, though. Her own heart had stopped beating when she'd run into Joe and Randy's room, finding Randy half hysterical and blood where Joe should have been. She feared the worst for Joe, having never gone through anything this terrible in her lifetime.

Midnight nodded. "Yeah, I'm fine," she said, a complete lie. She wasn't okay—she was sick with worry, her head was pounding, and a little while earlier she had noticed some spots of blood, probably from her uterine trauma. She knew it was related to all the surgeries they'd done on her, but she certainly didn't have time to worry about it now. What's the worst that could happen? she thought with a shrug. She already knew she'd never have another child.

Midnight dragged on through the day. They didn't hear anything. At five o'clock, Greg Dearborn had the audacity to walk onto the floor. Midnight looked up at him sharply when he approached her.

"I heard about Sinclair," he said. He almost looked concerned. Almost.

Midnight just nodded and walked away from him. He followed her to her office. At the doorway Midnight turned around, her eyes narrowed. "What do you want?" she said coldly.

Dearborn actually looked taken aback. "I wanted to find out what progress you'd made. Have you received a call yet?"

Midnight shook her head, the look in her eyes desolate.

Dearborn nodded, looking around and seeing a lot of people. "How many people have you got in here from your team?"

"All of them. Why?" Midnight replied, looking at him sharply.

"Well…" Dearborn shrugged. "That's a lot of overtime to burn when you've made no progress…" He trailed off, and Midnight knew he was thinking that Joe was already dead.

"Every one of my people stays on the clock until Joe's back. You got that?"

"I understand your position, Lieutenant, but I'm telling you right now—I am not burning up this quarter's overtime on a man who may not even be alive at this point."

Midnight's eyes became points of green fire as she looked up at him. Then she glanced over at the members of FORS, most of whom had stopped working and were watching her and the assistant chief.

Midnight gave Dearborn an "Oh yeah" look and walked to the middle of the room.

"Okay, people, listen up!" she said, her voice carrying easily. Spider took her hand and helped her up onto his desk, the most central one in the room. All thirty members of FORS swarmed around her, including Randy and Jessica. "It seems that there is an executive concern about the overtime we are utilizing. So…" Midnight's gaze trailed over to Greg Dearborn, staying on him as she continued. "Any of you that doesn't want to work past your work day—which, by the way, ends right about now—can leave. I will be unable to pay you if you stay." She didn't look at any of FORS, so there could be no way of saying she had tried to guilt, force, or otherwise coerce them into working without pay. Her eyes remained on Dearborn, who looked around the group. Nobody moved.

"I want you all to know," Dearborn said, raising his voice, "that Lieutenant Chevalier cannot take any disciplinary action whatsoever if any of you choose to leave. I will guarantee you personally that nothing will happen to you if you go."

There was silence among the members of FORS for a few moments, and then someone in the back said, "Fuck that!" Everyone else started to laugh and clap, and Midnight looked at Dearborn triumphantly. This time it was Tiny who took her by the waist and lifted her down from the desk. Midnight walked over to Dearborn, her arms folded, with Kana, Spider, Tiny, and Dibbs right behind her.

"I think you have your answer, Dearborn," she said, her expression indicating that she knew she had won this round hands down.

"Bitch," Dearborn muttered under his breath, and turned to leave. The four senior members of FORS blocked his way, each one of them looking like the fierce gang members they had been before joining the unit. Midnight stood off to the side, watching Dearborn's face.

"That wasn't a very nice thing to say to the lady," Spider said.

"Sure wasn't," Dibbs seconded.

"I think you should apologize," Kana said.

"Now." Tiny made the single word sound utterly deadly.

Dearborn looked over at Midnight, who was desperately trying to stifle a grin, which she barely managed. "I'm sorry," he said, sounding as if the words had been torn from his throat. Which was better than having his throat torn out, which was pretty much what the four members of FORS wanted to do to the guy right now. The apology given, Tiny and Kana moved to make a slim aisle for Dearborn to pass, eyeing him nastily all the while. When Dearborn had made his exit, the whole unit cheered, whooping and clapping. Midnight enjoyed the momentary relief of tension. Minutes later everyone was back to work.

They worked on through the evening and into the early hours of the next day. People were alternating sleeping in various places. Midnight had even found Spider sleeping on the table in the conference room; she'd shut off the light and left as quietly as she'd entered.

At three thirty in the morning, almost twenty-four hours after Randy had discovered Joe gone, Jessica and Tiny were working at the computer together. They were scanning for print matches and not having any luck. Tiny had just taken over looking again, and Jessica glanced over at Randy. She looked awful; she'd been a mess the morning before, but she'd managed to hold it together, offering whatever assistance she could to find her husband. Jessica knew it was doubly hard on Randy since the members of FORS still hadn't forgiven her for her dalliance with another police officer. Jessica's mind had circled the problem over and over. So many things didn't add up. How had the bad guys gotten into the house without setting off the alarm? Joe's system was so secure it was almost impossible to override, but since the partial fingerprint had been found on the keypad itself, it was assumed that they'd managed to do it somehow. They'd looked into the personnel who worked for the alarm company, but they'd gotten nowhere fast. Joe's system was top of the line, and even the company employees didn't have access to the security codes—and according to the manufacturer of the alarm, there was no way to override the system.

The police figured that the alarm company was lying because they didn't want to be held responsible if a police officer died because of their faulty system. But wouldn't that company want to help out if they thought they could? What if they weren't lying—what did that mean? It meant that someone did have Joe's security code. The limited personnel who had access to the codes were rechecked; FORS had even secured the fingerprints of every individual to cross-check against the partial. There were no dead-on matches, but partial prints were a tricky thing. One of them might have been match, but there just wasn't enough detail in the partial to be totally sure.

Okay, Jessica had thought, *so what if it wasn't someone from the alarm company? Who else had that code?* She'd checked—only Joe, Randy, Midnight, and Rick knew the code, and herself. But she had needed it to get in late at night; she'd even been careful to hide it when she'd keyed it in when Tiny was with her. It wasn't that she didn't trust him—she did—but Joe had trusted her to keep it confidential. Jessica took that kind of thing very seriously, having grown up in a cop family. She knew what the simplest mistake could cause. She'd had it drilled into her from early childhood that she didn't advertise what her father did, nor did she give out her address or phone number to anyone she didn't absolutely trust. It had caused a lot of friction in her youth, but she'd grown up understanding the meaning of confidentiality. She wondered if that was why she had a problem trusting people—she was even hesitant with Tiny, and he was a police officer. Everyone always trusted police officers. Something clicked in Jessica's mind as she looked at Randy. She turned to Tiny. "Hey, hon," she said. Tiny loved that she was already referring to him with an endearing term.

"Yeah?" he said, still scanning the prints on the screen.

"Do something for me?"

Tiny looked up at her, hearing a different tone in her voice and wondering what she was thinking. He was constantly amazed by her quick mind. "Okay."

"Look for the fingerprints of cops," she said quietly. She didn't want anyone to hear what she was doing until she was sure she was right.

"What!"

"Shh! Just check, hon. I've got an idea."

Twenty minutes later, Jessica and Tiny approached Midnight. They said they needed to talk to her, and that maybe the three of them should go into her office. Midnight looked at the two of them and nodded as she led the way. She was holding a cup of coffee; she had yet to sleep. Tiny and Jessica sat down, and Midnight set down her coffee and leaned against the front of her desk.

"What've you got?" she asked, seeing the hesitation in their faces.

"A cop," Jessica said simply.

"Huh?"

"A cop's in on it, Midnight," Tiny said.

"On Joe's abduction?" Midnight felt strange all of a sudden. Things started to fall into place even as Jessica began to nod.

"It's Dickerson," Jessica said, and Midnight abruptly felt sick. She paled visibly.

"Midnight!" Tiny stood, reaching out to steady her. He was worried that she was going to pass out.

"I'm okay," Midnight said weakly, holding up her hand to fend him off. She heard the door open and glanced around Tiny to see who it was. Her breath caught sharply in her throat. Rick stood in the doorway, his eyes on her.

"It's Dickerson," Rick said, his voice cutting through the fog in her brain.

Midnight nodded slowly. "You're about three minutes behind. Jessica figured that one out."

"Yeah?" Rick said, looking over to Jessica. Tiny had moved to stand behind her almost protectively. Jessica nodded. Rick looked back at Midnight. He was feeling the effects of seeing her again. His heart had skipped a number of beats when she peered around Tiny at him, and he was sure it was just going to stop altogether as she looked at him now.

Midnight was holding tightly on to her control. Seeing Rick again felt like someone had kicked her in the chest. She couldn't breathe.

"I think we should go…" Tiny said, and Jessica nodded. She and Tiny moved past Rick with some difficulty—he was standing stock still, staring at his wife. Tiny and Jessica realized as they walked out that everyone was staring in the direction of Midnight's office. They'd all seen Rick come in and head straight there. Now they were watching to see what would happen. Rick took one step inside the room, kicking the door closed with a booted foot. The office remained quiet, but people began to move around again, going back to what they were doing.

Meanwhile, their fearless leader was having great difficulty breathing, compounded by the sick feeling in her stomach caused by the shock of finding out that Dick Dickerson was involved in Joe's disappearance. Rick could tell she was very close to passing out. He took three long strides toward her, and without a word picked her up and carried her over to the couch. Midnight was shaking her head, as if trying to deny something.

"Midnight?" Rick said, wondering if she was going into shock for some reason.

"Oh Jesus, oh Jesus," she said, her voice a deathly whisper. She had just realized that by not telling anyone that Dickerson had attacked her, she had allowed the sonofabitch to be free—to possibly have killed her partner. She'd let him off the hook. She found herself up against Rick's chest as he embraced her. That's when the tears started.

"No, it's my fault," she moaned, over and over. Rick wondered if somehow she was relating all of this to her brother's death, or Tim's death four years before—those were the words she had uttered. She'd blamed herself for both.

"What's your fault, Night?" he asked gently.

Midnight looked up at him sharply. "It's my fault if Joe's dead," she said, her voice clear in the silent room.

"How?" Rick said, just as sharply.

Midnight took a deep breath, looking away from him then. "You wanted to know what happened the day I lost the baby?"

"Yeah…"

"It was Dickerson," Midnight said tonelessly.

Rick felt the blood leave his face. He reached out and turned her back to face him. "He's the one that—"

"Killed our baby. And I let the sonofabitch walk." Midnight shook her head, as if she didn't believe her own words.

"Why?" Rick asked, horrified.

Midnight looked him straight in the eye. "Because Randy was with him when he did it." The words dropped in the room, and Rick had to let them sink in before real understanding dawned.

"Randy?" he said, pure anger flooding his veins.

"Wait, Rick," Midnight said as he started to stand. "I don't think she planned on Dickerson ending up tangling with me. She was pissed because I had denied her application for a ride-along. Now that I think about it, I'll just bet Dickerson pumped her up to come and confront me."

Rick looked at her doubtfully.

"Let's find out." Midnight reached up to wipe her face with her hands. She closed her eyes, trying to regain her composure. Then she looked up at Rick. "Okay, go get her for me, will ya?"

Rick nodded and left.

He came back a few minutes later with Randy trailing him. Midnight was sitting behind her desk.

"Randy, come in. Have a seat." She motioned for Rick to close the door. "Look," she said, as evenly as possible. "I told Rick about you and Dickerson, but he doesn't believe me."

Randy looked from Midnight to Rick and then back at Midnight, obviously trying to figure out what Midnight had said. Her eyes showed her worry, and Midnight nodded. When Randy glanced at Rick again, she could see hatred in his eyes. "Oh, God," she said, closing her eyes and beginning to shake. She looked at Midnight, beseeching the other woman to understand. "I swear, I never meant any of it to happen. When I got the call that you'd denied my application I was mad, but Dick told me I should go and talk to you about it. He said that you were a bitch and you were trying to ruin my career. I decided to go and talk to you, but when we got there, I thought Dick would wait outside—it was my problem, after all. But he insisted he'd come in, and he swore he'd stand there quietly." She laughed ruefully. "If I had known what would end up happening, I never would have gone there. Sure, I was mad, and you know I was even stupid enough to take a swing at you, but I had no idea that he'd jump in…" There were tears in her eyes by the time she finished. She looked over at Rick, almost afraid of him now.

Midnight looked at Rick too, and he nodded to her. He believed Randy; she wasn't the kind of person who could act that well. She'd always been too genuine.

"We believe you, Randy," Midnight said calmly. "The reason we had to find out was that we think Dickerson has Joe."

"What!" Randy said, her face reflecting shock and horror. She started to shake her head, not wanting it to be true.

"Randy, it was Dickerson's partial print on the keypad at the house," Midnight said.

Randy became still as things started to fall into place. She remembered the day she and Dickerson had gone to Joe's house to pick up the rest of her things. Dick had been adamant about doing it that morning, even before the academy started at 8:00 a.m. She had punched in the security code without even thinking, and had actually stepped back on his feet when she moved to open the door. She had been surprised that he was that close, but she hadn't realized he'd been looking over her shoulder. She remembered the night he'd shown up when Joe wasn't home; she'd heard noises on the deck and by the front door, and Dickerson had shown up right after.

"Oh, God," she said, closing her eyes. "I told him so much about Joe." She shook her head, as if trying to clear it. "I don't even remember everything I told him. He was another cop—I never even imagined…" She trailed off as she realized that she may have gotten Joe killed.

"We know Dickerson's involved, Randy, but we don't know with whom, who's behind it," Midnight said.

"Yes, we do," Rick said.

Midnight looked at him as if he'd just lost it. She started to shake her head.

"It's the Riveras," Rick said.

Midnight stared at him for a long moment, as the memories of what the drug family had done years before came flooding back. "No," she said, wanting to be right this time. "We haven't gotten any threats, demands, or anything."

"So they're bein' real quiet about it this time," Rick said.

"How?" Midnight said, and Rick knew she wanted to know how he came by the information.

He shrugged. "A friend of Teddy's went out with Carlos Rivera. We were in a club and she was drillin' me on what I did for a living. We hit on FORS, and she told me that Carlos Rivera was planning a hit on a certain member of the unit. I just assumed it was Joe, because she said it was a he."

Midnight was nodding, purposely stepping past the fact that Rick had been out with Teddy only hours before.

"Where's Mikeyla?" She was suddenly terrified that he'd brought their daughter back with him.

"She's still in England. I figured she'd be safest there."

Midnight sighed with relief, nodding. "Good." Then she looked at Rick seriously. "They have our address."

"They what?" Rick replied sharply, wondering when the surprises for the morning would end.

"Have our address. Griff's group hit a house and found it with the Perros Locos, and I'll just bet that our boys have a pretty strong connection with the Riveras."

"Jesus," Rick said, moving to sit on the credenza behind Midnight's desk. "This is too fucking much for one morning."

Midnight called a meeting to tell everybody what they now knew. Randy was pointedly absent; she'd gone off to recover from what she'd done. The last place she wanted to be was in the room when Midnight told everyone that the guy she had cheated on Joe with was the one behind his disappearance.

"Okay," Midnight said. "We have some more information thanks to the help of some very able-bodied police officers." She glanced at Tiny and Jessica first, then looked over at Rick, who was leaning indolently against the window in the conference room with his arms crossed in front of his chest, pointedly distancing himself from the rest of FORS. He knew how they all felt about him, but he didn't care.

"We know that a cop is working with the bad guys on this one," Midnight said, and an outraged murmur started in the crowd. "Okay, people." Midnight raised her hand for silence. "The thing is, this cop has taken advantage of an awkward situation when all of our guards were down. The cop is Dick Dickerson, and"—she raised her voice— "before you all get your hackles up, let me tell you a little tidbit of information." She saw Rick look up at her sharply, but she shook her head, telling him she had to explain.

"I had the best reason of all to know that Dickerson was dirty. You see, my 'accident' wasn't an accident at all. Dickerson's the one that introduced my head to my entryway wall."

There was total silence in the room as everyone realized the implications of what she was saying. She could also see that they wanted to know why she hadn't done anything about it. "The reason the son-ofabitch isn't in jail right now is because of my weakness for Joe. You see, Randy was with Dickerson at the time. But before you all start in on her, you need to know that Randy had nothing to do with it, and if I didn't honestly believe that, she'd be in jail right now." The severity in her voice served to convince the unit. They knew that Midnight's instincts were just about always right, so they believed her. "Now look. Randy's as rattled about this as the rest of us, so let's try to give her the benefit of the doubt. She wants Joe back just as badly, if not more so than the rest of us."

The members of FORS started to nod and talk among themselves. The gist of what they were saying was Dickerson and what they'd do to the guy when they got to him.

"The other bit of information we have," Midnight continued a few minutes later, "is that our old friends the Riveras are behind this little shindig too." There was shocked silence in the room. Nobody could even fathom the nerve it took to try and hit a police unit not once or even twice, but now a third time. The possibilities were devastating. It also made them aware that any of them could be targets, but for the most part they were concerned about their leader.

"Could Dickerson's attack on you have been planned?" someone asked.

Midnight considered the thought, and after a moment began to nod. "It's possible. It may have been a quick attempt to get me out of the way." She looked over at Rick and saw a stricken expression on his face. If he hadn't been screwing around with Sheila, he would have been there to protect her. He'd known that, but the thought that it could have been an actual planned attempt to kill Midnight, with the secure knowledge that Rick was staying somewhere else with his girlfriend, made the impact of Rick's infidelity more significant.

"So Dickerson could have had his sights on Randy from way back," someone else said.

"Isn't Dickerson's sister the chick Randy was staying with?" Spider put in.

Midnight nodded, seeing the pieces fall together.

"Think his sister's part of it too?" Kana asked, looking at Midnight.

"Let's pick her up and find out."

Midnight lay on the couch in her office twenty minutes later, trying to get rid of her pounding headache, covering her eyes with her arm. She heard the door open but didn't want to use up the energy to open her eyes and see who'd come in. It was six o'clock in the morning, and she'd been awake for twenty-six hours. Her energy levels were dropping dangerously low. She sensed someone sitting next to her, and his scent came to her a moment later. She opened one eye. Rick was sitting on the floor right next to her. She closed her eye again, shaking her head. "I don't have the energy for a confrontation with you right now." Her voice was very weak, as if backing up her statement.

"Good," Rick said, very close to her ear. She could sense his face near hers. "Because I don't want to have a confrontation with you." His voice was very soft and sincere. His lips brushed her ear, and she shivered in response. "I'm sorry I wasn't there for you."

"Which time?"

"Every time," Rick said, refusing to rise to the bait. She felt him touch her hand, which was lying on her stomach. She tensed. She wasn't even close to being ready to deal with him yet; she was still reeling from the morning's revelations.

"Rick, don't," she said, softly but firmly. "Not here, not now."

When he didn't speak, she glanced over at him. He nodded, his face showing the pain of her rejection. She didn't have the energy to deal with that now either. She closed her eyes again, and must have dozed off, because she woke a little while later. Rick was still sitting on the floor next to her, his knees up to his chest, his ankles crossed, and his head down on his crossed arms resting on his knees.

The door opened, and Sarah Dickerson walked in, escorted by Tiny and Jessica. She looked afraid as Midnight and then Rick looked up at her with narrowed eyes. The two officers who had come pounding on her door at 5:20 in the morning had told her she was under suspicion of conspiracy to murder a police officer. Now, as she looked at Midnight, she was worried. Rick stood up and extended his hand to Midnight. She took it and moved to stand. Rick noticed her wincing and made a note to watch her the entire time they talked to Sarah.

They found out that other than disliking Joe and goading Randy into leaving him, Sarah had had no other involvement. They told her they had rock-solid proof that her brother was involved, and asked her about his associates. Sarah was able to tell them that he visited friends in Mexico a lot.

"Do you know where?" Rick said, his eyes shining intensely.

"Yeah. Well, sort of—it's down by Ensenada." Sarah shrugged helplessly. "They don't exactly mark the streets down there, but I'd know it if I saw it."

"What about a picture?" Midnight asked. Sarah nodded, and Midnight turned to Rick. "I'll bet that Griff can get the National Guard or even his own people to fly over a certain area and take pictures of the houses there."

Rick nodded. "Do it."

Midnight picked up the phone and dialed Griff's cell.

He answered almost immediately. Midnight explained what was happening, and Griff agreed to get ahold of the Guard. He explained that at this time of the morning, they were likely to have a faster response, since BNE's airplanes for southern California were stationed in Long Beach.

He called back twenty minutes later. "I can get you a C-26 out of North Island in twenty minutes. You did say these guys are drug dealers, right?" He sounded a little hesitant.

"Yeah, Griff. Coke, I think. Why?"

"I just didn't want to have to lie to the Guard and tell them it was a drug case, but I would have if necessary."

"Thanks, Griff. I owe ya."

They hung up, and Midnight got a call from the National Guard a few minutes later. She explained the situation and put Sarah on the phone. She told the guardsman what area the house was located in and then disconnected. She looked up at Midnight. "Lieutenant?" she said hesitantly.

Midnight looked at the younger girl, her mind already working through her plans for the next steps. "Yes?"

"I'm really sorry, ma'am. For everything." Sarah looked sincere, and Midnight couldn't help but smile. The kid looked absolutely terrified too.

"You'll make it up to me by finding the house they're holding my sergeant in."

Sarah nodded emphatically.

CHAPTER 5

Joe regained consciousness slowly. His head ached. Reaching up, he felt dry blood matting his hair. As his eyes grew accustomed to the darkness, he realized he was sitting on the floor. He tried to stand and was rewarded with excruciating pain in his side. Looking down, he saw that blood was still seeping from the gunshot wound in his side. He glanced around and knew he was not at home. "Shit," he muttered, resting his head against the wall again.

After a while he felt less groggy, so he once again attempted to stand. Eventually he made it to his feet. He looked around. There was one window and a door. The only furniture in the room was a chair. Joe tried the window but found that although it wasn't barred, it was nailed shut. He rapped on the glass and decided it was double-paned—no real hope of breaking it. He checked the chair and found that it was nailed to the floor. Moving back to the window, he looked out. The house he was in was on a beach, but he wasn't sure which one. He could also see men walking around outside, and he could tell they were guarding the house, even though they were trying to look casual about it.

He heard the door behind him open and turned around slowly, his side burning all the while. He was stunned to see Dick Dickerson. After a long moment, Joe started to shake his head, the look on his face one of disappointment.

"Bad cop?" he said derisively. "Isn't that just a bit too cliché?"

"Fuck you, Sinclair."

Joe just looked back at him, his eyes still reflecting disapproval.

"You think you're so ethical?" Dickerson said with a sneer.

"I know I wouldn't try to kill another cop," Joe said. A momentary look of surprise crossed Dickerson's face.

"It's too bad I didn't succeed," he mused.

Joe realized the man wasn't talking about him. "Yeah, well I guess you fucked up, didn't you?" he said, trying to draw him out.

"Next time," Dickerson said, his voice turning almost evil. "I know someone that wants to fuck her first."

"Yeah?" Joe narrowed his eyes. "Who?"

Dickerson looked at him sharply, suddenly realizing he was being played. "Don't try to play games with me, Sinclair," he said, gritting his teeth. "My associates may not want you dead just yet, but if you piss me off, I might just kill you accidentally."

Joe shrugged. "Probably shoot your own foot off in the process."

Dickerson produced a pistol and pointed it at Joe. "You wanna do some target shooting, Sinclair? 'Cause I could use some. Been a while since I've been to the range." The look on his face changed, becoming knowing. "'Bout three weeks, I'd say."

Joe did a quick calculation. That was when Randy had been there with the academy class. He looked back at Dickerson, his eyes narrowing once again.

"Guess you hadn't figured that one out yet, huh?" Dickerson clicked his tongue. "And I thought you were this great cop?"

"You put that heavy load in Randy's clip," Joe said, pulling a mocking expression. "Couldn't even do that right, could you?"

"I wanted it to be a hot load," Dickerson snapped. "I was hoping it'd blow up in her face." He sneered at the last, hoping to draw Joe out.

To his utter shock, Joe started to chuckle. "Like I said, you couldn't even do that right."

"You sonofabitch!" Dickerson took a step forward and raised the gun.

Joe tilted his head to the side. "You'd better get a little closer. I've seen your range scores."

Dickerson fired, but Joe had anticipated it and jumped out of the way before the shot went off. As he had predicted, it went wide. Dickerson didn't shoot well when he was pissed off. Joe made a mental note of that. He glanced up from where he lay on the floor; he'd landed on his sore side, and he was hoping that Dickerson hadn't managed to line up his next shot. He was surprised when two men entered the room and grabbed the gun from Dickerson's hands.

"Don't shoot him yet, muchacho. I want his friends too," said the short Mexican man closest to Dickerson, his accent thick. He handed the pistol to the other man and turned to Joe. "If you had any brains, you'd keep your mouth shut."

"And if you had any balls," Joe said, sitting up, "you'd face me head on yourself." He had recognized Carlos Rivera the moment he walked in the door. He was part of the cartel family who had sent the Scorpions after them four years before.

"Careful, English. I can still get to that pretty wife of yours," Carlos said, his look meaningful.

Joe said nothing. Inside he was rejoicing, of a sort. If they didn't have Randy, he was free to do whatever it took to get away without having to worry about trying to find her too. A thought nagged at him, though, as the three men left the room—if Dickerson was involved, just how much had Randy told them?

He dragged himself over to the nearest wall and leaned against it. The sun was coming up, and he was better able to see his surroundings. In a different scenario the room would be considered beautiful, even if all the furnishings had been removed. After resting for a while, Joe hauled himself up off the floor and went over to the window again. He couldn't see the men outside anymore, and he decided to keep watch to work out how often they appeared.

A couple of hours later, Dickerson walked back into the room. He found Joe sitting in the chair, looking out the window, his long legs stretched out in front of him. Joe glanced over and grinned sardonically when he saw Dickerson standing in the doorway.

Dickerson shut the door behind him. His eyes were glinting evilly. "So, Sinclair," he said, almost conversationally. "How does it feel?"

Joe didn't respond, just looked back at Dickerson with mild interest.

"I mean to have another guy fuck your wife and turn her against you."

"I wouldn't know," Joe said calmly.

"Sure you do, Sinclair. You think I knew the security alarm code all by myself? Randy was happy to supply it."

Joe gave a low laugh and shook his head.

"You don't believe me?" Dickerson said, his voice taking on an angry edge.

"I think you're an idiot."

"Well, I think you're a stupid fucking pansy who can't accept that his wife needs a real man around!"

Joe grinned. "I can accept it. That's why she's back with me."

Dickerson stared at Joe for a long minute. It was obvious he wanted to kill him now rather than wait, but he was afraid of Carlos Rivera too.

"You think you're so smart, Sinclair, but you wait. I'm gonna be the one to kill you, and believe me, it won't be pleasant. But first I'm gonna finish what I started with that bitch partner of yours." Joe tried to hide it, but Dickerson caught the slight look of surprise in his eyes. "So you didn't know, huh? Oh, yeah, it was me, Sinclair. I'm the one that fucked that little tease up. And ya know," he said, looking straight into Joe's eyes as he played his trump card, "your wife was standing right there when I did it."

Joe felt the words hit him as if they'd been a bullet from Dickerson's gun. He didn't bother to hide the shock. He felt sick suddenly, like everything had just turned upside down. Somehow he knew Dickerson was telling the truth. He wasn't sure how, but the looks that Midnight had given Randy, and the way Randy had acted the night Joe and she had gone to see her... the strange look that had crossed Randy's face when Joe had said he had been "wrong." It all fell into place, and Joe couldn't shake the cold feeling that settled in his stomach.

Dickerson was laughing, a cold, hateful laugh that rang in Joe's ears long after Dickerson had walked out of the room.

Shoving himself up out of the chair, Joe paced the room like a caged animal. Finally, his anger and frustration came to a head as he slammed his fist into the wall. He proceeded to take out all of his fury on it. When he was done, his hands were bloody and the wall had a fair-sized hole in it. Joe knew he was reacting to what Dickerson had said in just the way Dickerson wanted, but at that point he didn't care. He couldn't figure out why Randy hadn't told him, or why, for that matter, Midnight hadn't. He suspected Midnight had been trying to protect him, but he didn't have a clue why Randy hadn't said anything. Unless she was afraid of what he'd do. She'd been present when his partner and best friend had been brutally attacked. Joe couldn't imagine that Randy had actually been involved, only that she had stood by and watched. The mental picture that produced made him reel off another jab at the wall. Then he put his head against it, leaning heavily.

A tiny part of him wondered how much Randy really had to do with all of this. His heart told him that she hadn't known what Dickerson was doing, but his cynical side kept jeering at him for being so easy. He'd welcomed Randy back with open arms without any real discussion about Dickerson and why she had changed her mind. His heart latched on to the idea that Randy had returned to him after Midnight's attack—maybe she realized what kind of man Dickerson was. But if that was the case, why didn't she tell him? Why had she hidden it? Joe pondered the question over the next eight hours.

When Carlos Rivera walked into the room, Joe was leaning against the far wall with his back to Rivera. His arms were crossed against the wall, his head resting on them. He didn't even look up when the door opened.

148

"Hey," Carlos said, after waiting a full minute for Joe to turn around.

Joe looked up, his eyes taking in the man who had caused so much trouble for him and FORS. "What do you want?"

"Well, actually, English," Carlos said, his voice easygoing even as the look in his eyes belied the reality. "I want you dead, and your partner, and all your friends."

"We can't always get what we want, can we?" Joe said tonelessly.

Carlos frowned slightly, as if considering Joe's question. "No, but if I have to settle for you, that's muy bien too."

"So do it and get it over with."

"Oh, but that would take all the fun out of it." Carlos glanced at the wall Joe had beaten in. He scowled, then his eyes took on a knowing look. "Woman trouble?"

"Fuck you, Carlos."

Carlos clicked his tongue, shaking his head. "Terrible when a marriage goes bad, isn't it? The woman, she thinks she needs something more than your little English dick, so she goes looking for a real man."

"Yeah, too bad she found Dickerson instead."

Carlos shrugged, indicating he felt the same way about the other cop. "Yes, but she gets involved with him anyway, and he shows her how she can get back at her rich, estúpido husband." He shook his head in mock distress. "Next thing you know, her husband is dead and she inherits all those millions. It's a real fucking tragedy, it is."

"Yeah," Joe said, nodding. "A real American tragedy. So why don't we just get it over with and make Randy a millionaire?"

"Too easy, my friend, too easy. I want your friends to worry about you first. People get really stupid and careless when they're worried, and tired. They start making mistakes. They get into cars that just blow up, or they go to their house and find intruders who tragically end up killing these people. Terrible thing, this worry." Carlos' eyes had taken on an evil glint, and Joe found himself getting angry even though he knew that was what Carlos wanted.

Letting out an almost banshee-like cry, Joe threw himself at the other man. He struggled to wrest away the gun, gripping the cold metal. He didn't hear the men who came running into the room—he just felt the sharp concussion to the base of his neck as one of them drove home the butt of his rifle. He was hit two more times, both on the head, before he fell unconscious to the floor. He didn't see Carlos stand up, brushing off his pants, as he looked down at the blond Eng-lishman with disgust before walking out of the room with his men trailing him.

Joe remained unconscious for hours. When he woke it was dark outside. Again, he dragged himself from the floor, this time tasting blood in his mouth. His head was bleeding profusely from the gash that had been reopened. Joe pressed his hand to the cut, which caused a great amount of pain, but he was determined to stop the bleeding. Glancing down at the floor, he noticed a small pool of blood and re-alized that the gunshot wound in his side was bleeding again as well.

Yanking the tails of his shirt out of his jeans, Joe pressed the extra material to his side. He felt a bit nauseated from the pain, as well as lightheaded from the blood loss. He remembered why he had charged Carlos. He remembered the man's derision as he talked about car bombs and cops being killed in their own homes. He had to forcibly calm his nerves as they raged against the pictures that appeared in his head. He had thought about Midnight's classic red-and-white Corvette in a ball of fire. He thought about Tammy, who was by now due with her and Spider's first child. He thought about Jessica and Tiny, who were so gone over each other they might not think to be careful. The images kept piling up in his mind, and it made him shake with suppressed rage, with the knowledge that he couldn't do a damn thing about it. He strode over to the window and looked down. He couldn't see any of the men circling the house, but they had probably figured no one would be looking for him here anyway.

He heard the door open and turned as someone stepped inside. There was light from the hallway, although the room was dark. Joe knew it was Dickerson—he could almost smell him.

"You're awake again, I see," Dickerson said.

Joe said nothing. His eyes were adjusting to the dimness, and he saw Dickerson's eyes go to the hole in the wall. "I see you've decided to believe me about dear sweet Randy," Dickerson said, leering.

Joe nodded. "Yeah, I believe you. But tell me one thing."

"What's that?"

"How long have you been dirty?"

"Well," Dickerson said, his tone taking on an ironic lilt. "That's the funny thing. I had my eye on Randy for a long time… and things just finally worked out, ya know?"

"Long time?"

"Oh, yeah." Dickerson sounded quite proud of himself. "'Bout four years now, I'd say."

Joe was silent.

"Yeah, it's been four years now. First time I saw her was when she was with you. 'Course, she wasn't supposed to be with you that last time…" Dickerson trailed off, and Joe felt the hairs on the back of his neck stand up.

"Sergeant Dickerson," he said, his tone deadly.

Dickerson nodded, almost excitedly. "Yep, watch commander's back up."

"You're the one that sent me to San Ysidro."

"Uh-huh. Thought we'd finish you off that time."

Joe closed his eyes, shaking his head. He was astounded that he hadn't remembered Dickerson's name till just then. Midnight had asked him about it after the incident four years before, but he hadn't been able to remember. But now it had come back to him with total clarity. "So," he said, "it's taken so long, and you still can't get it right." He shook his head to emphasize his point.

"What's that supposed to mean?" Dickerson asked, rising to the bait nicely.

Joe shrugged. "Well, you said you've been watching Randy for four years now. You finally got her, and you couldn't keep her satisfied."

"I kept her plenty satisfied," Dickerson said, obviously trying to hold on to his control. "I sent her back to you to make you think everything was okay. She's just been faking it with you. She's had a taste of real man now, and she'll never go back to sloppy seconds again."

"Really?" Joe raised an eyebrow. "Faking it all this time now, eh?"

"That's right." Dickerson nodded, his ego puffing him up. "She's been mine since the day she walked out on you. I had to practically force her to go back to your bed for the time being."

Joe nodded, looking as if he was considering the thought as he paced over toward the window. Then his eyes pinned Dickerson. "Then why was she in my bed a week after she left?"

"Bullshit, Sinclair!" Dickerson yelled. His hand tightened on his gun.

Joe shrugged. "Don't believe it. But didn't you notice how late she came in the day she went to pick up some of her clothes? Didn't you notice that she smelled like she'd been fucked?" Joe's voice was full of mockery now, and Dickerson's face became suffused with fury.

"You fucking bastard!" he screamed as he fired his pistol over and over.

Three of the bullets slammed into the window just to Joe's right, and another hit Joe as he dove out the shattered window. When he hit the ground, he tucked into a roll as best he could. Then he was on his feet and running headlong down the beach. The pain was extreme, but the adrenaline flowing through him drove him up and over one of the nearby dunes and into some tall brush to the side. He dove to the ground as he heard shouts from the house. Thinking quickly, Joe threw sand over the bleeding wound in his side and the new one in his shoulder. He moved stealthily through the weeds, trying to make as little noise as possible.

He continued for what seemed like hours. Finally he couldn't go on, and he dropped to the ground, gasping for breath. His head was pounding; he imagined he'd caused some interesting new damage when he'd jumped through the only partially shattered glass of the double-paned window. He thanked the gods above that Dickerson had indeed been the lousy shot he'd expected he was. But now as he lay on the sand, breathing deep, nearly comatose, he wondered how he'd get anywhere, or whether he'd die out here in the weeds with no one ever even finding his body. He didn't know if he was badly injured, but the sand he'd thrown in the wounds to keep from leaving a blood trail ground against his skin painfully. His last conscious thought was of Randy as he passed out, face down in the sand.

****

Midnight sat in her chair, which was facing the far wall of her office. Her feet were up on her credenza, her eyes closed. When the phone rang, she woke with a start and grabbed it up from its cradle.

"Yeah?"

"Midnight," Griff said. "We've got some interesting information down here. I think you should come look at it."

"I'll be there in ten." Midnight hung up and stood, reaching for her gun.

"What's up?" Rick asked. He'd been sitting in one of the other chairs. She looked over at him as he got up, struck once again by the wrenching feeling she felt in her gut at the sight of him. "Griff's got the pictures from the Guard. I was gonna go down and see them."

Rick saw the exhaustion and worry etched deep in her eyes. "Let me drive you, okay? You look like hell."

Midnight looked at him for a long moment. "Always so charming."

"That's me."

Rick led the way out of the office. They were both surprised when an agent walked up to them as they exited the double doors.

"Lieutenant Chevalier?"

"Yes?" Midnight said impatiently.

"Phil Griffin sent me." The agent showed her his credentials, which Midnight looked over carefully. "He said you wouldn't be in any condition to drive at this point."

Midnight laughed. "That Griff, he's always thinking of me." She nodded. "Okay, let's go."

Ten minutes later they walked into the BNE building. The receptionist buzzed them through immediately. Midnight headed straight for Griff's office, with Rick right on her heels. Griff stood in his doorway and gestured across the hall. "We're in here." He stepped over to the door and shoved it open, standing back and indicating that Midnight should go first. She walked into the conference room, and the first thing she saw was one very bedraggled and damaged-looking six-foot-two-inch, dirty-blond-haired Englishman, grinning at her.

"Joe!" she screamed, launching herself at him. Joe stood, catching her up in a bear hug. He looked up at Rick in surprise as he walked in.

Midnight stepped back, her hand still touching his sleeve, as if to let go would be to lose him again. "Are you okay?" She knew it was a dumb question; she could see that he was wounded, her eyes narrowing as she noted the bandages at his side and shoulder. "Why aren't you in a hospital?"

Joe waved away her concern. "The Guard medics checked me out. I'm fine. We've got too much to do."

"Like hell—"

"Midnight!" Joe said, cutting through her rising anger. "People's lives are still in danger. Phil sent his people out to check on FORS, but we have to stop these guys. For real this time." He was angry, but it wasn't directed at her.

After a long minute, Midnight nodded, and they sat down to plan. Her hand frequently moved to touch his arm, or his leg, as if she were making sure she wasn't imagining him. She couldn't believe that he was okay.

She discovered that the National Guard had found him using their thermal imaging system—otherwise known as infrared—while trying to track the people they had noticed spreading out from a house down on the beach in Ensenada. They had been ready to call it in when they noticed a form lying prone in the tall weeds back from the ocean. They'd zeroed in, and utilizing the video capabilities of their aircraft had determined that this was the police officer everyone was looking for. They'd called in a medevac helicopter from the border and gotten Joe out as quickly as possible. He'd been checked out by the top medics, and although he'd lost a good deal of blood, his wounds were for the most part minor. Dickerson was indeed a lousy shot.

Two hours later they were prepared for the raid on the beach house. Since Midnight had already garnered an extensive amount of inter-agency assistance to get Joe out, they planned to utilize the same agencies to conduct the raid. They wanted the Riveras out of commission for good this time.

Joe stood at the window to the BNE conference room. He was alone, waiting. He heard the door open, and Randy's sharp intake of breath. He didn't turn around; he could almost feel Randy's hesitation. After a few moments he glanced over his shoulder. She was standing just inside the room, the door closed behind her. She was watching him, her face drawn and concerned. He turned to her, the look on his face very serious.

"Are you okay?" she asked hesitantly.

Joe nodded.

She walked over to him, reaching up to touch his cheek. He closed his eyes in response, but she could tell it wasn't out of any weakness for her. Randy realized she wasn't ready to have this confrontation with him. "Joe, I—"

"No," Joe said. He wasn't ready for the discussion they needed to have either. He held his arms out to her, and she moved into them. He held her to him, feeling very confused and lost. The look in Randy's eyes had told him that she was worried, dashing any hope he had had that what Dickerson had told him wasn't true. He knew he'd have to face that later, but right now he had a lot to prepare for mentally.

He pulled away. "Look, we're goin' out on the raid in a few minutes. I just wanted to... well, get a chance to see you, to talk to

157

you…" He trailed off, because he didn't know what he wanted to say to her.

"Joe," Randy said softly. "Please, just know that I love you, whatever else you might think."

"I know, Randy, I know," Joe said, stroking her hair. He leaned down to kiss her on the top of the head.

Midnight opened the door to the conference room, chagrined at having to interrupt. Joe glanced up at her, and she pointedly looked at her watch. He nodded, and she closed the door again. "I gotta go," he said, looking down at Randy.

"Can I ride along?"

"On the raid?" Joe said, sounding as if he thought her daft.

"Why not?" she said, eyeing him suspiciously.

Joe looked at her for a long moment. He knew he should tell her no, but part of him wanted her there. As if joining the raid and arresting Dickerson would mean that she really had no feelings for the man. Finally, he shrugged. "Fine with me."

"Absolutely not!" Midnight said, looking from Randy to Joe.

"Why not?" Joe felt strange that he was actually defending the idea of Randy going on the raid.

Midnight made a face. "Are you sure they checked that noggin of yours out thoroughly?" She eyed him suspiciously. "She's not even out of the academy yet. This isn't exactly an exercise, you know."

Joe shrugged. "So she can wait and go in with the cleanup crew."

Midnight considered it for a minute, narrowing her eyes at him as if to say he was pushing his luck. "Fine!" she said eventually. She looked past Joe. "Shit."

"What?" Joe turned to follow her line of sight. Dearborn was getting off the elevator. He glanced around, taking in all of the members of FORS as well as the BNE team and the National Guard, all gearing up for the raid. He was shaking his head as he approached Midnight. Joe narrowed his eyes at him. He was the only one who knew what Dearborn had said to Midnight about why her team was the top one in the department.

"Sergeant Sinclair," Dearborn said, extending his hand. Joe looked down at it as if it were a gun, and then back into the man's eyes. The look on his face told Dearborn that if he didn't remove his hand from Joe's reach, Joe would likely remove it for him.

Not missing a beat, Dearborn dropped his hand and looked around Joe at Midnight. "Lieutenant, can I speak to you in your office?"

Midnight eyed the man warily. She had no intention of having a private conversation with him ever again. "I'm busy, Dearborn, so whatever you have to tell me will either have to be here and now, or it'll have to wait."

"Well, it's this business you're attending to that I want to speak with you about." Dearborn sounded every bit the politician.

"It's a raid, Dearborn, not a meeting," Midnight said with a wilting look.

"Yes, I'm aware of that, Lieutenant, and I have to say there's a serious problem here."

"And what's that?" Midnight slipped a newly loaded clip into her Beretta and pulled back the slide, looking at Dearborn pointedly.

"Since Sinclair's back, I don't see the point in conducting a raid at this time. We're talking about over the border, not to mention all of the agencies involved. I just don't feel it's prudent at this point to carry out this tactical operation."

Midnight looked at him with an expression of boredom. "Are you finished?" she said, as if just waking up to find that he'd stopped talking.

Dearborn nodded, his eyes narrowed as he considered taking corrective action against her for her public insubordination.

"First of all, Dearborn, these people aren't your garden-variety criminals. They're a major drug cartel. Secondly, I find it necessary to take action on these people because they've tried to kill a number of my members not once but twice now. And frankly, they're starting to really piss me off." She smiled up at him sweetly. "Kinda like you."

"Lieutenant!" Dearborn yelled, all but losing control, more so when Midnight merely tilted her head to the side. "You are on report as of now for gross insubordination, and unless you'd like to be relieved of your command, I would suggest that you call off this raid—now."

"Nope." Midnight shook her head calmly.

"That's a direct order, Lieutenant. If you disobey it, I'll have your badge."

Midnight looked up at him complacently. Every eye in the place was on her. There wasn't a sound in the room. "Fire me." She moved around him, picking up her body armor and extra clips off the desk, and walked toward the elevator.

Dearborn stared at the spot where she'd stood, his mouth hanging open. He looked over at Joe, who was grinning.

"Fire me too," Joe said, and followed Midnight. All the members of FORS clapped as Joe, followed by Randy, headed toward the elevator. Some of the other agency people applauded as well, and the cheering got louder as Dearborn turned, totally red-faced, and headed for the stairwell.

The members of the raid, forty in all, were transported in National Guard UH-1 helicopters. Midnight, Rick, Spider, Tiny, Kana, Dibbins, and two BNE agents were designated as the entry team. Four in the front and four in back. The rest were split into follow-up and cleanup crews. They had plenty of air surveillance in case any of Riveras' people tried to make a run for it. It had only been three and half hours since Joe had made his escape, and since the Riveras had no idea that he'd been rescued or that the National Guard had taken pictures of the house from three thousand feet up, they couldn't have expected a raid to take place as early as this.

Dickerson was helping the Riveras pack up the house, stowing drugs, money, guns, everything. They were just being cautious. Dickerson had assured Carlos that he'd shot Joe Sinclair a few times before he got away. He told him it was just a matter of time before Riveras' men found him dead somewhere along the beach. Carlos didn't have as much faith in the cop as the cop had in himself, and he was being careful. The way he saw it, if FORS wanted to raid this house, on international soil, he had at least eight hours from the time Sinclair managed to get to them. It would take a long time first of all to get permission from the Mexican government, as well as the time it would take to draw up paperwork, get a raid team together, and drive down. San Diego PD couldn't afford aircraft or anything like that. Rivera knew that—considering how many of them were on his payroll, it was obvious San Diego PD couldn't even afford to pay their officers very well, let alone own any type of aircraft.

So Carlos Rivera was shocked when he heard the words "Police! Search warrant!" Then the doors at both the front and back of the house crashed open.

"What the?" Dickerson yelled as he reached for his gun. Carlos had already pulled out one of the AK47s he liked to keep around. There was a lot of shooting, and Carlos left Dickerson in the living room to head for the basement. There was an outside door down there that the cops wouldn't know about.

Joe had been told by Midnight that she didn't want him on the entry team because of his injuries. He'd nodded nonchalantly when she said it, and Randy knew better. As soon as Midnight went off with the rest of the team, Joe turned and kissed Randy quickly on the lips. He holstered his handgun and picked up one of the MP5s the Guard's people had left.

"Where're you going?" Randy asked.

"Goin' to pick a fight." Joe grinned at her, and then he was gone. Randy followed a few minutes later, a rifle in her own hands.

Joe got around the back of the house and headed up the stairs to the deck. As he got to the top, he heard breaking glass and ran in that direction. He reached the side of the house and saw Dickerson, but Dickerson wasn't looking at him—he was staring off to Joe's right. Joe glanced around the side of the house and saw Randy standing there with a rifle pointed at Dickerson.

"It was easy, Randy," Dickerson said. "You were easy. But now you're in the way."

Joe saw Dickerson bring up his pistol, and without hesitating he vaulted the railing and charged at him. Dickerson turned, bringing his gun around, and just as Joe hit him, he fired.

Randy screamed, but was surprised when she saw that Joe was still grappling with Dickerson. The rifle she was pointing at the two of them was useless. If she fired, Joe would be hit by the spray too. She dropped it, pulling out her duty weapon. She aimed at the two men and waited for a clear target. She was hoping that one of the other team members had heard the shot and would come around to help.

Not a minute later, as Joe fought for control of the gun, a chair was hurled through a window not ten feet from where Randy stood, and Midnight jumped to the ground moments later. She gave Randy a cavalier wink and headed toward the two men. She stopped a couple of feet from them. Dickerson managed to get up and pointed the pistol at Joe's head, intent on killing him once and for all. He was very surprised when he felt the cold metal of a Beretta muzzle pressed just behind his ear and a female voice say "I'll take that."

When Dickerson hesitated, Midnight pushed the gun against his head harder. "Think I won't shoot, Dickerson? Think I don't have any reason to?"

"You're a cop, Chevalier," Dickerson said, sounding sure of himself. "You won't do it."

"I quit today, Dickerson." Midnight almost felt his sharp intake of breath. "So, you wanna put that gun down now, or would you like me to ventilate your head for ya?"

"And if she misses," Randy said, having walked up with her gun pointed at Dickerson's head, "I won't."

Dickerson looked up at her, his eyes narrowed.

"Not so easy now, is she?" Joe said from the ground. He glanced up at Randy, then back to Dickerson.

Dickerson dropped his weapon, and Midnight shoved him to his knees and patted him down. She looked up at Randy. "Thought you were supposed to wait in the car," she said, a wry grin on her face.

"I had to go to the bathroom," Randy just as sardonically. She looked down at Joe and realized that he had indeed been hit when the gun went off—he was bleeding profusely. "Shit!" She grabbed her radio off her belt. "Ten-ninety-nine, officer down—get a medic in here, now!" Joe exchanged a look with Midnight at the authority in Randy's voice, then lay back and closed his eyes.

"Have 'em," Midnight said, standing as she saw four members of the raid team headed in their direction. "Take out the trash too, will ya?"

She went back toward the house to check on progress. All over, Riveras' men were being arrested. Midnight ended up on the deck, looking out at the ocean. She saw some movement just below her and decided to check it out. Putting her gun in her belt, she climbed onto the railing and jumped down. Immediately she saw that the movement had been a seagull, making a nest down below—the bird flew off, screeching.

Midnight glanced up to where she'd jumped from and realized she'd have to walk all the way back around the house. "Shit," she muttered, but then something caught her eye. Looking closer at the lower half of the deck, she saw seams that were vertical as well as horizontal. There was a door there. Reaching into her pocket, she pulled out the Spyderco knife she always carried on raids and opened it. She stuck the point into the area she figured would have the locking mechanism. It didn't take much work, and she managed to open the door. She waited three beats before stepping inside, gun out.

She was in a basement, and she could hear the sounds of the raid team upstairs. Then she heard talking in the back half of the room. She quietly moved toward the voice, careful to remain concealed. As she drew closer, she realized there two voices.

"...that fucking bitch of a wife of yours is always in my way." The voice was deep, with a Mexican accent.

"She does have that tendency." The second voice had an all-too-familiar English accent.

Midnight leaned back against the wall. Rick was standing there, and when she looked again she saw that Carlos had a gun pointed at him. Rick's gun lay on the floor between them. As Midnight started to move to get the drop on Carlos, she saw him raise the gun a little further and knew that if she watched a moment longer she would see him pull the trigger. She didn't have time to say "Freeze!"—she didn't have time to think. She just launched herself between them, bringing her gun up as Carlos' went off. She felt the impact of the bullet even as she squeezed the trigger, three times. All three of her shots found their mark, but she was already on the floor, unconscious.

When Midnight came to, she realized she was being held in someone's lap. She groaned.

"Night?" It was Rick.

She opened one eye. "Did I get him?"

Rick grinned down at her. "Yes, love. You got him."

"Goddamn it!" she said as she sat up. "Damn it, damn it, damn it," she muttered, over and over again.

Rick just stared at her as if she were the living dead. To his surprise she stood up and went to one of the walls. She reached up and ripped open her shirt to expose the body armor she wore over a T-shirt. Rick thought he'd collapse with relief. The body armor had a nasty hole in it, but it had stopped the forty-caliber round, even at close range. Midnight was shaking her head.

"What?" Rick stood and went over to her.

She reached up, pulling on the Velcro strips to release the vest. "That fucking hurt!" she said, sounding like a petulant child who had been told a shot wouldn't hurt.

Rick couldn't help but laugh. "Poor baby." He picked her up and carried her up the stairs he had come down earlier. It hadn't escaped him that she had just saved his life, but he could tell that with the mood she was in, sincere, deep gratitude would be wasted on her. As he got to the top of the stairs he looked at one of the officers on cleanup. "Got a body down there."

"Anyone we know?" the BNE agent asked wryly.

Rick shrugged casually, still holding Midnight. "Just the main man himself. No rush though, he's dead." He grinned down at the woman who was still his wife, whether she liked it or not.

Three hours later, Midnight had been checked out and was released from the hospital. She had two cracked ribs and was generally pissed off, but otherwise she was fine. She made Rick drive her to the office, where she verified that every vehicle owned by members of FORS had been checked thoroughly for car bombs. Some had indeed been planted, but all were deactivated safely. She stayed there for the next four hours, trying to assist with the massive amounts of paperwork that needed to be completed. Finally, at around one o'clock in the morning, she walked out to her Corvette. She was too tired to notice Rick leaving at the same time and following her out of the parking lot in his rental car.

Once on the freeway, Midnight spotted the same headlights following her. She continued to watch until she got off the freeway. At the first light, she figured out it was Rick behind her. In a way it irritated her; she knew he'd want to have the big nasty fight they were bound for, and it made her mad that he expected her to have it on the very few hours of sleep she'd had over the last couple of days. By the time she got to her house, she was really mad. She'd jammed the pedal down and arrived three full minutes before him. By the time he pulled into the driveway, she was at the front door, punching in the security code. His long stride brought him to the door as she went to open it. She turned to him, her eyes narrowed.

"What the hell do you want now?"

Rick stared down at her. "You."

Midnight gazed at him for a full thirty seconds before she could even formulate a response. Looking away, she shrugged. "That's too bad, because the feeling's not mutual."

Rick's lips twisted in a sardonic grin. Her voice was far too casual, belying her real feelings. He stepped closer to her, and she moved back, glaring up at him, but she had just backed up against the still-closed door. His close proximity affected her immediately.

"Really?" he said. Then he brought his lips down to hers, kissing her with all his pent-up passion. He reached behind her, shoving the door open. His lips never left hers, not even when he lifted her easily by the waist and stepped inside, just far enough to kick the door shut again. He pulled her body flush with his as he leaned back against the wall. Midnight's hands were clutching the front of his jacket, and when he pulled away, he felt her tighten her grip. They were both breathless, but Midnight's inner voice kicked in, and she tried to turn away.

"No, you don't!" Rick said forcefully as he pulled her back to him. "You're not putting me off again. I want you, and you know damned good and well that you want me, so let's just go with that for now. We'll work the rest out later." His voice brooked no argument, and Midnight knew what he was saying. Right now he would allow it to be just physical. She gave in, realizing she had no other real alternative. Her body was already screaming in protest at her attempted denial. She nodded as she looked up at him. Without another word he brought his lips down to hers again.

They continued to kiss passionately even as they backed toward her bedroom. But their progress was too slow, and Rick lifted her up in his arms, and with his lips still on hers, carried her the rest of the way down the hall and into the room. He broke the kiss to set her down. Then he lay back on the bed, pulling her with him so that she lay over him, taking into consideration her bruised and cracked ribs. Midnight wasn't even thinking logically; she didn't care about the pain in her chest. All she could think of was Rick's lips, body, hands, and other important parts.

Their physical reunion was for the most part earth-shaking, for both of them. Having never been apart for so long before, their bodies seemed to crave every caress, touch, and kiss. Hours later they fell into an exhausted sleep.

Rick woke to the feeling of someone stroking the palm of his hand. He opened his eyes and looked down at Midnight. His right arm was under her neck, and she held his left hand by the wrist. Her thumb was stroking absently at the now-healing cuts. She felt him stir and glanced up at him. "What happened here?" she asked mildly.

"A wedding ring," he replied, just as placidly.

"That's not where you're supposed to wear it, you know," Midnight said, a little chagrin in her voice as well as humor.

Rick shrugged. "Wasn't mine."

Midnight nodded. "I see."

But Rick knew she had known which ring he meant; she was just dancing around the discussion. She was silent for a long time, then she closed her hand in his. "I want Mikeyla back as soon as possible." Her voice was quiet, but he could hear the strength behind her words, and he knew she didn't expect him to argue with her.

"What about me?" he asked after a long hesitation. He hadn't been sure he wanted to ask her point-blank, but he figured he had to face it some time. Midnight's silence was almost tangible; he could feel her tensing.

"Forget I asked that," he said, not willing to hear her answer now. Midnight remained silent. Rick put his lips against her temple, closing his eyes. He knew that infidelity was one of the few things Midnight considered unforgivable. They had discussed it a number of times over the three and half years of their marriage. She had always jokingly told him that if he thought he wanted something better, he should go after it, but that he'd better not waste time looking around for her when he was done, because she wouldn't be there. He berated himself once again for testing her. Now he was afraid he was going to pay the price.

Rick knew their lovemaking didn't necessarily mean they were back together. Her silence only served to fortify that knowledge. Midnight was the only woman he had ever met who could have sex without entanglements. In fact, when she had been single, she'd made a point of getting any guy she picked up back to his place, so she could leave when they finished having sex and not have to explain anything. She didn't apologize for the way she was; she had told him a number of times that her heart and her sex drive were in two totally different locations. One didn't necessarily have to affect the other.

The phone rang, breaking the silence. Midnight reached over automatically and picked it up.

"Chevalier." Her voice came out almost hoarse. She listened for a few moments, then sat up. "When?" She nodded. "Okay, yeah, thanks." She sounded anything but grateful. Her eyes had taken on a look of sadness, and Rick became worried.

When she hung up, he looked at her. "What?"

Midnight shook her head, as if she couldn't believe the news herself. "They arrested Randy an hour ago. They're charging her with two counts of attempted murder of two police officers."

Rick stared at her, stunned. "You and Joe?" Midnight nodded. "Where's Joe?" He wasn't sure if he'd been released from the hospital yet.

"He's still at the hospital." Midnight stood up. "I have to tell him before he hears it from someone else."

Rick got up as well, and twenty minutes later they left. All discussion about their relationship was forgotten for the moment.

Midnight walked into Joe's hospital room. The doctors had told her he was fine; they just wanted to watch him for a couple of days to make sure no infection set in. Dickerson's bullet had caught him in the abdomen, and while it was very painful, it hadn't caused any real damage. Joe had been lucky once again.

He was awake when Midnight came in. He noted the look on her face, and he was sure he didn't want to hear what she was about to tell him.

"Joe…" she began, and the pain in her eyes was mirrored in his own.

Midnight blew her breath out. Rick reached out from behind, putting his hands on her shoulders reassuringly. She nodded, and then looked at Joe again. "They arrested Randy this morning." There were tears in her eyes. She knew she was hurting him, but also that he needed to hear it from her.

"The charges?" he asked, his voice a mere whisper.

"Attempted murder. Two counts."

Joe leaned back against the pillow, closing his eyes. He knew that what Midnight hadn't said was that it was the attempted murder of police officers—and the penalty for that was a minimum of twenty-five years without the possibility of parole. And since Randy herself was considered a police officer, she would likely get closer to the max-imum—life. He had known that Randy's indiscretion wouldn't go unnoticed by the department for long, but he had hoped to be able to talk to the powers that be on her behalf. Now that they'd actually for-mally charged her, things were much more serious.

"Where is she now?"

"County lock up." Midnight felt a sense of unrealism. This was Randy they were talking about, not some gang member or drug dealer. Randy, Joe's wife.

"Has bail been set?"

"Half a million." Joe looked shocked. "She's your wife, Joe. They know she has the financial means to come up with it."

"That's not supposed to matter," Joe said, his voice taking on an edge.

"I know, and it never does when it's a fucking drug dealer with millions, but they're trying to prove a point here." Midnight knew the anger in her voice wasn't helping, but the thought of what was happening made her mad.

"Get it," Joe said simply, his eyes on Rick.

"Joe," Midnight said with a note of caution. "You shouldn't be the one to bail her out—it won't look right."

"You think I fucking care? I want her the fuck out of there now! You know as well as I do that she didn't do it, and if the department doesn't like me bailing out my own wife, they can have my fucking badge."

"Okay!" Midnight held her hands up. "But will you listen to just a little bit of reason here?" She reached out and took his hand. "If you bail her out and take her home, it's going to look like she's snowed you. I think it would be better for her and you if you let me and Rick come up with bail, and I'll hide her away at my house, okay? Nobody really knows about my own place, and that way the press can't convict you of being the world's biggest sucker and convict her of being a whore. Okay?"

Joe knew she was right, but he hated the idea of having to distance himself from Randy when he knew she'd need him. It only strengthened his resolve to find proof of her innocence. Finally he nodded, and Midnight nodded back.

CHAPTER 6

A month later, Randy stood in a courtroom, her heart pounding as the judge entered and sat down at the bench. She sat next to her lawyer when the bailiff instructed them to. Her lawyer was Nicholas Kopanke, an ex-prosecutor for the District Attorney's office who now took on cases that he felt were unjust. He particularly liked cases like Randy's—a young cadet against a large, mean department. Nick didn't kid himself that the charges against his client weren't serious—they were, very much so—but he also knew his client was innocent. She had had an affair that had probably been a setup from day one, and it had put her in a compromising situation when her boyfriend and some friends of his wanted her husband dead.

Nick had met with every member of FORS, finding the unit very interesting and its leaders even more so. Midnight had told him that not only did she not believe that Randy was capable of what she was being accused of, but that she'd be happy to testify on the girl's behalf. Since Midnight had lost a child as a result of Dickerson's actions, and by way of her presence, Randy's, Midnight's words had surprised Nick. He knew that cops tended to close ranks to protect their own. The funny thing was, Randy wasn't really their own; she was only a cadet in the academy, from which she'd been suspended pending the outcome of the trial. Nick had also gotten the distinct impression that the members of FORS thoroughly disapproved of Randy's infidelity, but that disapproval didn't seem to extend to thinking that Randy had wanted Joe or Midnight dead.

The last person he'd talked to was Joseph Sinclair, Randy's husband and the man she was supposed to have wanted killed. Joe had told Nick first and foremost that he expected him to do everything within his power to get Randy acquitted. "No deals," he'd said, his expression showing how serious he was about it. "I don't want her doing any time—none, you hear me?" Nick had nodded, not even thinking about being offended by Joe's condescending tone. It was obvious that Joe, like most police officers, had a low opinion of lawyers, and usually that was for good reason. Nick had assured Joe that he used to work on their side of the law and that even now he didn't take any case in which he thought the defendant was guilty, deferring those to other lawyers who didn't care as long as the client had the money to pay them. Joe had nodded then, seeming satisfied with Nick's statements, and the interview had proceeded. Nick had come away feeling more determined than ever to get Randy Curtis-Sinclair acquitted. He had understood how much Joe loved his wife, and the terrible toll the accusations and subsequent separation were taking on both of them.

Now, as they sat in court, Nick could feel his client shaking. He reached over and put a calming hand over hers.

Randy looked at him, and from the confident look in his eyes drew the strength to calm her nerves. The last month had been the closest to hell she'd ever experienced. Fortunately, she'd been bailed out right away, although Nick hadn't been able to tell her where the money had come from—Rick and Midnight had been careful to hide that information from as many people as possible.

To Randy's surprise, when she walked out of the jail, Darrell and Donovan had been there. Darrell told her that he had heard what had happened and was aware she'd need a place to stay. She had gone with him happily. The following days had been difficult; the newspapers were calling her all kinds of names, trying to make more out of the story than there was. Making it sound like she and Dickerson had been a longtime thing, a claim that Dickerson, who was preparing for his own trial, didn't deny. He allowed the press to say what they wanted, and since he was always nice and easygoing with them, whereas Randy, in her humiliation, avoided them like the plague, the press made Dickerson into the poor love-struck cop who had let his girlfriend draw him into an evil plot. As usual, the media made as little as possible out of the fact that Dickerson was involved with a known drug cartel, and that he had actually been the one to almost fatally injure Lieutenant Midnight Chevalier.

Randy hadn't talked to Joe or heard from him since the raid. Midnight had been by to see her once. Randy had led Midnight out to the backyard of the Curtis home, where she perched uneasily on the retaining wall.

"How's Joe?" Randy had asked, her foremost concern his well-being.

"He's okay, Randy," Midnight had said softly. "You know why he can't see you, don't you? You understand all that, right?"

Randy had nodded, although she really didn't. She assumed Joe believed what everyone was saying. They'd never discussed it, and she knew he had been angry about it when he'd been rescued from the Riveras' compound. But they hadn't talked, so she'd never had a chance to explain. Now she just figured Joe didn't want to have any-thing to do with her, that if the police had found enough to charge her with, then she must be guilty. When she had faced Midnight, she hadn't had the courage to ask any real questions. Nick had told her that Joe was supportive of her, but she thought he was probably just trying to lessen the impact of the whole situation.

When she'd entered the courtroom that day, she had looked around, hoping to see Joe, but he wasn't there. The only people there that she knew were Darrell and Donovan.

The trial began with opening statements. Nick's was very compelling, weaving a tale of a young woman trying to find her independence and falling into a very bad situation. He stopped short of accusing Dick Dickerson of actually setting up the affair from the beginning, knowing that saying that, considering the press Dickerson was receiving, would only serve to turn the jurors off immediately. He wanted to let that information come out during the course of the trial. The opening statement given by Al Cruz, the Deputy District Attorney assigned to the prosecution, was just about the exact opposite, portraying Randy as some money-grabbing slut who wanted her husband's cash, and him out of the way. Every word Cruz said stung. By the end of his statements, Randy had tears in her eyes, which she tried valiantly to hide.

As the Deputy DA sat down, there was a ruckus at the back of the courthouse. Randy turned to see a number of the members of FORS coming into the courtroom. It was obvious they were attempting to do so as quietly as possible, but in their usual manner they attracted a lot of attention, particularly from the press. Especially when they all moved to the front of the courtroom and stationed themselves in the first two rows, right behind Randy. She looked back, catching Spider's eyes. He winked at her. When she looked at each of the rest of them in turn, they all gave her some kind of encouraging gesture. Nick felt his client sit up straighter, and he was glad that FORS had seen fit to attend the trial. Midnight and Joe, however, were not present.

The prosecution's part of the trial lasted a day. The DA's office called in witnesses from the academy class who had seen Randy's behavior toward Lieutenant Chevalier, as well as her friendliness with Dickerson. The DA also called Dickerson as a witness. He had woven a pattern of lies so thick that Randy couldn't believe he was even talking about her. She had been stunned as she listened, and had to hold down the desire to leap out of her chair and kill him barehanded.

"How did you meet Ms. Curtis?" the DA asked.

"She moved in with my sister after her husband kicked her out."

"He kicked her out?"

"Yeah. Randy said he was having an affair with his partner, and when she confronted him about it, he kicked her out."

"She told you that he kicked her out?" the DA said, wanting to emphasize Randy's alleged lies.

Dickerson looked straight at Randy. "Yes."

"When did she discuss killing her husband?"

"Objection!" Nick interjected. "Leading."

"Sustained," the judge said, and told the DA to reword the question.

"Did Ms. Curtis talk about her husband with you?"

"Yeah, she told me about how rich he was, and how she didn't want to leave the marriage without anything, you know."

"So what did she want to do?"

"She said it would be really nice if he'd have an accident, since she was the beneficiary on his life insurance policy as well as the main heir in his will…"

"What did she ask you to do?"

"She wanted me to pick a fight with Sinclair, so I could get him to draw down on me. That way I'd have reason to shoot him." Dickerson managed to make his answer seem so innocent, but Randy was ready to scream.

"Did you do as she asked?" The DA glanced scornfully over at Randy.

"I did one time." Dickerson shrugged. "But I couldn't do it. I mean, kill another cop? That's like killing a brother."

Randy was sure she was going to be sick. She closed her eyes and fought the desire to scream and yell and call Dickerson a lying sack of shit; she knew she had to maintain control, and a screaming defendant was usually a guilty defendant.

"You've been accused of attempting to murder Lieutenant Midnight Chevalier. Did this have anything to do with Ms. Curtis?"

Dickerson nodded, looking very apologetic. "She wanted Midnight—uh, Lieutenant Chevalier—out of the picture. She knew Joe and her were so close that Midnight would make getting to Joe difficult."

"So what happened?"

"Well, we went over to the lieutenant's house, and Randy picked a fight with her. Lieutenant Chevalier was winning at one point, but Randy told me to hold her so she could get a few good licks in."

"And did you do as she asked?"

"She didn't really ask, she yelled at me to do it, and I didn't know how bad she was going to hurt the lieutenant. I know it was a dumb thing to do, but I just let things get away from me." Dickerson shrugged.

"Now, going back to Sergeant Sinclair. How did you get the security code to get into their home?"

"Randy gave it to me. She wanted to make it easy."

"Did you personally accost Sergeant Sinclair?"

"No, I sent some guys to do it. I just couldn't." Again Dickerson looked chagrined.

"Did you tell them to shoot Sergeant Sinclair?"

"No, I think one of 'em just got carried away." He shrugged.

"What did you plan to do with Sergeant Sinclair?"

"I was just going to rough him up and tell him to leave Randy alone. 'Cause she told me that he was threatening her with divorce if she saw me anymore."

"And why did it matter to you that she continued to see you?"

Dickerson looked at Randy sadly. "Because I love her."

Now Randy was sure she was going to throw up, and she had to turn away to keep from doing just that. She shook her head, closing her eyes. She couldn't believe what was happening, and she was powerless to do anything about it. She felt Nick's hand on her shoulder, and knew that she needed to regain her composure. With a supreme effort born of her new independent streak, she turned and caught the merest hint of a nasty smile on Dickerson's face. She stared directly

180

back at him and shook her head just slightly, telling him he wouldn't win this time.

The DA asked a few more questions, and then indicated he had nothing further for the witness. The judge gave Nick the opportunity to cross-examine.

"With pleasure, Your Honor." Nick smiled confidently as he stood up. He looked at Dickerson, his disgust barely veiled. "Sergeant Dickerson—it is sergeant, isn't it?"

"Yes."

"You say that Randy Curtis told you her husband kicked her out?"

"Yes."

"And yet, Sinclair paid her half of the rent. Isn't that true?"

"Well, I don't know. It was my sister's apartment…"

"If it was her apartment, why were you there seemingly all the time?"

"Objection!" Cruz yelled. "Sergeant Dickerson's presence at the apartment hasn't been established."

"Sustained," the judge said. Nick nodded.

"Okay, how often would you say you were at your sister's apartment?"

"About once a week, until Randy moved in."

"And then?"

"All the time. I wanted to see her."

"How did you know that Randy was Sergeant Joseph Sinclair's wife?"

Dickerson paused, looking blank. "I... um... my sister told me, I think."

"You didn't know before that?"

"No."

"So you didn't see her name on the academy roster you received in a memo two weeks before Randy Curtis-Sinclair began the academy?"

"What memo?" Dickerson said, but he had started to perspire.

Nick walked over to the table and opened a folder, producing a document and holding it up for Dickerson. "I have here a copy of a memo addressed to you, as well as other speakers at the San Diego Police Department's hundred and tenth academy class schedule. It contains a roster. I believe this is Ms. Curtis-Sinclair's name listed, just below your sister's, isn't it?"

"Objection!" Cruz howled. "We weren't made aware of this memo in discovery!"

Nick calmly looked at the judge. "San Diego PD has a pretty heavy workload and a large shortage in their clerical staff. It took until just this morning to receive a copy of this memo."

The judge looked long and hard at Nick, but the lawyer's face revealed nothing. "Objection overruled. I take it, Mr. Kopanke, that you have copies for the prosecution? Or couldn't the overloaded clerical staff make copies either?" The judge's voice was wry, but it was a pointed way of saying that Nick better not pull too many more rabbits out of his hat.

"Of course I have copies, Your Honor. Made them myself, as a matter of fact." Nick's grin was wide, and some of the audience chuckled.

He handed a copy to the prosecution and then one to Dickerson. "Do you recognize this memo?"

"I get a lot of these. I don't read them anymore," Dickerson said wearily.

"I see," Nick said. "Isn't it mandated by your department that you read all memos directed to you?"

"I don't know that it's a mandate…"

"Sergeant, I can produce a manual section that says it is."

Dickerson hesitated for a moment, then nodded.

"So, did you read this memo?"

"I probably did."

"And you didn't notice Randy Curtis-Sinclair's name listed just below your sister's?"

"I probably noticed it, yes, but I didn't know her."

"But you got to know her, didn't you?"

"Objection!" Cruz yelled.

"I withdraw the question," Nick said, his eyes firmly on Dickerson. "Now, Sergeant, you said that Randy told you she didn't want to leave the marriage without anything. Is that correct?"

"Yeah, she said that Joe wouldn't give her anything in the divorce settlement."

"So the Sinclairs were getting a divorce?"

"Yeah. Why do you think Randy was worried? She was going to lose all those millions."

"Are you aware, Sergeant, that divorce papers were never filed for Joseph and Randissi Sinclair?"

"No." Dickerson paled just slightly. "I guess I assumed that Joe was filing…"

"Yes, I'm sure you did. Now, Sergeant, you said that Randy wanted to have you pick a fight with her husband. Is that correct?"

"Yes."

"And you said she wanted you to cause Sergeant Sinclair to 'draw down' on you?"

"Yes."

"What does that mean, to 'draw down' on someone?"

"Well, basically it means to draw your weapon and point it at someone."

"I see. And you said that you drew down on Sergeant Sinclair at one time?"

"Well…"

"I can have that part of the transcript read back to you, Sergeant, if you'd like, but as I recall, you were asked if you did as Ms. Curtis wanted and picked a fight with Sergeant Sinclair, to which you responded, and I quote, 'I did one time, but I couldn't do it,' indicating that you could not kill another police officer. I ask again, is that correct?"

"Yes, it is," Dickerson said, sounding flustered.

"What would you say if I told you I can produce witnesses from the apartment complex where Randy and your sister lived who will testify that it was you, and not Sergeant Sinclair, that drew his weapon first, and that Sergeant Sinclair could have easily shot you instead?"

Dickerson looked around at Cruz, his eyes worried now. "I… um… I don't remember, to be honest with you. It all happened so fast."

"I can call that witness and three or four more to refresh your memory, if you'd like."

"How can they remember from so long ago? Maybe they've just made things up according to what the press has been saying?"

"There's a police report on the occurrence, Sergeant."

"There is?" Dickerson's voice cracked ever so slightly.

"Yes. The apartment manager called the police during the occurrence, and she gave a statement as did a few other tenants, but nothing was ever done since they assumed it was police-related business. Let me ask you this, Sergeant. Do you recall Randy herself drawing Sergeant Sinclair's own backup weapon and pointing it at you?"

A murmur went through the courtroom, and Dickerson started to look really nervous. "I… No, I don't remember that."

"The witnesses do."

"Objection," Cruz snapped. "Your Honor, why don't we have a copy of the police report?"

The judge looked at Nick, who shrugged. "They should have it, sir. I listed it with all the other reports and information."

Cruz turned pale. He started to look frantically through his paperwork. Nick had taken a chance that Cruz wouldn't read the informal complaint, and he had been right. Cruz's plate was so full, since he was campaigning to become the next DA, that he didn't have time to be as thorough as he should be. Thoroughness hadn't ever been his strong point anyway. Nick grinned as Cruz found the two-page report buried in the mass of discovery paperwork. Nick wasn't even sure what all he had listed in discovery—he'd loaded it up with so much non-essential paperwork that he knew Cruz would miss a few things.

Nick turned to the judge and smiled. "See?"

The judge grinned. He had an idea what Nick was doing, but he'd liked the guy when he was in the DA's office, and he still did now.

Nick turned back to Dickerson. "Now, Sergeant, you say you don't remember Ms. Curtis pointing a gun at you?"

"No, I don't remember."

"If someone pointed a gun at me, I'd certainly remember." Nick sounded surprised.

"People point guns at me all the time."

"I see," Nick said, so deadpan that another chuckle went around the courtroom.

"I'm a cop."

"I'm aware of that," Nick said, his expression still nonplussed. "Moving on. The incident with Lieutenant Chevalier. You said that Ms. Curtis did all the hitting?"

"I didn't say that."

186

"You said that she picked the fight and instructed you to hold Lieutenant Chevalier so she could 'get her licks in' when she was starting to lose. Nowhere in that statement do I read that you struck Lieutenant Chevalier. Did you?"

"Did I what?" Dickerson said, trying to evade the question.

"Did you strike Lieutenant Chevalier?"

"No."

"Back to my original question. You said Ms. Curtis did all the hitting—is that correct?"

"Yes, I guess so."

"You guess so?" Nick looked at Dickerson cynically. "Sergeant, if you didn't hit Lieutenant Chevalier and Ms. Curtis was the only other person in the room, then it should be safe to say that Ms. Curtis did all the hitting."

"Okay, fine, yes. Randy did all the hitting."

"Okay." Nick walked back over to his table and looked down at Randy as he opened his folder again. He gave her a slight smile, and she returned it. She was thoroughly enjoying watching Dickerson squirm.

He turned back to Dickerson. "I have here a report from the hospital that treated Lieutenant Chevalier." He looked over at Cruz pointedly. "I trust, Deputy DA Cruz, that you have this report?"

Cruz shot him a nasty look and nodded.

"Good. Now, Sergeant, this report indicates that Lieutenant Chevalier sustained head trauma due to blunt force. It also indicates that her internal hemorrhaging resulted from the same. You're saying that Ms. Curtis managed to inflict these wounds with her hands?"

"I guess so. I'm not exactly a doctor."

"No." Nick pulled another sheet of paper from his folder and glanced over at Cruz before turning back to Dickerson. "Now, this report was completed by San Diego Police Department's crime scene investigators. They indicate a blood-spray pattern on the entryway wall to Lieutenant Chevalier's home. How do you suppose that blood got there?"

"I don't know."

"Okay. The crime scene investigators indicated that Lieutenant Chevalier was thrown against the wall. It had her handprint on it, where she tried to stop her forward motion, and the pattern of blood and subsequent pooling indicated that she had hit the wall and slid to the ground, probably unconscious. I checked this with the medical examiner, and he indicated that it would be consistent with her injuries. What do you have to say about that?"

"I don't know anything about any of that," Dickerson said warily.

"Did Ms. Curtis throw Lieutenant Chevalier into the wall?"

"Maybe."

Nick turned and looked at Randy, tilting his head to the side as if sizing her up. "My client looks like she might weigh a hundred and ten pounds soaking wet, and I've seen Lieutenant Chevalier—she's maybe a little bit bigger, but she looks a whole lot stronger. You've seen Lieutenant Chevalier, Sergeant. Wouldn't you say she's probably a lot more solid than my client?"

"I don't know," Dickerson said, his voice noncommittal.

"We could get experts in here to compare the two women."

"I guess so, yeah—Chevalier is probably more muscular. So? Randy was mad."

"Yes, but you said you were holding Lieutenant Chevalier. If that's so, how did Randy manage to throw the lieutenant against a wall?" Dickerson stared back at the attorney; he knew he'd been caught, and he was trying desperately to think of a way out. "You also stated that you had no idea that Randy planned to hurt the lieutenant that much, and yet you would allow her to throw the lieutenant against a wall?" Again, Dickerson didn't answer. "What did you do when you realized that the lieutenant was unconscious? Did you call the paramedics?"

"No. I didn't realize she was hurt that badly."

"She was unconscious, Sergeant." Nick's voice indicated his distaste for Dickerson's assessment of the situation.

"I... I guess I just panicked."

"Panicked?"

"Yeah. I mean, I knew Randy'd get into a lot of trouble, and I was so worried about her and all that I just panicked, and we left."

"So much for your love for your fellow officer—or is that just for the brother officers?" Again, a murmur started in the courtroom.

"No, I—" Dickerson started, but Nick cut him off.

"You said that Ms. Curtis gave you the security code to Sergeant Sinclair and her house. Is that correct?"

"Yes."

"Did she write it down for you?"

"What?"

"Did she write it down?"

"Yes."

"On what?"

"What?"

"What did she write it on?"

"I don't know what you mean."

"Did she write it on a napkin, a piece of paper, the back of your hand—what?"

"I, uh... I don't remember."

"Okay. You said that you didn't order the men who accosted Sergeant Sinclair to shoot him. Is that correct?"

"Right."

"Do you know how Sergeant Sinclair was injured in the shoulder?"

"What?"

"Sergeant Sinclair was shot in the shoulder. He said you did it. Is that true?"

"No."

"It's not?"

"No."

"Do you know how Sergeant Sinclair was injured in the abdomen?"

"No."

"He was shot, Sergeant. What kind of weapon do you carry?"

"I, uh, I carry a forty-five caliber Ruger. Why?"

"Let me ask the questions, Sergeant. What would you say if I told you that the bullet wounds to Sergeant Sinclair's shoulder and abdomen were a ballistic match for the bullets in your gun?"

"I'm sure I'm not the only person in the world to carry a forty-five Ruger," Dickerson said haughtily.

"No, but are you saying a ballistics match isn't proof?"

"I guess it is."

"You said you loved Randy Curtis-Sinclair. Is that true?"

"Yes."

"Do you still love her?"

"Not after all that's happened, no."

"But you loved her before?"

"Yes."

"Would you have married her?"

"What?"

"If she'd gotten a divorce from her husband, would you have married her?"

"I don't know."

"But you loved her."

"Yes."

"And you didn't know she wasn't getting divorced?"

"No."

"Even when she went back to her husband only two weeks after starting to date you?"

"I, well…" Dickerson's voice trailed off again as he realized that what he'd been telling the press hadn't convinced the important people. "I guess I kind of figured she wasn't getting a divorce."

"But Sergeant Sinclair was harassing her to stay away from you?"

"Yes."

"Why would he need to do that if she was with him?"

"I guess he was afraid she loved me too."

"Did she?"

"What?"

"Did she love you too?"

Dickerson looked over at Randy and saw the triumph in her eyes. "I thought so."

"But she left you to go back to her husband." Nick shook his head. "I have no further questions for this witness, Your Honor."

He sat back down next to Randy and was summarily patted on the back by many members of FORS. Randy smiled at him, inclining her head by way of thanks. Nick was pretty satisfied with himself.

When it came time for the defense, Nick called the members of FORS up one by one. Each of them told him that Randy wasn't the kind of person to go after Joe's money, that they honestly believed she loved Joe very much and she had just lost her way a little bit, and she had found the wrong guy to travel that path with.

Nick called Richard Debenshire to the stand. Rick looked very solemn as he sat in the witness chair. "Officer Debenshire, for the record, you're married to Lieutenant Chevalier. Is that correct?"

Rick nodded. "Yes."

"And it was your child that died in the incident with Sergeant Dickerson and Randy. Is that true?"

"Yes." Rick's eyes looked a little haunted.

"And who found the lieutenant?"

"Our three-year-old daughter did." Murmurs raced around the courtroom once again.

"I know this is difficult for you, but can you tell me what happened?"

Rick's eyes took on a distant look. "I had dropped our three-year-old daughter off at the house. She went into the bedroom and found her mother lying in a pool of her own blood. She called me, and when I got back to the house, I called the paramedics. Midnight was almost dead." Rick swallowed and closed his eyes briefly as the memories came back.

"And you found the blood on the entryway wall. Is that correct?"

"Yes, and I called the crime scene team in."

"Would you say your wife is strong, Officer Debenshire?"

"She can kick my ass if she's mad enough," Rick said, grinning. A laugh went up from the members of FORS.

"So you find it hard to believe that Randy could have inflicted the damage to your wife that she's accused of?"

Rick looked over at Randy, and then back to Nick. "Even if Randy was capable of it mentally, she couldn't take Midnight. Not many women can."

"So you think that Sergeant Dickerson had something to do with it?"

"Objection!" Cruz yelled. "Sergeant Dickerson isn't on trial here."

"Oh, no, that's next week—sorry." Nick didn't look the least bit apologetic. "I withdraw that question. Rick, do you think that Randy intended to kill your wife, at any time?"

"No."

"What is your relationship with Sergeant Sinclair?"

"He's been my best friend since I was five."

"So you two are pretty close?"

Rick grinned. "That's safe to say."

"And do you think that Randy had any intention of having your best friend killed?"

"No. I think she ended up with the wrong people, and they made things look the way they wanted them to."

"Do you think Sergeant Sinclair is gullible?"

"Joe?" Rick said, as if surprised by the question. "Hardly!"

"So you don't think he'd be fooled by insincere emotions?"

"Objection! Calls for speculation."

"Sustained," the judge said, eyeing Nick.

"Knowing your friend, has he been fooled in the past with insincere emotions or feminine wiles?"

"Joe's immune to 'em." Rick knew he was lying just a little bit; they didn't need to know that Joe wasn't immune to Randy.

"Thank you, Officer Debenshire. I have no further questions."

To many people's surprise, the DA had no questions for Rick. He had planned on asking him about his and Midnight's breakup, but had decided it would only make him look worse at this point.

When Nick called his next witness, it shocked many people, including Randy—Lieutenant Midnight Chevalier.

Midnight walked into the courtroom looking every bit the tough leader of a unit of gang members. She and Rick passed each other in the aisle, and they touched hands, giving each other a supportive look. Everyone in the courthouse caught it, as did a few members of the press, on film. Midnight wore all black—except for her badge, which she wore clipped to her belt as usual— slacks, her favorite dress boots, as she liked to call them, and a cotton shirt. Her hair was pulled back from her face with a black clip, and she wore the slightest bit of makeup. Many members of the press fell in love with her again. She made a striking figure as she raised her right hand to be sworn in. She had been discussed a lot in the proceedings, and now everyone was able to put a face—a beautiful, delicate one—to the woman who had been brutally beaten and left for dead.

"Lieutenant, thank you for coming," Nick said, and Midnight inclined her head slightly. She looked over at Randy and saw the surprise still in the girl's eyes. It occurred to her then that maybe Randy didn't know she believed her. She had danced around being specific at the Curtis home, not wanting to give Randy any false hope. But now she realized she should have been a little clearer. She caught Randy's eyes and smiled. Randy's eyes widened at the blatant support Midnight was offering her, and she smiled back.

"Lieutenant Chevalier, you run FORS—is that correct?"

"Yes."

"What does FORS stand for?"

"Former Organized Riot Seekers," Midnight said with a wry grin.

"And you hired Ms. Curtis?"

"Yes."

"Why?"

"I liked her."

"And she ended up marrying your partner?"

"Yes, the same time I married Rick, actually." Midnight glanced to the back of the courtroom, where Rick was leaning against the wall. Their eyes met for a moment, and then Midnight looked back at Nick.

"Let me get straight to the point, Lieutenant. Did Randy Curtis cause you the injuries that she is charged with?"

"No."

"Do you feel that Ms. Curtis in any way told Sergeant Dickerson to do what he did to you?"

"No. He was pissed because a woman was getting the better of him in a fight. So he fought dirty." Midnight's words fell like rocks in the courtroom. The murmuring started again, to the point that the judge had to bang his gavel and call for order.

"He was fighting you?"

"Oh yeah. Randy tried to take one swing, but she missed. I backed up, and Dickerson was there."

"What did he do?"

"Objection!" Cruz cried out. "I reiterate that Sergeant Dickerson is not on trial here!"

Nick looked up at the judge. "Your Honor, I'm trying to establish that my client had nothing to do with Sergeant Dickerson's actions. I need to get the whole story to do that."

"Objection overruled," the judge said.

Nick turned back to Midnight. "What did he do then?"

"He grabbed me from behind, and I jammed my boot heel down on his foot. We grappled some more, and then he got mad."

"What was Ms. Curtis doing?"

"She was just standing there. Looking absolutely horrified, I might add."

"How could you see that?"

"I turned to her at one point to jibe at her about the type of company she was keeping, but Dickerson grabbed me again before I could."

"Why didn't you report the assault to the department?"

"Because I knew that Joe wouldn't forgive Randy for something like that."

"Why did that bother you?"

"Because my partner is my best friend, and he loves his wife very much. I wanted them to get back together."

"So you withheld evidence so they could make up?"

"Yes."

"Are you close to your partner, Sergeant Sinclair?"

"Very. As I said, he's my best friend."

"Do you think my client wanted to have him killed?"

"No."

"Even after what happened to you, you still believe her?" Nick asked, disbelief in his voice.

"She loves Joe. She wouldn't do that."

"Not even for money?"

"Joe didn't want a divorce from her—she wouldn't have lost any money. He paid the bills the whole time she was on her own."

"Thank you, Lieutenant. I have no further questions." Nick went to sit down.

"Cross-examination?" the judge asked Cruz.

Cruz eyed Midnight. "Yes, Your Honor."

Midnight looked back at him calmly.

"Ms. Chevalier," Cruz said authoritatively as he stood.

"It's Lieutenant Chevalier or Mrs. Debenshire—choose one," Midnight said calmly, but her eyes were narrowed. She didn't see Rick's slow smile.

"My mistake, Lieutenant Chevalier." Cruz inclined his head to her. They were usually on the same side, and this was odd for him. "I know that this has all been a strain on you, and I don't want to compound that, so I have just a few questions."

Midnight said nothing, just looked back at him, waiting.

"You said that Ms. Curtis wasn't capable of wanting her husband killed. Is that correct?"

"No, it's not."

Cruz looked a little confused. "I'm sorry?"

"I said that Randy loves Joe and that she wouldn't do that. I believe that you're thinking of my husband—he said that Randy wasn't capable of it." There was subdued humor in Midnight's eyes. She had felt it necessary to help Cruz out a little bit—she felt almost sorry for him at this point. He was outmatched.

"Yes, okay," Cruz said, referring to his notes. "I'm sorry. Can I take that to mean that you do feel that Ms. Curtis is capable of hating her husband enough to want him dead?"

"No," Midnight said, not reacting to the way he twisted her words. She knew this was a lawyer's game. She did, after all, have a law degree too.

"Didn't you deny Ms. Curtis' request to ride along with your unit during her academy training, because you thought she had an attitude problem?"

"Yes, I did."

"But that attitude problem couldn't expand to include her husband?"

"There's a large difference between an attitude and all-out hate, Mr. Cruz," Midnight replied calmly.

"The attitude was directed at you?"

"Yes."

"And what occurred to make you feel that Ms. Curtis had an attitude?"

"She challenged my... agility when I was teaching in her academy class."

"Challenged your agility?"

"Yes, she indicated that when an officer in my unit got older, that officer probably sat at a desk and pushed paper a lot more." Midnight couldn't hide a sardonic grin.

"What did you do?"

"I proved her wrong."

"How?"

"By taking her down to the mat."

"How did she react to being humiliated in front of her academy class?"

"She didn't." Midnight knew where he was trying to go with this line of questioning, and wasn't willing to help him get there.

"She didn't react?"

"No."

"She wasn't angry?"

"Not to my knowledge."

"Are you sure you're telling me the truth, Lieutenant?"

"I don't need to lie to you, Cruz."

"So you don't feel that Randy could have been angry enough to consequently do what she did to you at your house?"

"She didn't do anything. I think we already covered that."

"But she was there."

"We covered that too. Yes, she was there."

"And you don't feel that lends itself to malice."

"No."

"Why not?"

"Mr. Cruz, I have dealt with hundreds of gang members, and I've been in a number of confrontations with gang leaders. Guilt by association isn't always plausible. People get swept up in what happens to them sometimes. I think that's what happened to Randy."

"But Ms. Curtis admittedly took one swing at you," Cruz said, playing the one card he had left.

"Yes, she did." Midnight shrugged. "She's a kid. She had to try it again."

"Oh, one last question. You admitted that you withheld evidence regarding this incident."

"Is that the question?"

"Is it correct that you withheld evidence?"

"Yes, I did."

"And what's to keep you from withholding more evidence to save your friend's wife from going to jail?"

"If I honestly believed Randy wanted him dead, do you think I'd want her around him?" Midnight raised an eyebrow at him, as if he were crazy.

Cruz stared back at her, realizing he'd be very happy when they were back on the same side. He didn't want to have to face her this way again. She was tough. "No further questions."

"Redirect, Mr. Kopanke?" the judge said.

"Yes, Your Honor. Lieutenant Chevalier, how serious is the penalty for withholding evidence?"

"It could cost me my shield," Midnight said calmly.

"How long have you been a police officer, Lieutenant?"

"Ten and a half years."

"That's a long time. You must be very sure of Randy's innocence if you're willing to give up your life's work."

"I am, just as sure as I am about her love for my partner." Midnight's voice carried across the courtroom; there weren't many dry eyes in the place. Especially not Randy's. She hadn't realized the risk Midnight had been taking by not handing her over to the authorities.

"Thank you, Lieutenant."

"Mr. Cruz?" the judge said. He knew the man wasn't foolish enough to try and attack Lieutenant Chevalier again, but he had to ask.

"No questions, Your Honor."

Midnight left the witness stand, and as she walked down toward the audience seating, she stopped behind Randy and leaned down to whisper in the girl's ear. "Hold it together, Curtis. It's worth the prize."

Randy laughed just a tiny bit, through her tears. She stood up and turned to Midnight, reaching out to hug the person she at one point had fooled herself into thinking she hated. "Thank you," she whispered. "Whatever else happens, please tell Joe that I love him."

"He knows," Midnight said. Randy cried harder, hugging Midnight again. Then she turned and sat down. Nick handed her his handkerchief, and she took it gratefully.

Court adjourned for the day shortly after that, with the judge giving the jury their admonishments.

Randy left the courtroom feeling a little bit better than she had that morning. "Nick, there's something I don't understand," she said as they walked down the hall.

"What?"

"Why was Dickerson stupid enough to lie, if he knew that Midnight would take the stand and tell the truth about what really happened?"

"Well, part of that had to do with a little last-minute... oh, gee, I forgot to tell Cruz till this morning that I was calling Midnight as a witness. Too late for Dickerson to change his bullshit story. And second, I think Dickerson figured that Midnight wouldn't testify for you, even if what he was saying was bullshit, because she might believe the stuff about Joe."

"That makes sense, I guess." She eyed him suspiciously. "You certainly know how to finagle them, don't you?"

"Hey," Nick said. "If I thought you were guilty, I wouldn't be doing all this. You're not, and I'm not letting them put away an innocent woman because she had an affair."

Midnight drove her Corvette home from the courthouse, with Rick in the passenger seat. He kept looking over at her, ever astounded.

"What?" Midnight said, glancing over at him. She made a face.

"You're incredible, you know."

"Yeah, I know." Midnight sounded like she thought anything but, but she was grinning.

"I mean it. You chewed that DA up and spit him out, and I think he enjoyed it."

"Funny." Midnight's cellular phone rang, and she reached over to hit the hands-free. "Yes?"

"Lieutenant Chevalier?"

"Dearborn?" As usual, she refused to use his rank.

"You and I need to meet."

"What for?" Midnight replied, surprising Rick with the quick anger in her voice.

"Frankly, for the disciplinary problems I seem to be having with you, Lieutenant."

"I see. And when will this little soiree take place?" She sounded overly casual, and Rick could see the anger on her face. It was amazing how quickly her mood could turn.

"Friday, in my office at oh nine hundred hours."

"This Friday?" Midnight said, surprised.

"Yes, this Friday, Lieutenant."

"Well, if this trial's not over, I won't be available."

"What do you mean, you won't be available? I thought you testified today?"

"I did, but the trial's not over yet."

"So what difference does that make?"

"One of my people's on trial. I'm gonna be there."

"Randy Curtis is not a member of FORS."

"No, but she's a member of this department, and she's my partner's wife," Midnight snapped.

"She's accused of trying to kill you and of trying to have your partner killed!" Dearborn exclaimed, as if she didn't know.

"And," Midnight said sharply, "she's innocent until proven guilty."

"Regardless, Lieutenant, I want you in my office at nine o'clock on Friday." His voice brooked no argument.

"And if I don't show?"

"Consider yourself on report."

"Add it to the list then." Midnight reached over and hung up. "Sonofabitch."

"My," Rick said, eyeing her. "Don't like the new guy much, do you?"

"That's an understatement."

Rick shook his head. "I can't believe he's still going to go after you about that raid."

"Wait till he hears about my testimony today. Withholding evidence—that'll be a good one for my file," she said derisively.

"Think he'll do that?"

Midnight looked over at him, and then started to shake her head. "You have no idea."

"So give me an idea."

"You missed a lot while you were vacationing across the pond, dear."

"Like what?"

"Like my first meeting with the assistant chief after the chief had his heart attack."

"What happened?"

"Oh, not much. He basically just told me that my unit had received far more special treatment than it deserved. And that I'd have to learn a new way of moving up in the world…"

Rick looked at her for a long moment, and suddenly, seeing the look in her eyes and how white her knuckles were as she gripped the steering wheel, he knew what she meant. "Was he saying what I think he was?"

Midnight laughed sardonically. "Oh, he didn't say it, but yeah, he basically thinks I laid anyone who would get me to the top. Some top!" She laughed again, but there was no humor in it.

"Jesus, Night. He said this to you and the guy's still breathin'?" He was serious; he knew Midnight's temper, that and the fact that she had probably told Joe. "Did you tell Joe?"

"Duh."

"I ask again—why is that guy still alive?"

Midnight laughed, this time with a little more humor. "I wouldn't let Joe kill him, that's why. I told him I needed him around to help me, not in jail somewhere."

Rick was silent for a long time, his face somber. "I should've been here for you," he said softly.

Midnight shrugged, not wanting to tell him that yes, he should have.

"Guess I've really left a lot to be desired where those marriage vows are concerned, haven't I?"

"Some, yes. I can't exactly remain blameless here either."

"What? Joe?" Rick said mildly, which surprised Midnight.

"That's what I was referring to, yes."

"Was it the same with him as it was before?" It was a question Rick had wanted to ask her for a long time.

Midnight looked over at him, her eyes narrowed just slightly. But he saw no anger there; it was if she was wondering how he knew. Her words confirmed that.

"No, it wasn't, but how...?" Midnight said, wondering how he knew.

"Let's just say I found that out for myself. No one is you. Hell, the way I look at it, you bein' with Joe, what, one time, was more like an afterthought than a real affair. Wasn't it?"

Midnight smiled. He knew her better than she had realized. She nodded slowly. She reached over and turned up the stereo, indicating that she didn't want to talk about it anymore. Rick knew to back off then. He felt a sense of relief that he'd been right about her and Joe. It made him feel like there was still some hope for them.

Over the last month, they hadn't really talked. Every time he had tried to get serious about a conversation, she'd get angry or just go quiet. He'd given up. They'd made love a few more times, each as intense as the first encounter after such a long time had been. He'd found himself wanting her more than he had in years. It was as if he was back to square one with her. When they'd first gotten together, things had been fiery from the start. But then he'd made the mistake of falling in love with her, and he'd decided that he didn't care if she loved him or not—he wanted to be with her no matter what. And here he was again, willing to be with her for whatever time she'd let him. It was strange; he had come full circle all over one woman. Midnight was the literal center of his life.

Now, as the song on the CD ended and another began, he realized what it was. "I Want You," the song that had affected him so much in England, the first night in the club. The one he had known she'd like. He started to grin, and Midnight saw it.

"What?"

Rick shook his head. "Nothin'." He hesitated. "I heard this song in England and thought of you. I knew you'd like it."

"You did, huh?" Midnight grinned at him.

Rick nodded, smiling.

They listened. Midnight sang the lyrics as Rick watched her, thinking how amazing it was that she could bounce back from so much in her life and still be so easygoing and happy. A little while later, the song ended and yet another began. Midnight looked over at him. "Did you hear this one too? 'Cause I like it a lot."

Somehow Rick knew what she meant, and as she turned the volume up, he knew why she liked it. It was called "Break Me Shake Me." The words were like a script of their thunderous relationship.

Rick noticed that she knew every word by heart, and she sang them like she really meant them. And he could tell that she did. It bothered him. When the song ended, he was still looking at her.

"Is that our relationship?" he asked, though he already knew the answer.

"Isn't it?" she said, raising an eyebrow.

"Yeah, I guess it is, but maybe that's the problem."

"Do you think we could be any other way?"

"If we wanted to."

But Midnight was already shaking her head. "Rick, we are who we are. You can't change something like that. Our relationship has always been fire and ice."

"I know." Rick leaned back against the headrest, feeling depressed suddenly.

"It's not bad, Rick. It's us."

"Yeah, but are we 'us' anymore? It's a moot point if we aren't together anymore."

She gave him a pointed look. "We're here together now, aren't we?"

Rick stared back at her, narrowing his eyes. "Wait a minute," he said hesitantly. "Are you saying…"

"Am I saying what?" Midnight said, twisting the knife just a little more. Then she started to laugh, and nodded.

Rick couldn't begin to quell the excitement that rose in his body. She had just restored his life with a simple laugh and a nod. It was damned dangerous, loving someone so much that such simple actions could all but kill him.

"In that case…" Rick reached into his jacket pocket. "I have something to return to you."

Midnight looked over at the diamond-and-emerald ring, laughing harder. She raised an eyebrow at him. "Have you been carrying that thing around with you all this time?"

Rick grinned sheepishly. "Yeah."

"Shame on you. Your grandmother would be appalled!"

"I doubt that. She'd know I was just trying to return it to its rightful owner."

"Is that what I am?" Midnight said. She'd just pulled up at a red light, and Rick reached over to take her left hand.

"No." Rick slipped the ring onto her finger, looking into her eyes. "You're my wife, and if that ring ever comes off your finger again, I will probably kill you." Midnight shook her head—he sounded half serious, and probably was, but she liked it.

CHAPTER 7

The next day in the courthouse, it was obvious to everyone that knew Rick and Midnight that they were estranged no longer. He watched her constantly, but in a deeply affectionate way. His deep blue eyes no longer held regret, but they were still ever possessive of his wife. And beware the foolish soul that tried to come between them again. Midnight had accepted that Rick was possessive of her, while Rick had accepted that he could never totally own her, because doing so would kill the fire that drew him to her. They had adjustments to make, but they'd do it, because they loved each other and wanted no one else in the world.

The bailiff called the court to order. As the trial proceeded, Nick pulled yet another astonishing rabbit out of his hat—he called Joseph Michael Sinclair the Fourth to the stand. A large ruckus went up as Joe walked in the back doors. Much as Midnight had been the day before, he was dressed in black from head to toe, the only color his gold shield glistening on his belt. Randy thought she'd die from the sight of him. He hadn't looked so incredible to her since the day they'd met. She knew it was from a combination of not seeing him for a full month, the stress of the trial, and the confident, calm look on his face as he raised his hand to be sworn in—or perhaps just the shock that he was there in her defense—but Randy felt almost faint. When Joe sat down, and his light blue eyes trailed over to her, she saw no accusation, no anger, no hate. She was sure she must be dreaming. There were tears in her eyes as she looked back at him. He shook his head at her, just slightly, as if to tell her not to cry, and a smile pulled at his lips as she cried harder because of it.

"For the record," Nick said, aware that he didn't need to clarify to anyone who Joe was, but doing it for effect, "you are Sergeant Joe Sinclair?"

"Yes," Joe said, his English accent clear in the courtroom.

"And you are married to the defendant."

"Yes." Joe looked straight at Randy. "Randy is my wife."

"How long have you and Randy been married?"

"Almost four years now."

"Did you ever intend to divorce your wife?"

"No."

"Even when you knew she was having an affair?"

"Yes, even then." Joe sounded slightly pained, and Randy closed her eyes.

"Did you intend to write your wife out of your will?"

Joe grinned, shaking his head. "No, I wouldn't want anyone else to have my family home but Randy."

"Your family home, Sergeant Sinclair—where is that?"

"In England."

"And your parents left you that home?"

"Yes."

"It would be safe to say that it means a lot to you?"

"Almost as much as Randy," Joe replied, eliciting sighs from a number of the women in the room, at which he grinned.

"So you never doubted your wife?"

"I'm in love, not deaf, dumb, and blind. I doubted her at one point, but after I had a chance to think about everything that surrounded this whole mess, I knew she had nothing to do with it."

"What kinds of things did you think about?"

"Well, there was the incident at the range."

"What happened there?"

"Randy was set to do a run-through of the obstacle course at Duffy Town, and I just happened to be there. She started the shoot, and I could see that she was having a rough time. Eventually the gun literally jumped out of her hand."

"Your Honor, I'd like to submit at this time that Sergeant Sinclair is a certified range master for the San Diego Police Department, and is being utilized as an expert witness in these types of incidents."

"Mr. Cruz?" The judge looked over at the Deputy DA.

"Stipulated," Cruz said, having used Joe in many cases himself. He couldn't fault his knowledge.

"Sergeant Sinclair, what does it usually mean when a gun does what you described?"

Joe scratched his forehead. "It means one of two things. Either the gun is too much for the shooter, or the gun has been loaded with ammunition that is too heavy for the gun."

"Which means what, 'too heavy'?"

"It means that the structure of the gun can't compensate for the strength or amount of powder used to fire the bullet."

"And which was it in this case?"

"The ammunition was too heavy. I checked it myself right there. I even argued with the sheriff's range master about it, until the man looked at the gun magazine himself and agreed."

"Why does that day stick in your mind?"

"Because Dickerson mentioned it when he and his friends had me. He said he'd loaded the ammunition himself, that he hoped the gun would blow up in Randy's face."

"Did he say why?"

"No, but I got the distinct impression that he wanted to get rid of her."

"He told you that she was involved in the scheme, didn't he?"

"Yes, he did, but he couldn't give me any proof. He just used it to make me mad."

"Did it work?"

"Partly, yes."

"Why partly?"

"Well, I didn't believe him about Randy giving him the security code, or any of that crap, but when he told me Randy had been there when he'd attacked Midnight… that got to me."

"Why?"

"Because Randy hadn't told me."

"Did your partner tell you?"

"No."

"Lieutenant Chevalier testified that she withheld the information from you and the department because she wanted you and Randy to get back together. Does that seem logical to you?"

Joe grinned. "For Midnight's screwed-up way of thinking, yes."

"You and your partner are very close?"

"That's a safe statement, yes."

"And your wife is aware of that?"

"She always has been, yes."

"So there's no reason for her to be suddenly worried that you were having an affair with your partner."

"Actually, I think she did manage to convince herself of that, but I think she had help there."

"And that help came from?"

"The Dickersons."

"Why do you say that?"

"Because Sarah Dickerson and Randy visited Midnight at her office one time. Sarah was goading Randy into accusing Midnight of sleeping with me."

"Objection!" Cruz interjected. "Hearsay."

"Your Honor, I will be recalling Lieutenant Chevalier to verify this story."

"Overruled. Continue, Mr. Kopanke."

"What other things have occurred to you since the raid, Sergeant Sinclair?"

"Well, Dickerson himself admitted to me that he was the one that just about killed Midnight. He only said that Randy had stood by while it was happening."

"Sergeant Dickerson told you he did it?"

"Oh yeah, he was real proud of himself."

"Charming. What else, Sergeant?"

"Well, there was the night that Dickerson showed up at our house, when he knew I was out."

"How do you know he knew you were out?"

"Because he knew that if he showed up at my house when I was home, I'd probably kill him." Joe's expression was completely serious.

"So what happened?"

"He confronted Randy and ended up trying to hurt her."

"Hurt her how?"

"He strong-armed her in the throat. She had a bruise for about a week."

"Not exactly an action for someone who claims to love her, you think?"

"Not exactly."

"Have you ever struck your wife?"

"Never."

"And you love her."

"Yes."

"Is there anything else, Sergeant?"

"Oh, yeah, there is one little detail that Dickerson let slip when he thought I'd be dead and no one would ever find out."

"And what detail was that?"

"That he'd been involved with the Riveras long before this."

"And how do you know that?"

"Objection! Your Honor, Sergeant Dickerson isn't on trial here." Cruz sounded exasperated at having to remind them over and over.

"Your Honor, at this juncture, establishing Sergeant Dickerson's longtime relationship with a drug cartel will set the pattern of planning and lies he has proliferated, thereby making my client a victim of his plot rather than a willing participant."

"Overruled."

Nick turned back to Joe. "Sergeant Sinclair, what did Dickerson say that made you aware of his longtime relationship with the Riveras?"

"He said he'd had his eye on Randy for a long time, that he'd seen her with me, about four years ago." Joe looked over at Randy to see how she was taking this revelation; she had started to pale.

"What happened four years ago?"

"A lot of things, actually, but one of them was my and Randy's kidnapping."

"The two of you were kidnapped? By who?"

"By a gang called the Scorpions. They were working for the Riveras and trying to wipe out FORS. They almost succeeded too. Did a lot of damage."

"How was Dickerson involved?"

"The day Randy and I were grabbed, I got a phone call. It was a sergeant saying that one of our people needed an okay to do a search. The guy gave me directions to the place. As it turned out, it was a setup—it was where the Scorpions were waiting to grab us. Dickerson's the sergeant that called me."

A number of angry voices shouted out in shock and fury. The judge called the room to order and indicated for Nick to continue.

"Sergeant Sinclair, you said that Sergeant Dickerson told you this, but do you have any proof?"

"Yes."

"And what is that?"

"Phone records. We managed to backtrack my cell phone records and, focusing in on that day and the approximate time, we traced the numbers for the phone line. And lo and behold," Joe finished triumphantly, "the call came from Dick Dickerson's office at the PD."

"You have those records to turn over to the District Attorney?"

"Yes, right here." Joe pulled out a sheaf of papers from the inner pocket of his jacket.

"And before you object, Mr. Cruz," Nick said, "we were only able to attain these records last night by overnight mail. I can have that verified by the cellular phone company."

He turned back to Joe. "There was one other thing, wasn't there, Sergeant?"

"Yeah. The other thing I can put my finger on is at the raid, when we went back to hit the house. I had told Randy to stay in the raid helicopter—I didn't want her involved because she isn't fully trained. Anyway, just like my partner, she didn't listen." He grinned at Randy, then looked back at Nick. "But the next thing I know, I hear Dickerson on the other side of the house. I look around the deck, and he's pointing his gun at Randy, telling her that she'd been easy, but now she was in the way…" Joe trailed off as he remembered the cold fear that had run through him, forcing him to charge Dickerson before he could shoot Randy.

"That's when you jumped Dickerson and he shot you. Is that correct?"

"Yes."

"So you saved Randy's life?"

"I guess so." Joe was never willing to take credit for his heroic deeds.

"Dickerson was aiming right for her, wasn't he?"

"Yes."

"And at that range, could he have shot her?"

"Even as bad a shot as he is, yes."

Nick grinned, as did many of the members of FORS. "So he could have killed your wife?"

"Yes."

"Then you saved her life."

When Joe hesitated again, someone in one of the front two rows—who interestingly enough sounded like Spider—said, "Just admit it already!" The courtroom burst into laughter as Joe grinned widely and nodded. There were bursts of applause, some even from the press.

When the courtroom had calmed down again, Nick continued. "A man doesn't save the life of a woman he doesn't trust."

"Not usually," Joe said.

"Do you think your wife had anything to do with the plot to kill you or Midnight Chevalier?"

"No," Joe said, his light blue eyes on his wife. No one in the room doubted him for a second.

"Thank you, Sergeant. No further questions."

"Mr. Cruz?" the judge said, aware that Cruz wanted to cross-examine this time.

"Yes, Your Honor. Joseph Michael Sinclair... the Fourth, is it?"

"Yes," Joe replied, his eyes cool.

"You come from a pretty prominent family back in England, don't you?"

"I guess so."

"I was told that your family is on the highest-regarded society rolls. It that true?"

Joe looked at Cruz as if the man were crazy, then shrugged. "I haven't been back there since Randy and I were married, and before that it had been over ten years."

"Well, then let me assure you, Sergeant, your family name is still intact on those rolls. That's pretty important in England, isn't it? Being on the society rolls?"

"In England, yes."

"What does it mean to you?"

"It means that my surname is on some damn piece of paper somewhere." Joe was getting irritated at the tactic the DA was taking.

"It doesn't mean anything to you?"

"No."

"You're an only child, aren't you?"

"Yes."

"So, the way I understand it, it's up to you to carry on your family name. Is that correct?"

"My father had siblings."

"I see. And are there any boys in the family yet?"

"Objection!" Nick called. "Sergeant Sinclair's family history isn't in question here."

The judge looked at Al Cruz. "He's right. Get to the point, counselor."

"It's your responsibility to carry on your family name as well as to uphold the level of aristocracy it has achieved. Is that correct?"

"No," Joe said, stunning the District Attorney.

"No?"

"You heard me."

"Why not?"

"Objection! The witness has answered the District Attorney's question. It isn't the sergeant's fault if the DA didn't get the answer he wanted."

"Sustained. Move on, counselor."

Al Cruz looked a little deflated, but he regained his composure as he looked over his notes. "Sergeant, you said that your wife was aware of your relationship with your partner. Is that correct?"

"Yes."

"Was she aware of your previous sexual relationship with your partner?"

Joe narrowed his eyes at the DA, not because of the question, but because the idea of this type of laundry being aired for the press pissed him off. "Yes."

Cruz once again looked surprised. It took him a full minute to recover this time. "Have you and your partner been together that way since you've been married?"

Joe looked to Midnight, who was sitting with Rick. She was looking straight at him, and when their eyes met, she gave him an imperceptible nod. Joe could see that she was holding tightly to Rick's hand, and he knew what her nod meant.

"Yes," he said calmly.

"You've had a sexual relationship with your partner while you were married to Randy Curtis?"

"Yes."

"Was Ms. Curtis aware of this?"

"When?"

"Excuse me?"

"Was she aware of it when?"

"Before Lieutenant Chevalier was attacked."

"No."

"Was she aware of it at any time before you were abducted?"

"Yes."

"When?"

"Three days after Midnight was assaulted."

"So it is plausible to say that your wife was angry enough then to want you dead?"

"No."

"She knew you had an affair with your partner, and you don't think that made her mad?"

"Mad, yes—murderous, no."

"Well, we don't really know that, do we?"

"Is that a question?"

"No. This incident at the range—you said that the range master wasn't aware of the ammunition loaded into Ms. Curtis' weapon?"

"That's correct."

"How would someone manage to load ammunition into a department-issued weapon without the range master knowing?"

Joe shook his head. "It's pretty easy, considering the cadets take their weapons home at night—since Dickerson was at the apartment constantly, it would have been easy to change the ammunition."

"Wouldn't it be fair to say that anyone could have done that, then?"

"I guess, but who else would want to?"

"Maybe Ms. Curtis herself?"

"Randy?" Joe said, having to hold back a laugh. "Until the academy, she barely knew which end of an ammunition magazine went into a gun, let alone how to load it and what ammunition to use to make the gun do what it did."

"But it's possible?"

"It's possible, but then you could have loaded it that way too," Joe said sarcastically.

"Let me assure you, I didn't. Now, Sergeant, you said that you didn't think Randy gave Sergeant Dickerson the security code to your house?"

"Yes."

"That's a pretty high-tech security system you have. How else would Sergeant Dickerson have gotten the code?"

"Well, there was the day I came home and found Randy and Dickerson at the house. He could have easily looked over her shoulder when she punched in the code to get in."

"What were they doing there?"

Joe shrugged. "Getting some of her things, I guess."

"Couldn't she have been showing him the layout of the house, to make it easier for him to have you abducted?"

"I guess."

"How did you react to your wife and her boyfriend in your house?"

"I threatened to kill him," Joe said tonelessly.

"That's a pretty strong statement to make."

"I felt pretty strongly about it when I made it."

"Do you still want to kill Sergeant Dickerson?"

Joe's eyes flicked over to Randy, then back to Cruz. "If he was putting your wife through what he's putting Randy through, wouldn't you?"

Cruz didn't answer, but Joe noted that many heads in the courtroom nodded. His eyes went to Randy again, and she smiled weakly at him.

"You said that it bothered you that Ms. Curtis hadn't told you about the attack on Lieutenant Chevalier?"

"Yes."

"Is it possible that she didn't tell you because she had a lot more to do with it than she wanted to admit to you?"

"If she'd had much more to do with it, Midnight would have told me. It was because Randy's participation in the incident was so inconsequential that my partner felt it wasn't important. I trust Midnight's judgement."

"With your life?" Cruz asked pointedly.

"Implicitly."

Joe and Midnight exchanged a look, and the rest of the courtroom watched.

"You said that Sergeant Dickerson admitted to trying to kill Lieutenant Chevalier. Why would he admit that to you?"

"Because he had a gun pointed at my head, and he figured I wouldn't be around to testify."

"Yet here you are."

"Yes."

"And how did you escape this drug cartel house? I thought it was a major cartel and that they had armed men guarding it, twenty-four hours a day."

"I guess they didn't figure on Dickerson."

"In what way?"

"That he's a lousy shot anyway, and when he gets mad, he's worse."

"Could you explain that to the court, Sergeant?" the judge asked, wanting this information clarified for the jury.

"The room they had me in down in Mexico had a window, but it was double-paned, too hard to break with my bare hands. Dickerson kept coming in and trying to push me, trying to make me mad. But the first time he tried to shoot me, I had turned the tables on him and his shot went wide and to the right. I noted that, and hours later when he was at it again, I goaded him into trying to shoot me again. That time he managed to shoot out the window, so I could dive through it."

The judge nodded, almost smiling at Joe's ingenuity.

"When you and your wife were abducted four years ago, did you at any time see Sergeant Dickerson with these people, the Scorpions?"

"No."

"And you just happened to remember now that Sergeant Dickerson was the one to call you, after all this time?"

"I didn't remember. Dickerson reminded me."

"Okay." Cruz nodded. "One last question, Sergeant. It's obvious to everyone in this room that you love your wife very much. Isn't it possible that your love of her is blinding you to the possibility that she wanted you dead?"

"I think if she wanted me dead, she had plenty of opportunities to do it herself."

"Thank you, Sergeant. No further questions."

Joe was dismissed. He stood and walked out. Outside the court-room, he leaned heavily against the wall. He heard the door open be-side him and glanced down. Midnight was there looking at him, with Rick right behind her.

"I'm sorry," Joe said to them both.

"About what?" Midnight said. "That we had sex, or that you had to admit it?"

Joe grinned at the wry tone in her voice. "Let me see," he said, looking up at the ceiling. "If I say both, I'm dead. If I say the first one, I'm dead. So I guess I'll go with number two, Your Honor."

Midnight laughed, shaking her head. "I figured it'd come out sooner or later. The people that should have known"—she glanced back at Rick—"knew long before now. No harm, no foul."

"I guess," Joe said uncertainly.

"You think it hurt Randy's case?" Midnight asked, raising an eyebrow.

"Don't you think so?"

"I think Cruz thought he was going to surprise someone with the information."

"Like who?"

"Like Nick," Midnight said. "Like you, so you'd stumble or lose your cool."

Joe nodded. "This court shit is certainly nasty business."

"Yes, it is, but fortunately we're usually on the other side."

"Yeah…" Joe trailed off, chagrined at having to be on the defense.

"I heard Nick's putting Randy on the stand next," Midnight said, her tone forcibly light.

"Where'd you hear that?"

"Nick."

"I don't want her up there. The DA'll crucify her."

"Joe, she got herself into this mess, and she's a big girl. She can get herself out."

Joe nodded slowly, hoping she was right.

The court adjourned after Joe's testimony. Randy declined Nick's offer to take her to lunch. She was too nervous. She knew she would be on the stand after the break, and it terrified her. She'd never been questioned before; more importantly, she'd never been cross-examined by a Deputy District Attorney. Nick had warned her that it would probably be brutal, but he was sure that if the jury could see how sincere Randy was in her regret, it would be the trick to turn the jury to their side.

Randy sat with her arms resting on the table as she looked over the questions Nick planned to ask her. They'd gone over them again and again, but she was still afraid she would freeze up. Her hands shook with her nervousness. She just wanted all of this to be over. She jumped when someone came up behind her and was further surprised when a hand wearing a distinctly familiar signet ring reached out to take hers.

Randy looked up, and Joe smiled down at her. He pulled her to her feet and took her in his arms. Randy couldn't believe he was holding her again. She buried her face against his chest, breathing in the smell of him. He kissed the top of her head, and she felt the urge to grab his hand and run out of the courtroom and never come back. But she knew the idea wasn't realistic.

"How're you doin'?" Joe asked softly.

Randy smiled. "Better now that you're here with me."

A pained look crossed Joe's face. "Randy, I'm sorry I couldn't be there over this last month, but they kept telling me it would prejudice your case, and I couldn't take that chance."

Randy shook her head, looking up into his light blue eyes. "You were here today, and that's something I never expected."

"Why?" Joe looked perplexed. "You didn't think I actually believed all that crap, did you?"

Randy shrugged, lowering her eyes from his. His finger under her chin brought them back up.

"I love you, Randy. I wasn't just saying that for the court reporter, you know."

Randy was silent for a moment, not sure what to say. "I just... When you got back from Ensenada the first time, when you looked at me, I knew he'd told you about Midnight, but you didn't say anything." She shrugged again. "I guess I figured you just didn't want to discuss it with me because you believed it."

229

Joe looked at her seriously for a moment. "I didn't talk to you about it because I didn't really know what I thought. I knew that you weren't a part of Dickerson's plan, but I also knew that for a while there you turned into someone I didn't know. I just wasn't sure, Randy."

Randy nodded, understanding what he was saying and loving him for being honest with her. "I guess I did leave a lot to be considered those days, didn't I?"

"You were a little weird, yes," he said, grinning down at her.

Randy returned the grin. "I know, and we're still looking for that pod, right?"

"You got it," Joe said, smiling brilliantly at her. He reached out and pulled her to him, hugging her close. He leaned down, his lips touching hers gently. Randy responded immediately, but in more of a soft, romantic way than with passion. They both knew this wasn't the place or the time. Their kiss lingered for a few long moments, and when it ended they stared into each other's eyes. Their look said all the things their minds didn't want to think about. Neither of them noticed the news camera operator sitting in the far corner of the courtroom, taping the whole exchange.

Eventually they sat down and talked about Randy being put on the stand.

"I'm scared, Joe," Randy said honestly.

Joe nodded, understanding her trepidation. "Look, the important thing is to stick to what you and Nick have talked about."

Randy nodded. "It's not Nick I'm worried about though."

"I know, but you have to keep one thing in mind when you're cross-examined."

"What's that?"

"Give the shortest answers possible. Don't give the guy any more information than he asks for."

"Like you?" she said, grinning.

"Yes," Joe said, as if demonstrating. "When he asks you the question, think to yourself, can I answer this with a yes or no? If you can, do it. Don't let him make you mad, don't let him get to you, because if he does, he's going to get you to say something you didn't mean to, and that's how he'll convict you. Okay?" Joe was watching her solemnly.

"I can do this," Randy said.

"I know you can."

"Will you be here?" she asked, suddenly concerned he'd leave.

"I'll be right there." Joe pointed to the bench behind them.

Randy nodded at him, her eyes wide.

"Baby, just remember you've been through worse."

"I have?"

"Randy! Remember San Ysidro? Daniel Robbins, all that?"

Randy closed her eyes, grinning, then looked at Joe. "I guess I didn't consider that as bad, because I knew you'd get us out of it. This time though…"

"You'll get out of it yourself, Randy."

This time it was Randy who drew hope from his faith in her. It had all come full circle.

Time seemed to pass in the blink of an eye, and before Randy knew it, court had reconvened. Joe did exactly as he had said he would and sat right behind her. She could feel his presence, and drew from it.

Nick recalled Midnight to ask her about the time Randy and Sarah had come to her office. Midnight explained that Randy had been asking about an accident she'd heard Joe had been involved in, but that Sarah Dickerson had tried to turn everything into an issue about her and Joe and the rest of FORS not being Randy's friends. She also told him that Sarah had insinuated that she knew all about her and Joe. Nick asked why Midnight hadn't brought this incident up when they had talked, and Midnight said that she'd actually forgotten about it until Joe brought it up. Cruz had no further questions.

Randy knew what was next. Even so, when the judge asked Nick to call his next witness and Nick said, "The defense calls Randissi Curtis-Sinclair," she felt her stomach tighten. Standing, she glanced back at Joe. His eyes were on her, and he nodded. She moved to the witness box. She was sworn in and sat down.

"Randy," Nick said, his voice friendly. "For the record, you are the wife of Sergeant Joseph Sinclair. Is that correct?"

"Yes."

"How long have the two of you been married?"

"Just under four years now."

"How old were you when you met Sergeant Sinclair?"

"Nineteen."

"And you worked for him—is that true?"

"Yes. I was hired as his secretary."

232

Nick looked surprised. Of course, he wasn't, but he wanted the jury to understand how young she had been when they'd met and married. He looked over at Joe and then back to Randy. "Sergeant Sinclair must have seemed larger than life to you then."

"He was, believe me," Randy said, sounding young still.

"Did he sweep you off your feet right away?"

"I would have liked him to, but no, he was already involved with someone else then."

"Lieutenant Chevalier?"

"No, someone totally different."

"So he wasn't dating his partner when you met? How did you find out about their relationship?"

"Well, it was obvious to me that she and Joe were very close. Joe was going through a very rough time when I met him—Midnight was trying to help him through it. But it was really Midnight that told me about her and Joe's unique relationship."

"Unique how?"

"Well, they were very close friends, and sometimes, when things got too intense, or one or the other of them needed someone, they'd be there for each other, in every way…" She trailed off, not wanting to cheapen Joe and Midnight's relationship.

"By every way, you mean in terms of sex?" Nick asked, his look pointed.

"No, not just sex. I realized that it meant just being there to reach out and hold each other, or offer the other a kiss, or a caress, when they needed it most. It wasn't just sex for them. In fact, Joe told me a lot later that it really didn't have to do with sex. Just that sometimes they needed to be as close as two people could get, because they had no one else that they trusted enough to open up to in that way."

"And what changed that?"

"Well, Midnight found Rick, and Joe found me."

"So they discontinued their relationship, at least sexually, right?"

"Yes."

"When did you think they were having an affair?"

"I only thought that when I applied at the department and Joe was against it."

"Let's address that, then. You said you applied with the department—as a police officer, right?"

"Yes."

"And your husband was against it?"

"Yes."

"Why?"

"Joe lost his parents to violence, and I guess he was afraid he'd lose me the same way."

"Did he threaten to leave you if you went through with your application?"

"No, he didn't."

"But you ended up leaving him. Why?"

"Because I thought he was having an affair with Midnight."

"And you decided that at what point?"

Randy nodded. "I guess I let Sarah talk me into the idea of them having an affair, but I don't want to say it was all her fault. She was reacting to my discontent over Joe's lack of support. I let her talk me into it. She didn't make me think it."

"So you don't think Sarah Dickerson was trying to set you up with her brother?"

"No, I think Dick just saw an opportunity and grabbed it."

"Randy, why did you want to become a police officer?"

"Because I wanted to do the important work that my husband, his partner, and their unit did."

"You didn't set out with the intention of having an affair?"

"Hardly. I just wanted to go to the academy and become…" She trailed off, as if she'd said more than she wanted to—and she had, even with her own lawyer.

"Wanted to become what, Randy?"

Randy thought about it for a moment, wondering how her answer would affect things, but aware that she needed to tell the truth now. "I wanted to be more like Midnight. I thought it would bring me closer to Joe." Randy looked over at Joe and saw the surprise in his eyes. She glanced at Midnight as well and saw chagrin reflected there.

"After everything that's happened, has your attending the police academy brought you closer to your husband?"

"Yes. Even after all that we've gone through, the anger, the hate, the lies, he and I have been closer than we were before. I'm more on his level now, instead of being the scared little girl he had to protect and watch constantly."

"Why did you have the affair with Dick Dickerson?"

"It just happened. I guess I had that old 'the grass is always greener' outlook at that point. I'd never been intimate with anyone but Joe, and I'd never shared as much of myself, and I guess I just figured that if Joe was great, then someone else might be even better. Dick pretended to support my decision to become a police officer, and with all that was happening, or not happening with Joe, I guess I just wanted a little bit of reassurance. Dick was there, conveniently enough, to give it to me."

"You said 'conveniently enough.' What makes you think that the relationship with Dickerson was contrived?"

"In hindsight, I can see that he was playing on my weaknesses. He told me that he'd think it was great to have any wife of his become a cop too. He talked Joe and Midnight down from day one. He told me that cops were basically sluts, and that I shouldn't doubt for a minute that Joe and Midnight were 'doing it.'"

"And you fell for it?"

"Hook, line, and sinker."

"But was it what you thought it would be?"

"Not even close. He was all gung-ho about my law enforcement career, and about bashing anything having to do with Joe, Midnight, or FORS, but otherwise, he lacked a lot of Joe's qualities. Then the thing with Midnight happened, and I was afraid, and I had a chance to see Dick's true colors, and they were violent."

"There was another incident beside the one with Midnight?"

"Yes. The day after Joe and I got back together, I went back to Sarah's apartment to get some of my things together and hopefully talk to Sarah. I didn't want to see Dick again. In fact, I hadn't since the day after we were at Midnight's house."

"Which was how long?"

"Three days."

"What happened at the apartment?"

"Dick was there. I told him I had seen Midnight."

"When did you see her?"

"Once with Joe, when he called me, needing my support, and then again the next day, when Midnight called me to the hospital."

"What did Lieutenant Chevalier say to you?"

"She had told Joe and Rick that she didn't remember what had happened to her, but she told me that she did indeed remember, and that I had better start remembering where my loyalties lay, or else she was going to bury me in the deepest hole she could find."

"Did she tell you why she didn't tell the police that you and Dickerson had attacked her?"

"She said that it was because she knew Joe still loved me and that she didn't want to be the one to put his wife behind bars."

"An interesting way of looking at things, wouldn't you say?" Nick said, more to the jury than to Randy.

"Midnight is like that. She puts things into perspective in terms of her priorities, and Joe is one of those priorities."

"So, getting back to the incident at the apartment, what did Dickerson do when you told him what Midnight had said?"

"He made light of it. I told him he was just lucky she wasn't pressing charges. That's when he told me that he'd tell everyone I had a lot more to do with Midnight being injured than I really did. He was standing behind me, threateningly, and I was afraid of what he'd do, so I jammed my elbow into his ribs. He grabbed me and threw me on the bed, but I got to the other side and threatened him with a bat."

"Did you hit him?"

"Yes, when he advanced on me, telling me he'd kill me if I hit him with it."

"What happened then?"

"I ran out of the apartment, and that's when I ran into Joe. Dickerson came out then, and when he saw Joe he went for his gun."

"Do you think he planned to kill your husband at that point?"

"I think that if he could have, he would have, yes."

"Is that why you backed your husband up?"

"Yes."

"You didn't trust his abilities?"

"No. I trusted his abilities, but I didn't trust Dick's underhanded way of handling things like this."

"Okay. So you were happy to be back together with your husband?"

"Very."

"And why didn't you tell him about the incident with Lieutenant Chevalier?"

"I knew that I needed to, that it would cause problems later, but I was always afraid it would irreparably damage our healing relationship. I wanted to tell him when the time was right. But we all know there's no such thing, right?"

"And when Sergeant Dickerson came to your house, did he threaten you again?"

"Yes, and he got physically violent again."

"What did he do?"

"He pinned me against a wall with his forearm pressed to my throat."

"Were you afraid of him then?"

"Yes."

"The night your husband was taken, you don't remember anything?"

"No. The doctors said I inhaled ether, and that it must have knocked me out."

"And when your husband returned from his captivity?"

"I knew that Dick had told him about my involvement with Midnight being hurt."

"Did he ask you about it?"

"No. I could just tell by the look in his eyes that he knew, but I don't think either of us wanted to talk about it just then."

"And at the raid, Sergeant Sinclair saved your life?"

"Yes."

"Is it true that you saved his once too?"

"I'm sorry?" Randy wasn't sure what he was referring to.

"Four years ago, when you and Sergeant Sinclair were abducted, a woman tried to kill your husband with a knife, and you shot her. Is that correct?"

Randy stared back at him dumbfounded, but then she remembered that Joe had talked to Nick before the break ended. She looked to Joe, and he nodded.

"Ms. Curtis, is that correct?"

"Yes, I guess it is."

"You guess?" Nick asked wryly. A chuckle went through the room. Randy seemed just as modest about the topic as her husband.

She smiled. "Yes."

"Randy, did you ever plot or request the murder of either Lieutenant Midnight Chevalier or your husband?"

"No."

"Thank you. No further questions."

Al Cruz stood, poised for the attack.

"Ms. Curtis, would you say your husband is very rich?"

"Yes."

"And is it true that you come from very modest means?"

"Yes."

"Being married to a rich man must be nice for you then?"

"Being married to Joe is fantastic, but it has nothing to do with money."

"But it does help, doesn't it?"

"No, it hinders us more."

"Why do you say that?"

"Because then jerks like you can make it sound like I married him for the money," Randy said calmly. She glanced at Joe and saw he had a sardonic grin on his face.

"So it wasn't the money then," Cruz said, nodding as if he'd been corrected. He was actually reeling just slightly from her response. "Did you envy Lieutenant Chevalier's relationship with your boss at the time?"

"Yes."

"And you still do, don't you?"

"No."

"What has changed that has made you less envious of Lieutenant Chevalier?"

"I have."

"You've changed. And was that change due to your relationship with Dick Dickerson?"

"No."

"But this change occurred during this time, isn't that correct?"

"No."

Cruz looked at her, perplexed. She wasn't answering his questions the way he had expected her to. "Did it bother you when Lieutenant Chevalier and her husband split up? Did you feel threatened by that?"

"Why would I?"

"Because she was free to go after your husband then. Did that bother you?"

Randy looked at him for a long moment. "If Midnight had wanted Joe, she could have had him all to herself any number of times before he and I were married. In fact, when Joe and I were engaged, I asked him if he loved her, and if he would rather be marrying her."

"And what was his response to that question?"

"He's married to me, isn't he?"

"For the moment," Cruz said snidely. "Moving on to your law enforcement career. If you love your husband so much, why would you decide to embark on a career you knew he wouldn't approve of?"

"Loving someone doesn't mean giving up your life for them and being everything they want you to be. I think the word you're looking for there is 'obsession.'"

"So even though you thought it might end your marriage, you continued to try to become a police officer. Did your husband change his mind during that time?"

"No, he just kept silent about his disapproval."

"But you knew he disapproved?"

"Yes."

"And your affair with Dick Dickerson—you knew your husband would find out about it, didn't you?"

"Yes, I knew."

"And yet you did it anyway?"

"Yes."

"Were you trying to hurt your husband?"

"Emotionally, yes."

"Why?"

"Because I had imagined that he'd hurt me."

"By sleeping with his partner?"

"Yes."

"But he hadn't, at that point?"

"Right."

"And you said that you felt that Dick Dickerson was trying to lure you into a relationship with him. Is that correct?"

"Yes."

"Isn't it possible that he had a man's natural reaction to a beautiful woman in distress?"

"It's possible, but he knew Joe, and he knew me, so I think there was more to it than that, considering his connections…"

"Ms. Curtis, isn't it true that you had numerous conversations with Mr. Dickerson about your husband's habits?"

"I don't know what you mean."

"I mean, for example, you told Mr. Dickerson that your husband likes to sit on the deck of your mutual home and watch the sunset with nothing but a glass of wine. Didn't you purposely tell him that so he would know that your husband would be unarmed at that time of day?"

"No, I told him that in a regular conversation, when I was trying to defend my relationship with Joe and how different he was away from the office."

"I see. And didn't you talk to Mr. Dickerson about your husband's negligence, on many occasions, about remembering to lock the rear sliding glass door in your home when he came in from the deck?"

"I don't remember the specific conversation, no, but it is possible." Randy looked over at Joe. She hadn't even thought about the conversations she'd had with Dick on the nights when they'd sat up drinking and talking. She had obviously told him too much. Joe's face was unreadable, but she could see that it was bothering him that so much had been said. She looked back at Cruz, narrowing her eyes slightly. He was making this into something it wasn't, but she knew it was his job.

"Isn't it true, then, that you were laying the groundwork for your husband's demise, and your return to his arms was merely another part of the plan?"

"No!" Randy snapped, her eyes narrowing angrily. "How can you stand there and—" she started, but she saw the quick shake of Joe's head. She looked over at him, and he shook it again. He was trying to tell her that she was doing exactly what Cruz wanted, and she shouldn't let him get to her. She took a deep breath and blew it out silently.

"What were you saying, Ms. Curtis? You were wondering how I could stand here and do my job, and keep a scheming, money-hungry adulteress from planning and administering the murder of one of San Diego's finest officers and getting away with it? Was that what you were asking, Ms. Curtis?"

Randy looked back at Cruz, her turquoise eyes unblinking. "I think you should know, Mr. Cruz, I am still a married woman, and my name is Randy Sinclair, not Curtis. And no, I don't want to know what you tell yourself at night so that you can live with your profession." Her voice was very calm, her eyes reflecting only serenity.

"Excuse me, I seem to be mistaking all sorts of names today." Cruz looked miffed. "Mrs. Sinclair, you said that you didn't tell your husband about the incident with Lieutenant Chevalier because you were afraid he'd leave you?"

"No."

"Excuse me?"

"I didn't say I was afraid Joe would leave me. I was afraid he wouldn't forgive me for it."

"What's the difference?"

"He may have been unable to forgive my lack of honesty in this instance, but he wouldn't leave me over it."

"How do you know that?"

"I know my husband, Mr. Cruz."

Cruz was silent for a moment. "Either way, isn't it true that you expected Lieutenant Chevalier to meet with a fate similar to your husband's, and for that reason you were unwilling to blow the whistle too soon?"

"Again, I don't know what you mean."

"There were car bombs and home invasions set up for many of the key members of FORS, including a bomb set for Lieutenant Chevalier at her and her husband's home. Didn't you expect that bomb to kill her so your little secret would remain safe forever?"

Randy was grinning openly now as she shook her head. "No, I didn't know about any bombs or home invasions."

"You seem awfully sure that this court will accept your word on it," Cruz replied, looking very cocky.

Randy looked over at the judge. "Your Honor, may I ask a question of the District Attorney, to clarify a minor point?"

"No, but you can ask your attorney to do so," the judge said, surprised by the request.

Nick stood and walked over to the witness stand. Randy whispered something to him, and Nick nodded, almost excitedly. He went across to talk with Cruz for a moment, and Cruz ended up searching for something in his massive files. A few minutes later, Nick made a request that he be allowed to redirect a question for his client. The judge asked Cruz if he was done with his cross-examination. Cruz checked his notes and shrugged, nodding.

Nick stood in front of Randy then. "Mrs. Sinclair, I have been told that the address of the home the District Attorney was referring to was in a Rosin Court. Do you know that house?"

"Yes, it's the house Rick and Midnight bought after they were married."

"They own another home as well, don't they?"

"Well, they don't, but Midnight does. Her house is farther into Pacific Beach. It's the house she owned by herself before she married Rick."

"And what is important about this information?"

"The DA said a bomb was set up at the house on Rosin Court, but Midnight wasn't staying at that house."

"Where was she staying?"

"At her own home. She'd gone there after she got out of the hospital, not back to the house on Rosin Court."

"And how did you know about this?"

"Because Joe and I went over to that house a few days after she got home."

"And the significance in this is?"

"That if I had really wanted Midnight dead, I wouldn't have had them set up a bomb in a house she wasn't likely to return to for a long, long time."

"Thank you, Randy. No further questions."

"Mr. Cruz?"

"Nothing, Your Honor." Cruz sat down.

An hour later, closing statements had been made. Nick had stressed that none of the members of FORS nor the two people that Randy was accused of trying to kill thought she had done it. He had pointed out the holes in the DA's theories, as well as the weak character of the man making the loudest accusations, Dick Dickerson. Cruz made his closing remarks as well, stressing the jealousy factor and the fact that people never wanted to believe the person they loved capable of any wrongdoing.

The case was given to the jury at 2:30 in the afternoon.

Joe stood outside the courthouse, leaning against one of the marble pillars, smoking. He had taken up the habit again since Randy had been arrested. Jessica walked out of the building and headed over to him. She leaned against the pillar as well, her shoulder touching his arm. She glanced up at him.

"So? What do you think?" she asked.

Joe shook his head, squinting in the bright sunlight. "Don't know."

"Have you thought about what you'd do if she's actually convicted?"

"Spend every penny I have appealing it."

"And if nothing works?"

Joe gave her a sharp look, then nodded. He knew she was just playing devil's advocate. He shrugged, taking another long drag of his cigarette, as if to calm his nerves. "I guess I'll break her out of jail, and we'll live on the lam for the rest of our lives."

"Cute," Jessica said, grinning. "Seriously though, I think that you and Midnight impressed a lot of people in that courtroom."

Joe guffawed. "Yeah, impressed 'em that we're better than any episode of Melrose Place."

"Bullshit, Joe." Jessica looked up at him as he gazed out over the marble steps. "I have news for you. By tonight you're gonna be a household name, just like Midnight and Randy will be."

Joe rolled his eyes. "That ought to put my undercover career safely in the basement."

"The price of fame. But in all honesty, I think people will change their opinion of law enforcement after this trial. I think your unit made a lot of people sit up and take notice. Your unit is worthwhile, and what you're doing is important. It's the kind of unit I'd like to be part of." She looked straight at him, pausing until he looked down at her. "So?" She gave him a pleading look. "Can I have a job?"

Joe laughed out loud, shaking his head as he pushed himself away from the pillar and turned to face at her. "I dunno. I've heard you're pretty skittish in a firefight."

"Shut up!" she said, grinning as she swatted him on the arm. Joe dodged out of the way, laughing. Jessica stood with her feet apart and her hands imperiously on her hips. "I'll have you know that I have the best range master in the country training me."

"Really? And this is as far as you've come..." He trailed off as he had to dodge her again. He clicked his tongue. "Maybe you should take up dogwalking, or somethin' a little less hazardous."

"And maybe I should just shoot you in the butt, to prove to you how much my aim's improved!"

"Okay!" Joe held up his hands in surrender. "You win. You got the job."

"Really?" Jessica said, stopping in her tracks.

"Really."

"You can do that?"

"Gee, thanks for your confidence in me," Joe said, grinning.

"Joe!" Midnight's voice came to them from the door to the courthouse. Joe looked over at her. "The jury's back."

Joe glanced at his watch. They'd only been out for an hour and a half. He and Jessica strode to the double doors, Joe stopping long enough to put out his cigarette.

They met up with Randy and Nick outside the courtroom. Midnight ushered Nick and Jessica in, giving Randy and Joe a chance to talk alone.

"Are you ready for this?" Joe asked, taking her into his arms.

Randy leaned heavily against him but nodded. She pulled away to look up at him, her eyes searching his. "No matter what happens in there, Joe, I want you to know that I love you and that I always will…" She trailed off as if she were thinking about what could happen to her.

Joe kissed her on the forehead. "Come on, let's get in there and get this over with."

Joe and Randy Sinclair entered the courtroom side by side, hand in hand, as if they were standing together against everyone there. They walked down the aisle, and Joe let go of her hand long enough for her to go around to her seat up front. She turned and looked at him as the judge walked in. Joe held his hand out to her again, his wedding band glistening in the lights. Randy focused on it as the jury entered from another room. She was afraid to look at them, afraid she'd see a guilty verdict in their eyes. Cameras were rolling and clicking away as they waited for the foreman to stand. Randy looked up into Joe's eyes and saw the confidence in them, and then she was brave enough to look at the jury. She waited for what seemed like forever.

"Has the jury reached a verdict?" the judge said.

An older man, the jury foreman, nodded. "Yes, we have, Your Honor."

"On the first count of attempted murder of Lieutenant Midnight Chevalier, how do you find?"

The foreman's gaze shifted to Randy, and she felt her heart skip a beat. "We find the defendant not guilty." A cheer went up from the observers as Randy smiled, with tears in her eyes, her hand clutching her husband's.

"On the second count of the attempted murder of Sergeant Joseph Sinclair, how do you find?"

"We find the defendant not guilty."

Randy let out a yell as she was caught up in Joe's arms. He lifted her over the barrier between them and hugged her to him, as if he'd never let her go again. "It's over, Randy. It's over," he murmured in her ear as she cried tears of relief and joy.

"Okay, give way here, Sergeant!" Midnight yelled over the din.

Joe obligingly released Randy, and she turned to Midnight. The women regarded each other for a fraction of a second, and then they both yelled triumphantly and caught each other up in a hug. Randy was congratulated and patted and hugged a number of times by the members of FORS and of course by her brothers, who had just come in that afternoon. Darrell had said that being at the trial would have made him too mad; he just wanted to be there when they acquitted her. He said he'd never had any doubt, and he hadn't. Randy never strayed far from Joe, always keeping within arm's reach.

CHAPTER 8

The drive home was almost unreal. Randy kept looking over at Joe as if expecting him to have disappeared. Her hand was gripped tightly in his.

"So, how do you feel?" he asked once they were on the freeway. They'd had a hard time even getting out of the courthouse. The press had been hard at their heels, wanting to know more about them, congratulating them, asking them question upon question. Joe had held her hand tightly and, lowering his head, basically bulldozed out of the courthouse to his Porsche, which was parked not too far away. The press were surrounding the car as well, but Joe managed to push his way through on the passenger's side and open the door for Randy, then shove through the throng to his side. He looked over at her now, waiting for an answer to his question, but aware that she was trying to decide.

"Better, but I just feel like we need to be together for a while before I know everything is really okay." She was hesitant, and Joe knew what she was talking about. Things had definitely changed between them, and some things couldn't be undone no matter how much they wanted them to be.

"We'll get through this," Joe said, his voice sure.

Randy just nodded, looking out the window.

Farther along the freeway they were overtaken by two TV news vans. Both were rolling, probably taping the happy couple going home. Joe glanced at the driver of the closest van, gave a quick salute, and proceeded to floor it. The Porsche, its turbo engine kicking easily into overdrive, sped away, leaving the much slower vehicles behind. Joe looked over at Randy and grinned. She returned it with one of her own.

"It's not going to be that easy, ya know," she said.

"Yeah." Joe grimaced. "Jess was already sayin' today that we'd probably be a household name tonight."

"She's probably right. I mean, here I was, the damsel in distress, and my handsome knight and his trusty companion came charging in to save me. Can't beat that for a news story."

"Yeah." Joe shook his head ruefully. "Guess you won't have to worry about me doin' UC for a while."

Randy looked chagrined. "I guess undercover work would be a little risky after all this, huh?"

"'Fraid so." He didn't sound too upset. "Have you thought about what you're gonna do now?" The question was simple enough, but it made Randy start to worry.

"I don't really know what my options are at this point. I guess I'll have to wait and see."

"Well, one of your options is to return to the academy and finish."

Randy looked at him for a long minute, trying to detect any inflection in his voice, but she knew he was keeping it neutral on purpose. "After everything that's happened," she said softly. "What do you want me to do?" It was an honest question. After everything he'd done for her, she wanted him to have his way on this. It was important to him, and she knew it.

"In court you said that if I had forbidden you to become a cop, you wouldn't have gone through with it. Is that true?"

"Yes." Randy nodded.

"But that was because it was the easy way out, and that way you didn't have to find out if you could cut it or not." His light blue eyes pinned her momentarily. "What about now?"

"What do you mean—do I think I can cut it?"

"Yeah, do you?" There was no accusation, no put-down in his voice, only the question.

Randy thought about it for a few moments, then nodded. "Yes, I think I can. I don't think I'll ever be the chase 'em down and hook 'em up kind of cop, but I think I could do some good out there. But it's a moot point, Joe. If you don't want me to do it, I won't. If I learned anything through all of this, it's that nothing is worth risking losing you."

Joe surprised her by pulling off the freeway and bringing the Porsche to a halt on a side street. He turned to her, taking her hands in his. "That's what I needed to hear," he said, his light blue eyes searching hers. "Through all of this, I've learned something too. I've learned that if I want to be happy with you, you have to be happy with you. What I'm saying, Randy, is that if being a cop is what you want, then I want it for you too."

Randy smiled as he pulled her into an embrace. She couldn't believe the change in him. And she was very happy that she hadn't been the only one to do a little bit of growing after everything. Knowing that Joe was behind her, Randy knew she could do anything in the world, and it made her feel very powerful.

After a few minutes, Joe put the car into gear and headed home. When they arrived, there were press people out front. Joe glanced over at her. The black Porsche sat at the entry to their driveway; they could see the press down the hill by the front of the house.

"Think we should run off for a while and try an' out wait them?" His grin was sly. "Or should I run a few of 'em over and make us real headline news?"

Randy smiled widely, shaking her head and clicking her tongue. "Sergeant Sinclair, run over innocent news personalities? I'm surprised at you! Maybe we should run over a few cameramen, just to make it seem unbiased."

Joe laughed, leaning back against the headrest. Randy laughed too, and it took them a few minutes to recover from their fit of hysteria. It was as if the intensity of the last month had finally gotten to them, and laughing was the way they worked through it. Randy would point out a cameraman, and Joe would nod, pointing to a reporter. They went a whole five minutes like that, eventually having to wipe tears from their eyes, they'd been laughing so hard. Finally, Joe drove down the short hill and pulled into the garage. They walked out hand in hand and were greeted by a hundred questions.

"Randy, will you go back and finish the academy?" asked a dark-haired female reporter.

Randy looked at the woman, remembering her as one of the reporters who had recounted her side of the story most accurately. She smiled. "Yes, provided the police department still wants me after all the bad PR I seem to have caused them."

"You didn't cause it, Dickerson did!" yelled one of the cameramen in the back.

Joe and Randy laughed.

"Sergeant Sinclair, how are your wounds healing? Are you back at work yet?"

Joe grinned. "Well, like I told the jury, Dickerson's a really lousy shot, so no major damage was done. Yes, I've been working since the week after it happened."

"Randy," said another female reporter, though she was looking at Joe almost dreamily. "Is your relationship with your husband really as romantic as it sounded in the courtroom?"

Randy turned to look up at Joe as she answered. "More." She reached up, and in front of twenty reporters and assorted news crew, kissed her husband passionately. Joe swept her up into his arms, kissing her forehead as he looked out at the press.

"You'll excuse us. Up until this morning in court we hadn't seen each other for a month." With that, he walked up to the front door, punched in the new security code, and opened it. Inside, he kicked it closed with one booted foot. The entire press corps seemed to sigh, the women reporters continuing their reports about the happy couple while the men exclaimed over what a lucky man Joe Sinclair was to have two such beautiful women to take care of him.

That evening, Midnight, Rick, Jessica, Tiny, Spider, Tammy, and their new baby boy, Joseph Nguyen, joined the Sinclairs in celebrating their victory. They ordered a lot of takeout, the men drank a lot of beer, and the women a lot of wine and mixed drinks—except for Tammy, who was breastfeeding. They turned on the news and watched as each and every station told the story. Joe and Randy were surprised when they saw their conversation in the courtroom during the lunch break. The reporter talked about the two of them as if they were Romeo and Juliet and had had to overcome incredible obstacles to be together.

The story of Joe and Randy's early romance and subsequent marriage was told over and over. Midnight and Rick were portrayed as a very intense but very much in-love couple. There were shots of their testimony, and more importantly the touching moment when, as Rick left the stand and Midnight took it, they touched hands. The press weaved a story of love, commitment, loyalty, and dedication, and Midnight and Joe were portrayed as the heads of one of the most important organizations in the country. The members of FORS, although not shown—Midnight had strictly forbidden it, threatening a huge lawsuit if even one of her people appeared on any news cast—had been described as one-time hoodlums turned police officers. The program was discussed—although in very little detail, again under Midnight's strict admonishment—and was touted as the premiere gang interdiction operation in the country.

"Great," Rick said when he heard that description, but he was grinning all the while. He pulled Midnight closer to him. "I'll never see you after this."

Midnight laughed and looked over at Joe. "Well, since you are now the fair prince of San Diego and worth zilch in the undercover field, maybe you can help with the program setup stuff, huh?"

"Oh goody." Joe sounded very unenthusiastic.

"We have more immediate issues to deal with." Rick looked pointedly at Midnight. She nodded seriously.

Joe glanced at them. "What?"

When Midnight didn't answer, Rick gave Joe a sour look. "Dearborn wants Midnight in his office at nine tomorrow."

"What for?" Joe asked suspiciously, his eyes narrowing.

"He wants to ream me for disobeying his direct order about the raid."

"At least that's what he says," Rick said angrily. "I think his intent is a little more about the first part than the last."

Spider, Tammy, and Tiny were listening intently. Jessica and Randy already knew about what the assistant chief had said to Midnight in their earlier meeting, so they caught Rick's meaning easily.

"What's goin' on?" Tiny asked darkly, not liking the tone of the conversation at all. He was looking at Midnight over the top of Jessica's head; she was sitting on the floor in front of him.

Midnight looked at Rick and Joe, and then over to Tiny. "The assistant chief has, uh, different opinions about the way I achieved my lieutenantship…" She trailed off as Tiny caught her meaning.

"That bastard, who the fuck—" Tiny started, then looked a little embarrassed at using such language in front of the ladies, but he knew Midnight was used to it.

Midnight held up her hand, nodding as she saw Spider's expression mirroring Tiny's. "I know, I know, but the point is, how do we call him on it?"

The men looked at each other. It was obvious what they wanted to do to call Dearborn on his possibly fatal mistake.

"Okay, okay!" Tammy said, laughing. "Let's just bring the testosterone down to a manageable level here." She was holding her new son, grinning as she patted her husband on the head. "Beating the assistant chief to a bloody pulp, although in theory sounds wonderful, in reality is a felony. Let's just attempt to be a little more proactive here. What can we do to put the sonofabitch away for good without breaking many major laws?"

"We could take him to Mexico and do it," Rick said darkly.

"Canada would be effective there too," Joe said.

"If we kill him in an aircraft, would that be considered on American soil?" Spider asked.

"I don't know, but we could test it out," Tiny said.

All four women were laughing by this time.

"My heroes!" Midnight said, still grinning widely. "But I have a better idea."

The next morning at 8:50 a.m., Midnight was escorted into Greg Dearborn's office by his secretary. Midnight thanked the young woman and sat down across from Dearborn.

"Thank you for coming, Lieutenant. I hear there was good news for your friend."

"Yes," Midnight said, as if still responding to a lawyer.

Dearborn picked up a folder. "I've been looking over your file."

Midnight nodded, saying nothing.

"Your record is impressive, considering…"

Midnight refused to rise to the bait. She just waited.

"Well, anyway, the reason I called you here today was to discuss the incident of a month or so ago. The only reason I haven't done so

259

sooner was that I have been so busy trying to run this department, and I knew your unit was caught up with the trial."

Again, Midnight nodded.

"I want to explain to you why I didn't want you to do the raid that day. I don't think you fully understood the big picture. And your disobedience of my orders was insubordination in its purest form." Dearborn paused, expecting Midnight to rebut his words, but most disconcertingly she remained silent. He could detect no anger in her expression, and she certainly wasn't acting defensively. Maybe she's finally coming around to my way of thinking, he thought. "Lieutenant?"

"I'm listening," she said calmly. "You were going to explain to me the big picture."

"Yes, well, in these days of political correctness, we have to be much more careful about the way we handle certain situations. This is not the Old West, Lieutenant, and we don't hang our prisoners in lynch mobs. Charging off after Sinclair's alleged abductors could have caused an international incident. Our position with the Mexican government is very precarious. One bad incident and it could easily crumble. Do you understand?"

"Yes, sir," Midnight said, her voice almost tinged with actual respect.

"You see, I have an entire department to look out for here, and I can't let one of my units go off half-cocked and cause a major disaster. I appreciated your angst over your partner's abduction, but when he returned virtually unharmed, it was a time to proceed with caution. I understand that in this case things turned out fairly well, although Carlos Rivera was killed under questionable circumstances with no witnesses to prove that he had a gun, except of course for your husband…"

"I understand, sir."

"Do you, Lieutenant? I'd really rather not put such a dark blot on such an exemplary record, if it's not necessary. I know you'd like to make captain, and something like this wouldn't bode well for that hope."

"I'm aware of that, sir, and I'd be very appreciative of anything you could do."

"Well, I find your attitude refreshing, Lieutenant, and I'm sure that we could work something out to keep this off your record."

"That would be wonderful, sir," Midnight said, lowering her eyes almost demurely.

Greg Dearborn was astonished at the change in her. His phone buzzed, and, still watching Midnight, he reached over and hit the intercom button. "Yes?"

"Sir, I have a gentleman out here to see you. He says it's important."

"Fine, I'll come right out." He switched off the intercom. "I'll be right back, Lieutenant. Make yourself comfortable while you wait." His tone was inviting, and she nodded, looking up at him as he stood.

When he returned to the office, Midnight was standing by the window, looking down at the scenery below. She had removed her jacket. Greg Dearborn had to admit, she was indeed beautiful. She was wearing a straight black skirt cut four inches above the knee, without any stockings—with her tan, she didn't need them. She had been wearing a tailored jacket but had removed it so he could see her lace-and-satin camisole. She also wore three-inch black heels. Greg Dearborn had never been attracted to a female as much as he was at that moment, and to know that he had her basically over a barrel on this one, holding over her the blot to her record and a denial of a promotion she seemed to want very much… Yes, she was indeed over a barrel. In fact, Greg decided, he'd rather have her over his desk. He locked his inner office door. Enjoying his new power, he walked over and stood just behind her at the window.

"It's a nice view, isn't it?" he said, his lips close to her ear. She even smelled sexy, he reflected as his excitement grew.

"Yes, it is," Midnight said softly.

Greg moved a step closer, just a hair's breadth away from touching her. "So tell me, Lieutenant. What would getting the captain's position mean to you?"

Midnight was silent for a moment. "It's very important to me, sir. It would give me the opportunity to command my own bureau, not just one unit."

"And that would be very good for your career, wouldn't it, Lieutenant?" He closed the tiny distance between them and felt her sharp intake of breath. A moment later she seemed to relax against him. His hands closed on her narrow waist, tightening as he tried to contain his excitement.

"Yes, sir. It would be very good for my career," Midnight said huskily.

"I'm sure it would be very good for me as well," Dearborn said, savoring his power.

"Most definitely, sir." Midnight turned around to face him. Her eyes were points of green fire. "Do it."

Dearborn thought she meant her, but he found he was very wrong a moment later when the door to his office was kicked open, the wood shattering. Rick and Joe entered, and Rick moved to Midnight, standing behind her almost protectively. He put his hands on her shoulders as she looked daggers of victory at Dearborn, her chin raised just slightly.

Dearborn was stunned, but it didn't take him long to start trying to cover his ass. "What's going on here?"

"Oh, I think you know that one," Joe said, leaning against the partially shattered door jamb.

"Maybe he doesn't," said a voice from just outside. Chief TJ Grant stepped inside, his eyes on Dearborn. "Perhaps we need to read him his rights, so he'll be aware of just what is going on."

"Rights? I don't know what you think you've come into, but it's certainly not what you imagine." Dearborn sounded every bit the politician.

"We heard," Rick said, his eyes narrowed, his expression telling Dearborn he was lucky the chief was there. "Everything." He reached over and turned off the intercom light.

Midnight was grinning evilly. "I guess your career ladder'll be closed for business for a while, huh?" Her eyes trailed down to his crotch as she said it.

"Yeah, and a whole new one will open up," Joe said.

The chief nodded, glancing to Spider and Tiny as they moved past him toward Dearborn, both looking very menacing. "Take the assistant chief into custody."

"What should we book him for?" Spider asked wryly.

"Sexual misconduct, sexual harassment, and anything else I can throw at him and make stick."

Tiny and Spider nodded and walked over to the assistant chief. They "took him into custody" in a less than gentle manner, but the chief didn't seem to mind. They led him from the room a few minutes later. Midnight was sure from the looks on their faces that Dearborn wouldn't make it downstairs without tripping a couple of times.

As Midnight watched them go, she felt a weight lift from her. She turned, glancing up at Rick. He was looking down at her, his expression a little concerned.

"Are you okay?" he asked as the chief and Joe politely left them alone.

Midnight leaned against him as she nodded. "I was sure I was going to lose it when he actually touched me, but I made it."

"I wish you would've let us handle it our way. Beating the hell out of him would have been much more satisfying."

"You and me both, babe, but we're cops and we have to act like it, even if it's a real challenge sometimes."

****

The next couple of weeks were hectic at FORS. Within a week of Randy's acquittal, Dickerson had rolled over on the Riveras. Although he would still do jail time, it would be less likely to be hard time. It had been suspected that Dickerson had been getting information from the assistant chief about FORS' status as well as other, more minor details. It turned out Dickerson and Dearborn had been such good buddies that Dearborn had been less than discreet about his opinions of Midnight and her crew. Dickerson had just been sly about garnering information he wanted from Dearborn by getting the man started about Midnight. DMV records had been found that Joe's late ex-girlfriend Tasha had had, as well as some new information Dickerson had pulled. Fortunately, he hadn't been able to access all of FORS' records due to an extra security measure put there by Midnight after the previous attack on the unit. Dickerson had actually used Dearborn's computer to get Midnight's address, but even Dearborn hadn't had access to Midnight's members' information.

As far as Dearborn went, he was fired from the department and brought up on charges of sexual harassment. No one even thought to contest it, since the chief stood behind Midnight all the way. Midnight had contacted him the night she and the crew had worked out the idea of trapping Dearborn. He had been happy to help, having been very offended by Dearborn's accusations of his own misconduct. Midnight had always had a special place in Chief Grant's heart, but it had never extended to anything beyond a sincere appreciation for abilities.

Randy had gone back to the academy, although she met with a great deal of attitude from the instructors and the recruits she attended with. She hadn't returned to the same class, since she had missed too much to be able to graduate on her original date. Her new class was set to graduate in three weeks, and she managed to get back into the routine without much trouble. Her classmates' attitude was, however, very troubling. The department may have been behind her on paper, but that did not extend to the people who worked there. She told Joe about it, saying that she knew she should have expected it, but it was still difficult to take.

Joe had called his friend the training sergeant, asking what was going on. It had been an interesting conversation.

"I've heard that Randy's gettin' the black-ball treatment there. That true?"

"What the hell did you expect, Sinclair?" Jones had replied. "She was tried for trying to kill two cops."

"Tried and acquitted."

"And we both know that don't always mean shit."

"It does in this case, Jones."

"Well, I don't know what you think I can do." Jones had sighed, aware that he was being unfair but unable to help himself. He believed too that the whole thing had been a headquarters whitewash for Joe's sake.

"I think you can make sure nothin' happens to her, because if somethin' does, I'm holdin' you responsible." Joe's voice had taken on a superior tone, even though he was the same rank as the man he was addressing.

"I promise you, I won't let anything happen to her, but I can't change people's opinions. Everyone has a right to think what they want, Sinclair."

"Yeah, even if they know they're wrong."

Things had improved a little for Randy at that point, but she was more than ready to graduate. Although, she was worried that whoever might be her FTO or her partner would think the same way. She didn't talk to Joe about it; she knew he'd extended himself by calling the training sergeant, and didn't want him to have to fight all her battles. She knew that if she wanted this career, she was going to have to learn to stand up for herself. That was what she intended to do.

****

A week after Randy's trial was over, Midnight and Rick were finally reunited with their daughter. Deborah and Susan brought the child home, saying they were stopping back in New York to do some shopping. Midnight was in tears the moment she saw her daughter get off the plane. Mikeyla launched herself at her, squealing in delight. Mother and daughter hugged fiercely, and Mikeyla refused to allow herself to be put down—not that Midnight wanted to, but Rick was adamant that she not overdo it just yet.

Midnight had been seen during the week by her doctor. She was having minor cramping and trouble sleeping. The doctor told her she needed to try and take things a little easier, maybe go on a vacation. Rick, who had taken her to the doctor knowing she wouldn't go any other way, had shaken his head at the man, rolling his eyes. Obviously, the doctor had no idea to whom he was speaking when he suggested time off to recuperate. Midnight had grinned at her husband but had said nothing to the doctor other than to thank him. Rick had been after her ever since to slow down a little bit. Sometimes she listened, other times she didn't.

Rick eventually took Mikeyla into his own arms, telling her that Mommy needed a rest. Mikeyla kept a watchful eye on her mother all the way through the airport and out to the car. They spent that weekend getting reacquainted. Midnight explained to her daughter why

267

they'd been apart for so long. Mikeyla was thrilled that everything between her parents seemed better and that Daddy smiled a lot more now. She also noticed that both Daddy and Mommy seemed to be more playful with each other, as well as cuddling a lot more. They included her in the cuddling too, enjoying their time with their child much more now.

Midnight had eventually come clean with Rick, telling him she couldn't have any more children. Rick had been surprised, but he had in turn surprised her by looking at the positive side. "Now I don't have to worry about you risking your life again, do I?" he had said softly, his ever-present concern prevalent in his eyes. Midnight had nodded, not looking directly at him. She was still unhappy about the diagnosis. Rick had reached out, touching her softly under the chin and making her look at him. "Midnight, I want you in my life forever, and if that means that we just have Keyla, that's still better than most people have. I love you, I love Keyla, and that's enough." His voice was soft and sincere, and it had brought tears to Midnight's eyes.

"I just…" Her voice had caught in her throat. "I wanted you to have a son."

"Night." Rick had taken her into his arms. "I don't need a son. I need you, okay?"

Midnight had finally nodded, knowing she'd get used to the idea eventually. They had talked briefly about adoption, but it was too soon for Midnight to even think about. Rick had dropped the subject for the time being, figuring that if she wanted to talk about it she would bring it up. There were no secrets between them now. Things weren't exactly perfect between them yet, but they were getting close to being back to themselves again.

A call from Sheila at the house the following Monday served to separate them ever so slightly again. She had called to tell Rick, needlessly, that she was not pregnant. She sounded curt and angry, but Rick hadn't even cared. He even talked to Angela briefly. Angela was very happy to hear that he and Midnight were back together. She told him privately that she had known all along that her daughter would never make him feel the way his wife obviously did. Rick thanked her for all the support she'd lent him during Midnight's "accident," and assured her that he'd be more than happy to let her see Mikeyla anytime she wanted. "As long as it's over here or on neutral territory." Angela had laughed, understanding his meaning fully. She told him that he'd better take good care of his family. Rick assured her that was his intention from now on.

Rick hung up, feeling better about the situation with Sheila. He really hadn't cared about her being pregnant. He had never considered for a second giving Midnight up, even if they hadn't gotten back together, to marry Sheila. But knowing that she wasn't pregnant made it even easier for him to try and put the whole affair behind him. Midnight wasn't as easygoing at that. She was quiet that evening. Her attitude wasn't openly hostile, just sedate. Rick knew it would take some time for them to be normal with each other again. He just wondered how long that would be. He didn't push her to talk about what she was feeling, understanding that she was just trying to overcome her feelings of anger at his infidelity. After a few days she seemed to come around; they never discussed it.

****

Joe, Midnight, Rick, and the rest of FORS attended Randy's graduation. When her name was announced, Joe was pleasantly surprised that she was addressed as Randy Sinclair. She had dropped her maiden name altogether. She looked directly at him as her badge was pinned on, and his smile was proud. The chief himself did the honors, and in respect of Midnight and FORS he gave Randy a longer salute than the other candidates. It wasn't a major difference, but Midnight and Joe noticed it and appreciated it.

After the graduation, Randy moved through the crowd toward Joe. He got to her first and grabbed her up in a bear hug, lifting her off her feet.

"I was proud of you up there, love," he said softly in her ear.

"I was nervous as hell up there," Randy replied, laughing.

Darrell and Donovan were there as well. They both hugged her.

"You look pretty good in that uniform," Darrell said grudgingly. He was almost bursting with pride.

"Yeah," Donovan said, eyeing his sister enviously. "Maybe when I'm old enough I'll apply for the police force too."

Darrell rolled his eyes. "Oh God, three cops in the family. My friends'll never come to the house again!" He had automatically included Joe as part of the family, a fact that was not lost on either Joe or Randy.

The other members of FORS crowded around her, congratulating her and patting her on the back. Randy laughed and enjoyed all of it. Ever since the trial, she had been accepted back into the fold of the unit. No one had any lingering doubts. It was as if seeing Joe, Midnight, and Rick testify for her meant she had to be innocent.

Later that day they had a celebration at Joe and Randy's house. They barbecued, drank, and played football on the beach. Oddly enough, everyone wanted to be on the same team as Tiny and Kana. Dibbins quarterbacked for one team, Spider for the other. Randy and Midnight made a point of being on the same team, on opposing sides to their husbands, saying they wanted the opportunity to tackle them. Which they did frequently.

After the game, Joe took Randy's hand and led her into the house, back to their room. He sat her on the bed, then pulled out a box from under it and handed it to her.

"What's this?" she asked, looking at the box in surprise.

Joe shrugged. "Just a kind of graduation gift."

Randy grinned up at him as she unwrapped the box, which was rich mahogany, a foot in length and eight inches wide. When she opened it, she found nestled in hunter-green velvet a gun. It was black stainless steel, with beautifully crafted mahogany grips. There was even elegant tooling in the metal itself. It was the most incredible gun Randy had ever seen. There were also two spare magazines in their own spaces. Setting the box down, Randy ran her hand over the grips of the gun, touching the slide gently. Finally, she lifted it. She'd expected it to weigh more than it did. Careful to point it away from Joe, she looked down the sights. The weapon felt perfect in her hands, as if it had been made for her. She looked at her husband as she lowered it. He had a very proud smile on his face. She had handled the gun properly, and he was secretly thrilled that she had reacted to it the way he would have reacted to a weapon like it.

Randy was turning it over in her hands, looking at it from every angle. Then she glanced up at him, pointing to the gun's sights. "Tritium?"

Joe's grin widened as he nodded. She had recognized the night sights his own weapon had, a particular type that basically glowed in the dark, to help an officer line up a sight even at night. He had told her about them when he was helping her at the range, and he was glad that she had remembered.

Randy pointed to the magazines. "Single stack, because my hands are small?"

"Right again," Joe said.

"But you got me on the gun itself," Randy said, pretending to look like a failed student.

"It's a Smith and Wesson, my personal favorite, model 4013. It's forty caliber, which will give you some serious knock-down power, but the weight of the stainless steel slide will help with the kick."

Randy stared up at him, shivering as if he were talking dirty to her. "I love it when you talk guns." She smiled. "It's almost like foreplay."

Joe raised an eyebrow. "Now, if that's what you're lookin' for... Put the gun down, Officer, and I can show you that too." He leered at her, his eyes glittering with humor.

Randy carefully tossed the gun aside and held her arms out to her husband. "C'mere, you." She pulled him down over her as she lay back. She kissed him, burying her hands in his hair. A few minutes later they were breathless.

Joe rolled over, pulling her with him, and lay looking up at her. "I love you."

"And I love you," Randy said. "Thank you for letting me do this. It's really important to me."

"Then it's important to me too, because you are everything."

"What can a girl say to that?" Randy said softly.

"Just that you'll never leave again." His voice caught in his throat, and Randy realized the depths to which she had hurt him. The thought stabbed at her, and she knew she would spend the rest of her life happily making it up to him.

"That's easy enough to promise." Randy kissed him and then pulled back to look down at him. "Because even wild horses couldn't drag me away from you again."

Joe hugged her close, and they kissed for a while longer. Eventually they rejoined the party and proceeded to get fairly drunk. It was the first time Randy had ever actually gotten buzzed around these people; it was an eye-opening experience.

It was a loud, happy party, and the members of FORS ended up passing out or falling asleep all around Joe and Randy's house. Rick and Midnight wound up in one of the guest bedrooms. Midnight was just a little bit tipsy; Rick was too.

"I'm gonna take a shower," Midnight said.

"Be careful."

Midnight nodded as she walked toward the bathroom luckily located within the bedroom. She stripped off her jeans, tossing them over her shoulder. Rick sat on the bed, leaning against the headboard.

He laughed when her shirt was also tossed over her shoulder, then piece by piece the rest of her clothing.

Twenty minutes later, when she climbed out of the shower, Midnight saw that her husband was standing in the doorway, watching her. Rick had been getting ready to lie down when he caught her movements in the shower. He was still wearing his jeans, but nothing else. Midnight grinned at him as his eyes travelled down her body appreciatively.

"You," he said huskily, "are an incredibly beautiful woman."

Midnight smiled, strolling over to him. "You're not too bad yourself," she said, her voice just as sultry. She slid her hands slowly up his body, bringing her lips down to kiss his chest. Rick buried one of his hands in her hair. The other slid down her still wet back, pulling her to him. He released his hold on her long enough to grab a towel to wrap her in, then swept her up in his arms and carried her over to the bed. He began kissing her, and any thoughts she might have had about sleep went right out the window.

They made love for hours and wound up sleeping comfortably in each other's arms, all of the troubles of the past months totally forgotten.

****

A week later, Rick and Midnight were on their way to the office. Midnight was driving her Corvette; she had told him she needed to on that particular day, because she needed to take the edge off her nerves. Rick glanced over at her. She had managed to shock him again. She was wearing a hunter-green dress with a tiny print on it and gold buttons all the way down the front. It was open just above the knees, although the dress itself fell to halfway down her calves. And since her car was a stick shift, she had hiked it up a little bit farther so as not to catch it with the three-inch black heels she wore. The lower halves of two very shapely, perfectly tanned thighs were drawing his attention constantly. Her hair was pulled up loosely on the sides with a green clip, tendrils of curls escaping to frame her face. She wore actual makeup this time; she'd brought out her cat-like green eyes with ivory and brown eye shadow and dark green eyeliner. Her cheek bones were accented with an auburn shade of brown, and her lips were touched with a similar color.

Rick had been sure his heart had stopped when she'd walked out of the bathroom that morning. He had wanted her immediately, but she had danced just out of his reach. She'd chided him for his lack of control and, with a grin, had told him she'd let him take the dress off her later. Rick had warned her playfully that it had better not be too much later, or he'd probably die. It was an important day for her, and he knew she wanted to look her best. She had accomplished that with seeming ease.

Rick watched her as she sang along to the Def Leppard CD. He was surprised; Def Leppard wasn't usually her thing. But she seemed to know every word. It struck him that the song called "I Wanna Touch U" was very fitting for the moment. He did very much want to touch her, and much, much more. When the song ended, he grinned. "Do you realize that you just sang a Def Leppard song word for word?" he said, raising an eyebrow.

Midnight glanced over at him, her eyes twinkling. "Did I?" She sounded surprised.

"Yes." Rick reached out to touch her bare leg. "Have I told you that you look incredible?"

Midnight smiled. "Yes, a couple of times now."

"Can I tell you again?" he said, grinning rakishly.

"I think you just did," Midnight said, laughing now. She reached over to turn the radio down a little bit. Rick could see her hands were shaking. He reached out and took her hand in his.

"Nervous?" he asked, eyeing her.

"No," Midnight said, not sounding sincere in the slightest. Rick raised his eyebrow at her again. "Okay, maybe a little. Captain's a big deal, you know."

"I know. But you can do it."

Midnight looked over at him and shook her head slowly. "I don't know, Rick. It's a lot. It's… it's a whole bureau of my own. Not just my little corner of the world—a whole bureau."

"You can do this, babe. I know you can."

"Promise?" Midnight said, sounding very much like Mikeyla.

"Promise."

Midnight drew in a deep breath and blew it out slowly. She nodded. "Okay."

An hour later, Midnight's single-bar insignia for the rank of lieutenant was taken from her hand and the double bar indicating the rank of captain was pinned in its place. The chief was very proud of her, especially her exemplary behavior in handling Dearborn. She had brought to fruition a program conceived, developed, and run by herself. She had maintained a level of professionalism and influenced her own members to act in much the same manner. Spider and Tiny had both made sergeant, and the chief was hinting that he'd like to make Joe a lieutenant if Joe was so inclined. Joe's response was lukewarm. He wasn't really into the whole rank thing; he just wanted to do the job. He had, however, assured the chief that he appreciated the thought and that he would definitely consider the promotion. The chief hadn't been very surprised by Joe's attitude; he hadn't even been offended. He'd grown very fond of many of the members of FORS. Jessica had been hired strictly as a law enforcement member of the unit—Midnight had called in a favor with the chief. Jessica was very happy to be part of the family now, although everyone had already accepted her because of her quick thinking during Joe's abduction as well as her ever-growing relationship with Tiny.

Things in the unit were moving along nicely, though Midnight felt very melancholy about having to release some of her control over it. Managing a whole bureau for the department would involve the supervision of other investigative units as well. She wasn't sure how their lieutenants would take her promotion, but she was determined to do a good job.

Sitting in her office, Midnight watched as her mother admired her wall of achievements. It was still unreal to Midnight that her mother was there. Carrie had insisted on coming to the promotional ceremony. Even Jack had come, but he had had to leave right afterwards to get to his new job. Midnight had been astounded by their presence, and in a remote way happy that her father had seen fit to attend. She'd long since realized that her relationship with her father was never going to be a close one, but she was happy that he had at least acknowledged her accomplishment.

Now, as Carrie exclaimed over yet another award that Midnight had received over the years, she sat at her desk, her crossed ankles resting on a bottom drawer that she'd opened just for that purpose. She was trying to adjust to the idea that she might have to pack up her office and move in the coming weeks. She had requested to be allowed to stay where she was, since the two other units she was to supervise were located on the same floor and her current office was, after all, centrally located.

Joe walked in a few minutes later, a wry look on his face. "I can't believe I have to ask this, but do you have any street clothes with you?"

"Why?" Midnight sat up to face him.

"Well," Joe said, leaning casually against the door jamb, "it seems that a couple of your personal favorites have decided to make your promotion a real event…" He trailed off, and Midnight narrowed her eyes at him.

"What's goin' on?" she asked. She knew he was referring to the B Street Boys and Perros Locos, two particularly nasty gangs that tended to clash on a frequent basis, causing a great deal of damage to passersby, personal property, and each other.

"They're on the move. Word's out they're gonna rumble," Joe said, watching Midnight expectantly.

"You did this, didn't you? Somehow, you did this," Midnight said with mock accusation. "Yeah, I have street clothes." She looked down at her dress, shrugging. "Hell, I think I was freaking everyone out in this anyway. I looked too captainly."

Joe laughed and left the office.

"What's that mean?" Carrie asked, eyeing her daughter. "These people are going to fight?" Midnight nodded as she stood up. "And what are you going to do?"

"Stop 'em, hopefully. I'll be back in a few minutes, okay?"

Carrie nodded as Midnight walked out. Ten minutes later, she returned clad in her usual uniform of jeans, boots, and a black cotton shirt. She was carrying her holstered weapon. "Mom, you can hang around and watch the briefing, or I can get one of the uniforms to take you home…"

"That's okay, I'd like to see this briefing." Carrie was interested in every aspect of her daughter's job now.

Midnight nodded as she walked over to her desk and reached around to fit the holster flaps over her belt, the muzzle of the gun pointing down into the small of her back. Joe walked by. "Briefing?" he said, and Midnight nodded, beckoning her mother as she walked out of the office and toward the conference room.

Carrie was shocked by the number of people there. Midnight was a little surprised herself, but she recognized some of the extra faces in the room as members of the two units she was taking over command of. Midnight stopped by the officers who weren't part of FORS, making good eye contact and keeping a firm-but-not-too-firm grip as she shook hands with them. Then she made her way to the front of the room.

"Okay, let's get this rolling here, boys and girls!" she shouted over the raised voices. Everyone quieted right away. "It seems that two of our social clubs have a little territorial dispute going on, and it looks like it's gonna be an all-out fight this time. So as you can guess, it's our turn to go in and shut 'em down."

"Who're we lookin' at?" one of the younger members of FORS asked.

"The B Street Boys and Perros Locos. Now, a lot of you know these gangs, and you know they like to pack heavy and they have no problem with killing a cop, or even one of us." She smiled at that. The members of FORS had always considered themselves outsiders in the department, and for that reason Midnight had always put herself on their level when referring to them as a group. They started to chuckle at her inference. "So I want body armor on, weapons loaded heavy, and extra trimmings for everyone. Joe, have you got us a stock of MP5s?"

Joe nodded. "We got twenty."

"Good. I want my best shotgun handlers on those twenty. Spider, you get 'em set up."

Spider nodded.

"It's my intention here to hit 'em head on, unless anyone has any better ideas?"

"Head on?" asked one of the officers from the vice unit. "Isn't that a little risky?"

Midnight inclined her head slightly, acknowledging that yes, it was. "Yeah, but a lot of times that's the only thing these kids respond to—a show of force. A bigger, badder gang, as it were." Midnight grinned. Many of her team cheered, and the officer seemed happy with her answer. Midnight had said it in a way that allowed him to be right, but for her to be right too. That was her style. Many of the non-

FORS members in the room began to think that working for this woman might not be so bad.

"Who's gonna lead us in?" one of the other non-FORS officers asked, obviously not familiar with the fact that Midnight was a "working supervisor" in every sense of the word.

"I am," she said. The officer stared back at her, but was smart enough to nod rather than voice the protest that showed on his face. Midnight didn't take it personally. She knew that a lot of police officers were of the opinion that women didn't belong in the field, because most women didn't have the physical strength to handle real attackers. Midnight had the strength and agility to handle just about anyone, and anyone she couldn't manage would be dealt with by any other member of her unit.

Two hours later, FORS and a few members of the department's vice and investigative units arrived at the scene. They were in east San Diego, in a semi-commercial area, although you wouldn't have known it from the deserted streets. There was a gathering of youths farther down the street, and another off to the left. It was obvious that these were the two gangs set to fight each other. The law enforcement group was easily equal in numbers to one of the groups, and many of them looked much more fierce than the kids in the real gangs—not counting the particularly lethal-looking weapons they loaded and slid into various holsters or, in the case of the rifles, slung over their shoulders.

There were police cars stationed around the area, and the officers were standing in front of their vehicles, keeping an eye on things. The uniformed officers had been given orders to maintain the peace until FORS got there. So far the two gangs had only yelled insults and flashed gang signs at both each other and the police. No guns had been shown as of yet, but Midnight did not doubt for a minute that they were carrying.

Joe noticed that the car down the street they were on was the one Randy was assigned to for her field training. He stifled the worry that jumped into his heart. Randy could take care of herself; she'd done pretty well so far. She'd been in a couple of scuffles, which she'd come out of fairly well. She'd been working with Midnight to improve her hand-to-hand combat skills, and Midnight said she had been doing well. Now, as he looked down the street, he caught sight of Randy, and she spotted him. She turned to her field training officer and said something, and the man nodded. She walked down the street toward Joe.

"Fancy meeting you here," she said, grinning.

"Tell me," Joe said, returning the smile. "Are our little friends being good?"

Randy shrugged. "They haven't tried to shoot anyone yet, if that's what you mean. On the other hand, I've been propositioned by about four of them so far."

"It's nice to see they have taste."

"No real luck though." Randy sighed. "I'd better get back. I just wanted to tell you to be careful."

"Aren't I always?"

He was hailed with four cries of "No!", one from Midnight, one from Jessica, another from Rick, and the last from Randy. Joe laughed, as did the others. "I guess not, eh?" He glanced down the street and, like a conspirator, pulled Randy further into the knot of people. He grinned as he leaned down to give her a quick kiss on the lips.

"Why, Sergeant Sinclair, I think that could be considered sexual harassment!" Jessica said with a grin.

"Shut up, you," Joe said, still smiling. He looked down at Randy. "And you. Be careful yourself, okay?"

"I will." She smiled as she turned to head back to her post. Halfway there, she glanced over her shoulder and saw that he was still watching her. She flipped him a wave and continued down the street.

When everyone was set, Midnight called out, "Mount up!"

Joe and Rick fell in behind her, with Tiny, Spider, Dibbins, and Kana flanking them just to the rear. The other members of FORS fell in behind their leaders. Coming down the street, they did indeed look like a gang. Midnight's strides were long and purposeful. She looked every bit the gang leader, and Randy imagined it was much how she'd looked when she'd led her original gang, the Vettes. Randy's eyes fell on Joe as they came toward her squad car. It was obvious he was focused on what they were heading into, and she could see in him, too, the gang leader he had been. Randy reflected on the change in him again. He had been ever supportive since her return to the academy, and even more so when she got to the training part of her job. He was always offering ideas to help her with her problems, but he never pushed them on her. He made suggestions and she decided the best way. Reaching down, she touched the grips of her duty weapon, the gun he had given her. He'd told her later that he wanted her to have the best gun he could get her, and the idea that he had taken the time to figure out what would be best for her warmed her heart again. It was a far different relationship than they had had less than eight months ago, but it was better.

Midnight kept watch on the two gangs as she walked down the street. She could feel the presence of her husband behind her and to her right, and she could also sense Joe's strong presence. She knew she was lucky have such strong, supportive men there for her when she needed them. FORS was her extended family, for a long time her only family; it meant everything to her, and she was glad that Rick had finally come to understand that. He'd learned that taking her away from FORS would be taking away a part of her, and that she wouldn't be the woman he loved without that integral part of herself.

As they got closer, the two gangs moved toward them, their leaders heading them up. Midnight was surprised when she caught sight of the Perros Locos leader; she knew the man. He recognized her too.

"Juarita," Javier Reséndez said, nodding.

"Javi." Midnight nodded back, still looking guarded. Whether she knew him or not had no bearing on how she planned to handle this situation.

"You know this puta?" one of Javier's members asked him, referring to Midnight in not very polite terms, but she was used to it. She raised an eyebrow at Javier, her face schooled in an ever-confident expression.

"Yeah, I used to run with her set," Javier said, looking Midnight over. "But she didn't look that good then."

Midnight felt Rick tense behind her, but she didn't look back at him. She hoped he wouldn't say anything, and he didn't.

"Yeah, but now she's a cop," the leader of the B Street Boys said. "You a fuckin' snitch now, Javi?"

"Hey, fuck you, puto. You come over here and I'll show you somethin'!" Javi stepped toward the other gang leader.

"Whoa, whoa, hold up there, Javi!" Midnight reached up and shoved the gang leader back. Javi slapped her hand away but made no move to go toward the other man again. "You know I can't let you two kill each other," she said.

"And who the fuck's gonna stop us?" one of the members of the B Street Boys yelled.

Joe lifted his shotgun, drawing back the stock. "We are."

There was murmuring and some rude comments, but no one else spoke up.

"So what's your fuckin problem, eh?" Javi snapped. "Why do you care if we fight?"

"Look," Midnight said calmly. "You guys want to kill each other, fine, but my problem is that you never manage to kill each other. You kill innocent bystanders, you kill kids on their way to school and what not, and I can't have it, not on my watch!"

"Fuck you, puta!" the leader of the B Street Boys spat as he lifted his T-shirt. He pulled a gun from his waistband and started to point it at Midnight. Before he even knew what was happening, the gun was knocked from his hand and he was lying flat on the ground with Midnight standing over him. He also had a nasty-looking gun pointed at his head by a brown-haired Englishman. Midnight and Rick had reacted at the same time.

"I'm a cop, kid, not an idiot," she said angrily. "Someone else want to try that?" She looked up at the B Street Boys, her eyes narrowed, then glanced at Javier. "You wanna try me?"

"I don't fight chicks," Javier said, leering at her. His gang laughed.

"No?" Joe stepped forward. "How 'bout me then?"

"Shit," Javi said, giving Joe a dismissive look. "Not with that fucking shotgun in your hands."

Without looking, Joe tossed it to Rick, who caught it without looking away from the guy his own gun was trained on.

"Come on," Joe said scornfully. "Try me now."

Javi looked at Joe as if sizing him up. He stepped to his right, his hands down at his sides in a badass way, like he didn't have to worry about someone like Joe. He paced Joe off, stepping to his right again and then back to his left. Joe's eyes followed him, but he didn't react to the younger man's tactics. He waited and watched.

Randy and a few of the officers nearest to the confrontation had come in close enough to see what was happening. Randy watched her husband, holding down the urge to shoot the young man pacing back and forth, trying to bait him. She realized suddenly how dangerous Joe's job really could be. She hadn't been so close to it since she'd had training, and now she knew what Joe's limitations were in terms of the law, and it was scary. She knew the younger man had basically all the rights and laws on his side.

Javier was still trying to throw Joe off. Midnight eyed him warily, but she stayed where she was. Joe had thrown down the challenge, and it was up to him to take Javi out. The other members of FORS split their attention between Joe's encounter and the rest of the gang members watching. They knew better than to assume they would fight fair. Suddenly, it had become FORS against the other two gangs, pretty much what Midnight had wanted.

In a flash, Javier lashed out, trying to catch Joe in the face. But Joe was just as fast and moved deftly to the side, grabbing Javi's fist as it went past. Utilizing the younger man's momentum, Joe flipped him easily, taking him to the ground. Javier let out a grunt of anger as he knocked Joe's arm aside, and with surprising agility got to his feet again. This time he pulled out a switchblade, depressing the button. The blade locked with a resounding click. The other gang members made "Ooooh" sounds and yelled out obscenities. FORS remained silent; they knew better than to distract Joe

Javier crouched, his eyes on Joe. He was obviously angry about being shown up once and didn't intend to lose this round. Joe could see the determination in the younger man's eyes. He took a few slow, deep breaths, his eyes never leaving his opponent's as he centered himself, focusing on Javier alone. He knew FORS was watching the others; he had no concerns but the young man in front of him. "C'mon, kid, try it," he goaded. "Or are you all bluster and no balls?"

"You'll see, puto," Javier chanted, shifting his weight back and forth. "You'll see."

"Bring it on, big man. Let's go, I got a date," Joe said, his grin sardonic.

"Yeah? Well I'll fuck her for you after you're dead."

"She don't do wetbacks." Joe had used the right words to push Javier past his limits. Javi charged at him with surprising speed. Joe managed to step aside, but the youth's knife curved around in a wide left arc, catching Joe's arm. He winced, but brought the injured arm up and knocked the blade aside so it couldn't do any more damage. Javier once again surprised Joe by spinning around and bringing the knife up, intent on driving it home in Joe's chest, but Joe reached up and grabbed his wrist. After that it was a battle of who was stronger. Javier was trying to push the knife home using both hands now, as Joe held him off with one unfortunately weaker arm. He held his injured right arm to his side. It was bleeding pretty badly by now, but he paid no attention to it. He heard Randy yell his name, but he couldn't take the time to look at her. He was concentrating on Javier's red face, and he noted movement behind him. He knew that Midnight was most likely drawing her weapon, preparing to shoot the man who had been part of her own gang years before if it looked like he might actually win this battle.

"Javier!" Midnight howled, but the fight went on, because Joe gave a quick shake of his head. Midnight knew he meant for her to hold off. He knew that beating Javier was important; at this point, it could be a quick end to the whole show.

With an effort born of years of discipline, he tensed his bleeding arm and caught Javier in the upper-left rib cage with an unexpected blow. Both men cried out at the contact, but Javier crouched down in pain. Using his advantage, Joe drove his fist home on the side of the younger man's head, knocking him down. FORS cheered, and the members of the other two gangs looked a little stunned. If these people could knock down their leaders...

Rick gestured to Spider with his head, indicating the guy he was still covering while Midnight's attention was diverted. Spider moved to cover the downed leader of the B Street Boys as Rick went toward Joe, whose back was to him as he looked down at Javier. Rick backed up to his lifetime friend, putting his shoulders firmly against Joe's, lending him support without it looking like he was doing just that. He could feel Joe's weight relax against his back, and he knew Joe was hurt pretty badly. He nodded to Tiny, who moved to cover Javier with his rifle as Rick turned around slowly. "You alright?"

Joe nodded, but it was obvious he really wasn't. He glanced around, trying to locate Randy. He saw her at the edge of the group; she was watching him worriedly. He gave her a cavalier grin.

There was movement from the other two gangs then. Someone shouted, and someone else pulled out a gun. Things got confused from there. FORS, who had stood so calmly by moments before, mobilized into a well-organized gang. They moved into the other two gangs, knocking people to the ground, backing each other up. Joe moved to the side, catching a guy Dibbins had just shoved back and taking him to the ground.

"Joe!" he heard Randy call out, and as his head snapped up he saw her launch a kick at a gang member who had been coming up on his flank. The guy started to turn on Randy, but she grabbed a handful of the back of his shirt and a handful of his hair. Looking very much like Midnight, she took him to the ground and cuffed him.

As she stood, Randy saw Joe was watching her, even as he took yet another gang member down. He gave her a salute and she smiled, feeling very much a part of his life now. She turned to watch for any others trying to take advantage of any of her friends' split attention.

She didn't see Joe again for twenty or so minutes. By then it was over. Many of the members of the B Street Boys and Perros Locos lay on the ground, either cuffed or out cold. Some of the others had run off, only to get caught by the waiting squad cars. The FORS members and the other officers were for the most part uninjured. A couple of them had gotten cut or bruised, but they'd done the job they'd been trained to do, and no innocent citizens had been hurt.

As FORS regrouped around their leaders, people started to come out of the nearby stores. Several police cars had pulled up, as well as two Paddy wagons, for all the gang members to be arrested. Uniformed officers were taking them into custody, reading them their rights and leading them away. Randy was assisting her field training officer, but he could see that she really wanted to be with the group gathering around Joe and Midnight.

"Go on, I got it," Sergeant Grunwald said, grinning as he nodded toward FORS.

"Thanks!" Randy smiled at the older man. She finished putting her prisoner in the Paddy wagon and walked over to the group. The members of FORS made an aisle for her, knowing she wanted to get to Joe. "Hey!" she said as she broke into the inner circle.

Joe was sitting on the ground, and he looked up at her, his light blue eyes squinting in the sunlight. "Hey, yourself," he said, grinning.

She sat next to him, touching his arm gingerly. Someone had given him a bandana to press against the wound to stem the flow of blood. "You okay?"

"Bloody as ever. You?"

"Unharmed," she said, her tone indicating that he'd made the mistake, not her.

"Funny."

The members of FORS laughed. Midnight stood in the circle of Rick's arms, looking down at her second. "I called for the paramedics—I want you checked out," she said, her voice no-nonsense.

"Yes, ma'am." Joe saluted with his injured arm and winced at the pain that shot through it.

"See," Midnight chided.

"Yes, Captain."

"Hey, yeah," Spider said. "We probably have the only captain in the history of the department to ever lead a gang fight, ya think?"

"At least!" someone yelled.

"Maybe the first captain in the history of the State," someone else said.

"Maybe in the country!" Tiny put in.

"Maybe the world!" Dibbs yelled.

"Alright, shut up!" Midnight smiled. "Don't you guys start on me now. I expect no trouble from this motley crew when I take over command."

Many of the crowd laughed, others issuing catcalls.

Spider eyed her. "You still gonna go out with us?"

"On shit like this?" Midnight said, and Spider nodded. "Hell yes! I'm promoted, not dead!" She yelled out a banshee war cry and was joined by many other voices.

Later, at the Pit, FORS celebrated their victory. They both celebrated and mourned Midnight's promotion. At one point Joe raised his bandaged arm, signaling for silence, and everyone quieted eventually. Joe had his other arm around Randy, and Midnight and Rick were sitting in a booth very close by. Rick had his back to the wall, with Midnight leaning comfortably against him. His arms were stretched out on either side of her, a bottle of beer in one hand. Midnight had a glass of Southern Comfort. Tiny sat on the bar, with Jessica on a stool between his legs. Spider and Tammy were at a table close by, his arms around her. Kana stood with one of the guys she'd been seeing recently; he looked just as tough as her, but she seemed to be having a good time. Dibbs sat on the bar next to Tiny, telling him over and over that if he took his eyes off Jessica for a minute, he was going to grab her. Tiny would hold up a meaty fist and tell him to go ahead and try. The other members of FORS were sitting or standing in a large semi-circle around Joe and Randy.

"I want to offer a toast," Joe said, looking over at Midnight. "To my partner, my boss, my best friend. For all the shit she's put up with, for all the times she held my hand or dragged my sorry ass out of a bottle. I know that all of you have something you could pin on her and make stick—she's been there for all of us. And now we have to share her with the rest of the department, with those other guys…" The members of FORS laughed at his derision. "We want you to know, Midnight, that even if they bust you back down to lieutenant for any unpolitically correct gem you bring up at the executive staff meeting, we at FORS will always be your followers. We are your family, and we're the ones who love you." He was sincere, and as Midnight looked around at everyone else's faces, she knew they all felt the same.

After a moment, she lifted her glass. "To all of you, and to all of us," she said, her voice carrying. "To FORS."

Everyone raised their drinks. "To FORS!"

You can find more information about the author and series here:

www.sherrylhancock.com

www.facebook.com/SherrylDHancock

www.vulpine-press.com/midknight-blue-series

Also by Sherryl D. Hancock:

The *WeHo* series follows a group of women from Los Angeles as they navigate the ups and downs of love, life, work, and everything in between.

www.vulpine-press.com/we-ho

The *Wild Irish Silence* series. Escape into the world of BJ Sparks and discover how he went from the small-town boy to the world-famous rock star.

www.vulpine-press.com/wild-irish-silence-series